CHAINS

ROYAL BASTARDS MC

KRISTINE ALLEN

MW01193700

I'm Nico "Chains" Trinidad—Tail-Gunner for the Ankeny RBMC. I'm not a good man, but I'm loyal to the core. I won't hesitate to protect my club.

I wanted Jasmine more than my next breath. Just one night, and she was a fire in my blood I couldn't extinguish. It didn't matter that she was forbidden.

When my chapter stumbled into the middle of a sinister organization, it put us all in their crosshairs. Chaos ensued, and she became a casualty.

Damaged and scarred, she used me, and I let her. My need to possess her overrode common sense. Until we got caught and I was shipped off to keep her brother from carving out my heart.

Months later, I came back to secrets and lies that blew up in our face. Now, I need to find a way to save her from one of our deadliest enemies or lose everything.

I'm going to prove I'm the right man for her and unleash the hounds of hell on them—even if it kills me.

CHAINS, 1st Edition Copyright 2021 by Kristine Allen, Demented Sons Publishing, LLC.
All Rights Reserved.

ISBN-13: 978-1-953318-02-2

Published in the United States of America. First published August 3, 2021.

Cover Design: Gray Creations
Photographer: Wander Aguiar
Cover Model: Chris Fleming
Editing: Olivia Ventura, Hot Tree Editing, www.hottreepublishing.com

The purchase of this e-book, or book, allows you one legal copy for your own personal reading enjoyment on your personal computer or device. This does not include the right to resell, distribute, print or transfer this book, in whole or in part to anyone, in any format, via methods either currently known or yet to be invented, or upload to a file sharing peer to peer program, except in the case of brief quotations embodied in critical reviews and certain other noncommercial uses. It may not be re-sold or given away to other people. Such action is illegal and in violation of the U.S. Copyright Law. Criminal copyright infringement, including infringement without monetary gain, is investigated by the FBI and is punishable by up to 5 years in federal prison and a fine of $250,000 (www.fbi.gov/ipr). Thank you for respecting the hard work of this author.

This is a work of fiction. Names, characters, businesses, places, events, and incidents are either the product of the author's imagination or used in a fictitious manner. Any resemblance to actual persons, living or dead, or actual events is purely coincidental. The publisher does not have any control and does not assume any responsibility for author or third-party websites or their content. For information, contact the author at kristine.allen.author@gmail.com. Thank you for supporting this author and her rights.

Warning: This book may contain offensive language, violence, adult, and sexual situations. Mature audiences only, 18+ years of age.

To Chris Fleming.
You were a bright star that burned out entirely too fast.

Angelia
Happy Reading!
Kristine Allen

ROYAL BASTARDS MC SERIES

Featured Characters:

Declan, Wolfman, Bones, Axel, Throttle, Brick, Doc, Kane and ol' ladies from the Flagstaff RBMC Chapter by M. Merin

Patriot, Rael, Grim, Bodie and their ol' ladies from the Tonopah RBMC Chapter by Nikki Landis

Spark and Croc from the South Australia RBMC Chapter by Khloe Wren

Tarak, Edge, and their ol' ladies from the Santa Fe RBMC Chapter by Jax Hart

Jameson and Sadie from the RBMC National Chapter in New Orleans by Crimson Syn

Void, Toxin, Nycto, and Eva from the Tampa RBMC Chapter by KE Osborn

Lean and Mani from the Pittsburgh RBMC Chapter by Deja Voss

ROYAL BASTARDS CODE

PROTECT: The club and your brothers come before anything else and must be protected at all costs. CLUB is FAMILY.

RESPECT: Earn it & Give it. Respect club law. Respect the patch. Respect your brothers. Disrespect a member and there will be hell to pay.

HONOR: Being patched in is an honor, not a right. Your colors are sacred, not to be left alone, and NEVER let them touch the ground.

OL' LADIES: Never disrespect a member's or brother's ol' lady. PERIOD.

CHURCH is MANDATORY.

LOYALTY: Takes precedence over all, including well-being.

HONESTY: Never LIE, CHEAT, or STEAL from another member or the club.

TERRITORY: You are to respect your brothers' property and follow their Chapter's club rules.

TRUST: Years to earn it… seconds to lose it.

NEVER RIDE OFF: Brothers do not abandon their family.

PROLOGUE

'd never admit it to a living soul, but I was fucking terrified. It was getting dark, and it would be my third night sleeping out on the street. Glancing around, it seemed like there was movement in every shadow. Sounds seemed amplified. My senses were on overload, and paranoia was tight on my heels.

Not close to being tired, I decided to walk downtown for a bit. More people, less shadows.

After adjusting my backpack, I pulled my beanie down over my eyebrows, then darted across the street and down a few blocks. Weaving in and out of the growing throngs, I shoved my hands in the pockets of my jeans.

As the sun set, the temperatures began to drop. My hoodie wouldn't ward off the late fall chill well by the time full night hit. I'd pull out my jacket later.

Pretending to belong, I leaned my shoulder against the brick of an old building. Hands shaking, I dug in the side pocket of my bag and pulled out a smashed pack of cigarettes. Extracting one, I lit it and took a satisfying drag before blowing the smoke into the air. Then I shoved the pack back in and zipped the pocket shut.

A few people gave me dirty looks, because smoking wasn't

really cool anymore, but most ignored me. Kind of the story of my life.

"You got another one of those?"

I glanced over and into the hazel eyes of a girl who didn't look old enough to be out by herself, let alone asking to bum a cigarette. Taking another drag, I stared at her but didn't reply.

"Well, fuck you very much too," she grouched. Then she simply stared at me. "You're new."

"What the hell are you talking about?" I asked, unable to resist after her cryptic remark.

"You think I don't know everyone who hangs out down here? Besides, no one our age is down here at this time, carrying a bag that looks stuffed with all your worldly possessions, and looking lost—unless they are. Welcome to Never Never Land, Lost Boy." She smirked, and the way she seemed to look through my entire existence was unnerving.

"Yeah, I'm just passing through." I tried to sound cool, hoping to blow her off.

She snorted. "Okay. I'll play along. Where you headed, tall, dark, and handsome?"

I shrugged. "California."

In truth, I had no idea where I was going. I'd been cut loose from foster care when I aged out of the system a week ago. I'd spent too much of the money I had on a bus ticket to Des Moines and a hotel room for the first four nights. Realizing how dumb that was, I'd packed up my bag and hit the street.

She laughed, and my hackles rose a little at her attitude. "California, huh? How you gonna get there? Fly in your private jet? I got news for you—dreams are for the foolish. The only way you're gonna survive out here is if you toughen up and learn the only one who's gonna look out for you is you. If you make a few close friends, you'll have someone to watch your back. But don't trust too easily. That'll get you burned too."

As I studied her, I sucked deep on the cigarette. Then as I blew the smoke out, I held it out in a… a peace offering of sorts?

She gave me a half-grin and reached for it. When our fingers touched, I was slammed with visions that had me gasping for breath and stumbling backward.

"You okay?" She appeared concerned, but she took a drag, then held her hand out to give it back.

"You keep it," I choked out, trying to make the visions of her being repeatedly raped by an older man get out of my head. "I think I just quit."

Her melodic laughter rang out. "Thanks. I'll see you around, Lost Boy."

It took a minute to fully get my breath back as I watched her walk off smoking the rest of my cigarette. Despite the cool temperatures, she had on a short denim skirt, a pair of combat boots, and a lightweight denim jacket. Her curly dark hair was blowing around her face as she smiled up at a small group of what I guessed were college-aged guys.

They chatted for a bit, one of them slipped a hand in her jacket, and she stepped back. Then I saw her shake her head and say something. He smirked, reached in his pocket, and handed her some money. It shouldn't have surprised me when she sauntered off around the corner of the building with him as his friends yelled out taunts, but it did.

It didn't take long before he came strutting back out tucking his shirt in. His friends laughed with him, and they all walked off and into one of the small bars. She still hadn't come out.

Right when I was getting ready to go check on her, she came around the corner wiping under her eyes. She looked up and saw me still standing there. A huge smile that was fake as fuck spread across her face as she approached me.

"You eaten yet?"

Like an idiot, I stood there and blinked at her.

"Earth to Lost Boy," she said as she waved a hand in front of my face. "You in there? Are you some kind of special kid, or what? I asked you a question."

"Um, no," I finally replied, realizing I was starving as my stomach rumbled.

"Well, come on. I know this little twenty-four-hour diner a couple blocks away that serves a cheap but good breakfast all day. My treat."

Without answering, I shuffled along beside her, careful not to brush against her hand that was swinging along between us. She chattered the entire way there until my head was about to explode.

We sat in the corner, and I shoved my bag in the booth next to me. "You're gonna wanna get a locker at the bus depot for that. You keep carrying it around, someone's gonna take your shit. Carry the minimum with you at all times. Two waters and two of the breakfast specials." She ordered for both of us, and I twisted the straw paper in my fingers as I waited for the food to arrive. I could tell she was staring at me, but I didn't look up.

"What's your name?" I finally asked her, chancing a quick glance up at her.

"Monique. What's yours?"

"Nico."

"So what's your story, Nico? Get kicked out? Runaway? Sprouted up out of the flowerbeds in city park?" She chuckled, and I couldn't believe that she could be so sunny after what I'd seen both in my head and on the street ten minutes ago.

"Aged out of the foster system," I mumbled.

"Mmm, tough break. Didn't you have a job?" she asked before taking a drink of her water.

"Yeah, I did, but I got fired a few weeks ago." No clue why I'd told her the truth, but I did. I looked away. It was a shit job at a fast-food restaurant, and I didn't regret beating the shit out of my coworker. When we were clocking in, I had bumped into him and accidentally touched his arm. He was using date-rape drugs on girls and had planned to use it on one of our other coworkers who was only sixteen.

Thankfully, no one pressed charges against me, but part of that could've been the boot I'd buried in his nuts. Well, along with the warning that the next time I'd crush them under my boot heel. It was part of the reason I left our small town and headed toward a bigger city.

"Bummer. You got papers?"

"Huh?"

"Papers." She said it like she was talking to a toddler. "Birth certificate, social security card, driver's license? That shit. Papers."

"Oh. Yeah, they gave me everything when I left."

"Guard it with your life. That will be like gold. You can get another job. You mind fast food? Gas stations? They're usually hiring, especially if you'll work the shitty shifts." She glanced at the waitress as she put two plates on the table and gave her a smile of thanks.

The waitress gave a tired smile back, and after making sure we didn't need anything else, she left.

"So why don't you get one of those jobs? You know, instead of…." I trailed off, uncertain of what to say and feeling stupid for pointing out that I had an idea of what she'd done in that alley.

Pursing her lips, she seemed intent on smearing jelly on her toast.

"Sorry," I muttered.

She shrugged but still didn't make eye contact. Then she took a bite and said, "No papers," with her mouth full.

Though I'd been starving, my stomach churned at the thought of her selling herself to survive. She was pretty in an understated way. Her creamy latte-colored skin was smooth and makeup free, but she didn't really need it. Thick dark lashes fanned over her hazel eyes as she looked down. Perfectly shaped lips were full but marred by a tiny sliver of a scar through the top one. Not enough to detract from her beauty, but enough to give her character.

A strange need to protect her surged through me, and I shook my head at the feeling. We ate our food in silence after that.

"You got anywhere to sleep tonight?" she finally asked me.

"I haven't slept much in the last couple of nights," I muttered. I'd crashed the first night in the bushes behind the hotel I'd stayed at. The next night, I'd snuck in the pool area of the hotel and slept on one of the lounge chairs, but a security guard chased me off at about two in the morning.

She twisted her lips off to the side, appearing to think. "I don't know why, but I like you, Lost Boy." She'd gone back to calling me that over my name. I wanted to correct her, but I didn't want to piss her off since she actually was being nice to me. And she'd offered to buy my food—though I wasn't about to let her pay for it. Especially not the way she'd earned it. It didn't feel right having her do that to feed me.

"Mmm," I grunted.

"Well, I can show you a few places that are safe to sleep, but you gotta ditch that bag somewhere safe. You hear?"

My eyes darted up at her from my plate that was almost wiped clean. "Okay," I said cautiously.

When the waitress came back with our ticket, Monique tried to pay, but I wouldn't let her. She glared at me. Then she muttered, "I'm not fucking you."

"What?" I asked with wide-eyed shock. "I never asked you to!"

She continued to glare. "Well, okay. Good. Then thanks for dinner."

After we left, she showed me the places she knew of that I could sleep and used one hand to push her hair out of her face. "You be careful tonight. I'll be seeing you around, but I got, uh, work to do."

I blinked at her before I cleared my throat. "Um, okay. Thanks again."

Appearing to consider me further, she shook off her thoughts and gave me a wave as she walked off. "Later, Lost Boy."

"Sure," I said as I watched her disappear into the crowd on the sidewalk.

We weren't far from the river, and I prayed she wouldn't hook up with the wrong guy and end up floating in it. She was playing a dangerous game, but I wasn't one to talk. If I didn't figure something out, who knew where I might end up.

Suddenly exhausted, I made my way back to the alley she'd pointed out behind several of the bars. There were a bunch of motorcycles parked behind one, and I stopped to drool for a minute. I'd always wanted one but knew I'd probably never be in a position to own one.

"Don't fucking touch them," a voice said from the shadows, and I belatedly noticed the cherry of his cigarette.

Holding up my hands in surrender, I stepped back. "Easy, man, I wasn't planning on touching them. Just admiring them; that's all."

The guy stepped from the shadows, and his eyes raked me from head to toe. He actually didn't look much older than me in the dim light of the alley. I noticed the leather vest he wore had a small patch I couldn't make out, but otherwise was blank. The back door of the bar opened, and another guy stuck his head out.

"Hey, prospect! Here." He tossed him a bottle of water that the guy caught with a "Thank you."

The dude in the door glanced my way but addressed the man he called prospect. "Everything okay?"

The guy outside turned to look at him, and that's when I saw the patch on the back that said PROSPECT.

"Yeah, it's all good."

"Good," the guy in the door replied. "You need anything, holler."

"Roger that," he said.

While they were talking, I slipped off and went behind the dumpster of the place next door. There was some cardboard stacked against the dented metal, and I quietly spread some of it in the small space between the building and the metal bin.

Once I was satisfied with how it was situated, I shoved my bag under the dumpster where it wasn't visible and laid my head on my folded arm. The faint sounds of music and laughter that carried out of the bars were my lullaby for the night.

Little to no sleep for over forty-eight hours had me quickly dropping off.

I had no idea how long I'd slept before I was startled awake by someone trying to take my pants off. "What the fuck?" I muttered, trying to get my bearings.

A shadowed figure was over me, pulling at my pants, and the smell coming from it was horrendous. In my sleep-addled mind, he was a demon straight from hell coming for me. The truth was possibly worse.

"You're real pretty, ain't you?" The demon creature cooed with fetid breath as I fought for all I was worth. The problem was, though I was tall for my age, I wasn't a very big guy. He had a good fifty pounds or more on me.

Finally getting my hand around his neck, I pushed him back.

When I made contact with his grimy skin, it was like being hit by lightning, and I gasped. Visions of the things he'd done horrified me and had me reaching blindly for something I could use as a weapon.

My fingertips were damn near raw by the time they curled around something cold and hard under the dumpster. The rasping sound of metal on asphalt startled the guy enough that he paused. It gave me a slight advantage, and I kneed him twice in quick succession. He reared back in surprised pain, allowing me to kick him off and scramble to my feet.

When he came at me again, I swung the chain in my hand wildly.

"You little fucker!" the guy grunted out when it made contact. "I'm going to kill you for that, then I'm gonna fuck your pretty ass as you bleed out on the ground!"

Panic and terror like I'd never experienced swept through me, and I began to blindly swing the heavy chain over and over. The roaring in my ears didn't register as being from my own lips until a light was shining in my eyes. In straight up fight mode, I spun and savagely swung the chain again.

"Easy boy! Fuck! We ain't gonna hurt you! Chill out, it's okay," the voice said. Eyes darting around wildly, I realized I was surrounded by a bunch of bikers. My heart was beating so fast, I thought it might either explode or burst from my chest.

"He's dead," one of the other guys said from where he was crouching over the crumpled heap of the man I'd initially believed to be a demon and then known to be worse.

"He—" I gasped. "He was gonna—" Backed against the wall, I wanted to cry. I was going to go to jail for murder, and I was only eighteen years old. Fuck.

The man who had spoken to me first glanced from me to the piece of shit on the ground. Then he looked to the men with him.

One of them stepped forward and said something in his ear that I couldn't hear.

"We ain't gonna call the cops. Okay?" he said to me.

I swallowed hard, and my eyes searched around for an avenue of escape. Panic burned through me when I didn't see one.

"Kid, we're gonna clean this up. We know what he was gonna do. We won't let anything happen to you, but you gotta trust us, okay?"

Shaking uncontrollably, I dropped the chain that I realized was covered in blood and things I didn't want to think about. Then I started to hyperventilate when I saw the blood splattered on my clothes and the wall. My vision started to get spotty, and I dropped to my knees before I blacked out.

The day the Royal Bastards found me in that alley may have been one of the worst days of my life, but it was also probably the best.

The then president, Rowdy, had been true to his word. They had cleaned up what had become a crime scene, and no one ever knew about what I'd done. The crazy thing was, they never expected anything for it. At the time I hadn't understood why.

They even given me a job cleaning up their tattoo studio and their strip club. I would go in every morning before they opened and clean for a few hours at each place. I only made minimum wage, but it was enough to get a tiny efficiency apartment for me and Monique.

As soon as I'd saved enough for the deposit, I moved us in. We weren't in a relationship, but she'd been the first person in ages to treat me like a human being instead of a check for fostering me. She'd kinda become the sister I never had.

They were even letting me make payments on an older-than-dirt bike so I had transportation I could afford.

"Boy, I need to talk to you," Rowdy said, and I looked over my shoulder as I dumped the trash can in the dumpster.

"Okay?" I asked, suddenly wary.

He motioned inside, and I followed him, the heavy metal door slamming once we were in.

"Hey, baby," Cookie said as she passed us on her way to the dressing room. I guessed she was working the lunch shift. Barely older than I was, she was one of the dancers. She also gave me a blowjob for helping her moving her shit to a bigger apartment. After that, she and I hooked up occasionally, but we were on the same page and that's all it was.

She also didn't give me shit for wearing gloves or not touching her when we fucked. I let her think it was a kink. That was easier than explaining the truth.

Rowdy went in the office and pointed to the chair. He closed the door and took the seat behind the desk. He liked to make people wait, and this time wasn't an exception. He steepled his fingers and studied me.

Patiently, I waited.

Finally he got to what he'd called me in for. "What do you think of being a member of the Royal Bastards?"

He couldn't have shocked me more if he'd said Mother Theresa had given birth to him and the Pope was his father. "Excuse me?"

"You deaf?"

"No, sir," I said with a rapid shake of my head. "I just thought I heard you wrong. You asking if I'm interested in becoming a member of your club was, well, unexpected."

"That didn't answer my question, boy."

"Yes. The answer is yes."

"Good. There's something you need to do before you can prospect though," he said cryptically, and my guts churned. It could be anything, and I hoped they didn't want me to kill someone again. I had no idea if they had some kind of gang-like initiation or something. They were tight-lipped about their club.

And I *really* didn't want to go to jail at eighteen.

"What would that be?" I said, cursing the slight tremor in my voice.

"You need to learn specific skills." He leaned back in his chair and locked his hands behind his head.

"Like?"

"You're gonna join the army and become a Ranger or Spec Ops. Then come talk to me."

PART I

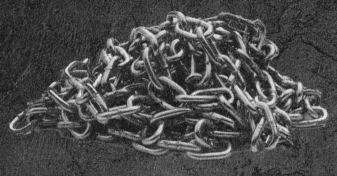

ONE

Chains

"CAT AND MOUSE"—THE RED JUMPSUIT APPARATUS

Six years later…

"Welcome home!" I'd heard that a million times since the party started. Sure, I'd seen everyone when I came back on leave, but I was finally home for good. I'd done what Rowdy had asked, and I'd become one of the best snipers on my team. Yeah, I made it into special operations, and I'd been a killing machine. That part of the military didn't bother me; it was some of the shit I saw that I had no control over that haunted me at night.

During my first deployment, Monique had dropped off a note at the clubhouse and disappeared. Rowdy had told me when I called home. I'd tried to find her, but without a last name or social, she might as well have been a ghost. I'd often wondered what happened to her.

The party was heating up, the drinks were flowing, bass was thumping, the bonfire was lighting up the night sky, and the women were hot. It should've been exactly what I needed to lose myself before I took on the title of "prospect" tomorrow and a year of shit-work began. The thing was, I needed a minute to myself. I grabbed a bucket off one of the tables and filled it with ice and several beers. Quietly, I snagged a chair in the shadows. After I popped the top, I lifted a cold bottle to my lips and surveyed the party. That's when I saw the two chicks on the edge of the crowd, not far from where I sat. It was obvious they were out of their element, but they were gorgeous. They also didn't notice me, so it gave me time to study them.

One was blonde, short, but curvy—the other was the one I couldn't keep my eyes off. Mink-colored hair rippled over her shoulders. Eyes that flashed gold in the firelight scanned the crowd. My eyes traveled over the banging body I could already see myself bending over the nearest stable object.

"You need a beer?" I asked from my shadowy hiding place. Both girls squealed a little, and I chuckled.

"Fucking hell, you scared the shit out of us!" the blonde said as she pressed her splayed hand over her chest. The brunette studied me without saying a word. When she stepped closer, her eyes caught the light of the bonfire and reminded me of a tiger's eye stone. They were stunning. They also eerily seemed to be able to see right through me.

"Yeah, I'll take one," she boldly said as she approached me with cat-like grace. Her lips were full and ruby red, and her tits, not too big, not too small, stretched the black fabric of her sliced-up shirt.

A crooked grin lifted the corner of my mouth as I reached into my bucket and popped the top off with one of my rings. "Here you go," I said as I handed her the dripping bottle, careful not to make contact with her slender fingers.

Her pink tongue wet her bottom lip as she took the cold bottle from me. That sultry gaze of hers locked on mine as she took a drink.

"Why are you hiding over here in the dark?" she asked.

I shrugged. "Needed a minute. Why were you two hiding on the edge instead of joining the party? Isn't that why you're here?"

They cast uneasy glances at each other before they schooled their features. "Just checking things out," the brunette smoothly replied.

"You want one?" I held my beer up to the other girl just as Ghost popped up behind them.

"Boo!" he said with a laugh and placed an arm around the blonde. He tried to do it with both, but the brunette dropped her head and stepped closer to me, hiding behind her hair. Her body language screamed she wasn't comfortable with Ghost's bold manner. Immediately, I wanted to rescue her, but had to remind myself it wasn't my place.

"Thanks, but I don't drink beer," the blonde said to me with a wrinkle to her nose.

"Then how about we leave this broody asshole here in the dark and I take you two pretty ladies to the bar for something you do like?" Ghost said with his usual charm.

"I'm good with my beer," the brunette said in a soft tone.

"You okay here, J—" the blonde started.

"Yep!" the brunette immediately piped in before her friend could finish her question. Ghost cocked his head as he looked at her with a narrowed gaze, but the blonde slid a hand up his chest, and he looked down at her with a grin.

"Cool, cool. Be good, Nico." Done with our brief interaction, he steered the blonde through the crowd.

"Sorry about him. So what's your name?" I asked her as she sat on the bench of the picnic table under the tree.

"He's okay. Call me Jay," she said as she boldly held my gaze. Funny, but she hadn't seemed okay when Ghost was there.

"Has he bothered you before?" If he had made the golden-eyed beauty uncomfortable in any way, I'd throttle him. That would end my prospect time before it started, but something told me, for her, I'd be okay with that.

She shook her head rapidly and raised the bottle. Her slender hands shook slightly, but I was sure she thought I didn't notice. The thing was, I noticed everything. Hell, my life had depended on it for years.

"First time here," she said after she lowered the beer but dropped her gaze. The pulse in her slender throat was pounding. *Interesting.*

"What do you think so far?" I asked her as I watched every little nuance of her movements.

"It's all right. Not exactly what I thought it was going to be like," she said as she scanned the crowd. It was pretty wild, and I wasn't sure if she and her friend had known what they were in for when they came. There were all levels of debauchery going on that she quickly looked away from. A flush tinted her bronze skin.

"You in the military?" she asked as she glanced at my high-and-tight haircut.

I ran a hand over the short length causing a rasping sound. "No." It wasn't a lie. That part of my life was over.

"Oh," she said before she took another drink of liquid courage.

We made small talk, and I was quickly mesmerized by the cadence of her voice and her rich, throaty laugh. Each time she spoke, my cock jumped in my jeans until it was damn near painful. Something about her screamed to me on a primitive level.

"So Jay, you wanna go somewhere quieter?" I asked, knowing exactly what I wanted to do with her. Patiently, I waited and casually finished the last beer. I'd had three to her two. She might be feeling mellow, but there was no way she was drunk. That's something I wouldn't do no matter how horny I was—take advantage of a woman.

Again she wet her lips, and I had to adjust my dick. Her honey-colored gaze watched me, and I didn't make excuses. We both knew what I was asking. She glanced out into the crowd, locating her friend as she danced and made out with Ghost. Her gaze nervously scanned the party-goers, then she returned those beautiful eyes to me.

"She's safe. He's a bit forward, but he's a good guy." For the most part anyway, but what she didn't know wouldn't hurt her. Ghost would never hurt a chick.

She set her empty bottle on the table next to the others and stood. "Lead the way, Nico."

My grin widened, and I stood. Carefully avoiding touching her bare skin that peeked between her shirt and her denim skirt, I placed my hand at the small of her back. We went around the building and in the back door. The music played inside, but not as loud. Down the hall we could hear the party that had moved inside, but in the back hall where the rooms were, it was muted.

Slipping my key into the lock, I opened the room I'd been given to use for the night. Normally prospects wouldn't get their own room, but for tonight this one was mine. Rowdy told me to have fun and to enjoy it while I could, because I'd be sleeping in the bunkhouse when I put on that prospect cut.

"It's pretty sparse in here," she said as she walked the small room, trailing her fingers along the dresser, then sat on the end of the bed. Her hands were next to her hips as she leaned slightly forward, causing cleavage to show through the cuts in the front of the T-shirt.

I shrugged, not wanting to discuss the room.

For a second she looked nervous, but that bold gleam quickly returned. "Come here," she whispered in that sexy, husky tone. My balls tightened at the sound, and I had to tell them to calm the fuck down. I set my empty bottle on the dresser and stepped between her legs.

Without another word, she worked my belt loose and unfastened my jeans. She shoved them down, and my cock sprang out, happy as you please. "How many girls have you fucked in here, Nico?" she asked before she gripped my shaft in her hand and slowly worked the length.

All I could do was shake my head.

Anyone would've thought I was a kid getting his first hand job. I sucked in a breath and fought to keep from shooting my load in her face. "Goddamn," I groaned as she leaned forward and licked the end of my cock, swiping the clear bead off the tip. Immediately, my heart began to hammer against my ribs, and I thought for sure she could hear it thumping like the telltale heart as it pumped all the blood in my brain to my engorged cock.

Jay was fucking beautiful, but when she wrapped her lips around the head of my cock and worked it farther into her mouth, she was stunning.

"Fuuuck," I moaned. I had to lace my hands at the back of my neck so I wouldn't grab her head and shove my cock down her throat. Touching her might ruin everything, but fuck, my hands tingled to feel her—ached to run through the silky strands of her mocha-colored hair and cradle her face.

Inside a voice screamed at me. *Just once.* Take off those sexy-as-fuck clothes, fuck her mouth, then run my hands and tongue over every inch of her golden skin until I was hard again. Didn't matter that I knew that was impossible. This primal roar filled my ears as each beat of my heart chanted *she's mine, she's mine, she's mine.*

That mouth was pure magic. Like nothing I'd ever experienced in my life. Mind-blowing and evidently load-blowing, because I had to grip her hair and pull her off so I didn't shoot down her throat before I drove into her pussy. It had been so long since

I'd actually fucked a woman, I was dying to feel her tight sheath squeeze my cock.

"Why did you stop me?" she panted as she gripped my thighs. I was careful not to touch anything but her hair, and even that I was getting ripples off, but nothing solid.

That was manageable.

"On the bed. On your knees," I demanded. For a split second, I regretted treating her like a patch chaser—though I didn't have one yet. Why? Because possessiveness spread through my blood like thick poison. A tiny whisper in the back of my mind told me she was meant for me and me alone.

That she really was mine.

Except I knew better. I'd never have a woman of my own. It was impossible.

Still, the perfect fucking woman, she did as I said and turned to her hands and knees with her ass facing me.

"Don't question me, and don't touch me unless I tell you to," I said. Eyes hooded, she looked over her shoulder and nodded.

Pure adrenaline zipping through my veins, I gripped her skirt in my hands and wadded it up to her waist. Her thong barely covered her swollen pussy, and I could see it was drenched. It was my undoing. Knowing I might be fucking up, I needed a taste. Reverently, I knelt behind her. My fingers tightly gripped her skirt, and I pulled her hips back so I could lick her through the satin.

"Fuck," I muttered to myself at the first burst of her unique flavor over my tongue. If only I could bury my face in there as I gripped her bare hips in my hands, I'd be in heaven. Yet, in truth, I knew it would possibly be hell.

Still, she tasted divine. Like a sweet and tangy elixir of the gods, handed to me on a satin-covered platter. Being unable to fully devour her as my fingers dug in with a bruising grip like I wanted pissed me off. It had me wanting to howl in frustration and gnash my teeth at the unfairness of my life.

Using one thick, chunky ring, I teased over her clit. She whimpered and pushed back toward me. Her scent filled the room and damn near made me high as I inhaled deeply. Slowly, I trailed the cold metal along the skin I ached to stroke. Finally, I hooked the point of the ring in the side of her panties, and with a flick of my wrist, I snapped the delicate fabric.

She gasped, and I did the other side. The tiny scrap fell forgotten to the floor, baring her glistening folds to my hungry gaze. Tempted beyond control, I slipped the tip of my tongue into the center and quickly lapped the creamy wetness. Hazy images began to form when my hands brushed her satiny skin, and I pulled away with a frustrated growl.

I tried again, careful to grip the fabric of her skirt, hoping the images wouldn't solidify if I slipped. When they stayed a fuzzy blur, I fucked her with my tongue, much as I planned to do with my cock. She whimpered and moaned with each swipe. Not able to get enough of her, I pressed on her back so her chest was flat to the bed. That tipped her pelvis enough that I had access to her swollen little clit. I licked from her dripping wet center, then down around that bundle of sensitivity before I sucked on it as she panted into the comforter.

Her entire body began to quiver as I sensed her orgasm approaching. Relentless, I held that pink pearl with my teeth and lashed at it with the tip of my tongue. One last deep pull on it, and she exploded. Not wasting a drop, I licked every bit of it as she pulsed around my tongue. Her pussy was addictive, and I didn't want to ever stop, but my cock was demanding its due.

"I'm going to fuck you so hard, you'll never forget me," I growled out and bit her ass cheek playfully. Then, I stood and pulled a condom from my pocket. Deftly, I made quick work of the wrapper and rolled it down my straining shaft. Then I clutched the denim of her skirt in my hands, wishing it was the smooth, bare globes of her ass.

My hips worked to line my desperately bobbing cock up with that soaking wet core. When I was there, I pushed in slowly, inch by inch, and a moan escaped as she instinctively clutched at me. "Damn baby, your pussy is tight but needy," I said in a husky tone.

"I want you to fuck me, Nico," she pleaded, and I lost my goddamn mind. With a groan, I drove my cock home. The momentary resistance and her sharp cry registered as my momentum drove me to the hilt.

"Jay?" I asked in confusion through panicked gasps. I'd never in my life fucked a virgin, but I knew one when I felt it. Instinct had me jerking free of her at the same time my inner beast snarled at the loss of her heat. Blood was thinly smeared on the surface of the condom, and that beast within gave a possessive shout.

"Did I hurt you?" I gasped, worried because I hadn't been easy.

"I'm fine. Please, Nico. Don't stop. Please," she begged, and I heard the tears in her voice.

Gripping her hair, I pulled her up to her knees to make her look at me. "You should've told me!" I cried, still reeling.

"I was afraid you'd say no if you knew," she whimpered, and my anger gave way to regret as I released my hold on her silken tresses.

"Jay, I don't want to hurt you. You're a virgin. I like it rough, but not at a woman's expense."

"Not anymore. And I want that. I want you," she said in a soft whisper.

"Why? You don't even know me," I asked, incredulous even as my cock wept at being withheld from her hot, wet core.

"When I saw you tonight, I knew it was going to be you," she admitted as she dropped her head and hid in the thick waves of her hair.

"Fucking hell," I muttered, running a shaking hand over my mouth. I was torn. The unnaturally aware part of my soul ached for her, as if she was created to be my other half. But I didn't know how a relationship could work. My rational side yelled *abort, abort, abort!*

Too bad I didn't listen to that side. I knew I should, but the primitive beast in my soul drove me. With gently pressure to her back, I pushed her back to her hands and knees. Clenching my jaw, I hissed through my teeth and pushed back inside. Pausing to allow her to adjust, I asked, "Are you okay?"

"Yes," she gasped out. When she did, her sheath gripped me tight.

It was so good, my eyes rolled back and my heart stuttered. My stomach rippled with the flutter of a million mad butterflies, and a tremor shot through my body.

Hands back on that denim, I gave in to the beast and her pleading. "This is mine," I growled as I thrust deep. She whimpered, and her walls gripped me like a vise. "Say it!" I demanded with another stroke.

"Yours, fuck yes, Nico, it's yours," she cried as her fingers twisted the linens and she dropped her chest back to the bed. I hadn't even seen her completely naked, yet I knew she was mine. Somehow, I'd find a way.

"Yessss," I ground out through each animalistic thrust into her perfect body. I wished for my leather gloves so I could strum her clit, but they were in my jacket in the closet, and I wasn't stopping. I needn't have worried.

The second I grunted out "I'm coming," she screamed my name and her tight cunt milked every drop of the cum that shot into the wretched but necessary condom. One last shudder and a deep plunge into her sheath had me shaking. I dropped my head to her back.

"Are you still okay?" I panted out.

"Mmm-hmm," she languidly hummed into the navy-blue comforter.

Gently, I withdrew as I held the condom at the base. She whimpered. The diluted blood was still smeared, and I wanted to pound on my chest like a caveman. *Mine.* I quickly slid it off and tossed it in the trash. When I returned from the bathroom, she was sitting up.

We needed to talk. Without thinking, I reached out to help her up so she could clean off in the bathroom. The second our fingers touched, I was slammed with visions of a young Angel on his knees as his father held his hair so another man could violate him. Jay hid where Angel had shoved her before his father brought the man in but watched with tears in her eyes.

With a shout, I released her hand and stumbled back. Though the bond had been severed, I tasted her horror and her fear.

"Nico?" she asked with worry filling her tiger's eyes.

"Who is Angel to you?" I demanded, my voice hoarse as if I'd been screaming for hours.

"What?"

"Who. Is. Angel. To. You?" I shouted.

"He's my brother," she admitted as she bit her bottom lip and stared at me with worry. "You're not going to tell him, are you?"

"Oh my fucking God. I'm a dead man. You—I—I saw. Oh shit," I stammered as I shook my head over and over.

She stood and reached for me beseechingly.

"No!" I shouted. "Don't touch me!"

I watched as worry morphed to hurt on her beautiful face, and I hated myself.

"Holy shit. I saw what happened to Angel as a boy. Fuck, Jay, I can't touch you. You are so off-limits, it's not even funny. And now

I know... oh shit... Angel...." My stomach churned as bile hovered in my throat at what I'd seen.

"What do you know, Nico?" she whispered as her eyes widened and her face went ashen.

"Too much," I admitted.

"Oh my God. You can never tell him," she begged before she quickly straightened her clothes. "Promise me you won't breathe a word of it."

I nodded. No one needed to know what I'd seen.

She winced as she moved toward the door. I wanted to reach for her. I wanted to ask her if she was okay. I wanted to comfort her. I wanted to hold on to her and never let go.

But my reality was, I let her walk away.

TWO

Jasmine

"DOUBT"—THROUGH FIRE

"This is bad," I muttered to myself as I raced out of the room and down the hall, ignoring the soreness between my legs. *Holy shit. Fuck, fuck, fuck. What did I do?*

How was I supposed to know that the man I'd dreamed about was going to be at my brother's clubhouse? Not that I cared that he was part of my brother's club. Jude, now known as Angel, was okay with me hanging around his club, but he didn't want me hooking up with the guys in his club. He'd made that *very* clear, but I figured if he was a member, then the rest of the guys couldn't be *that* bad.

The problem was, I didn't know he'd have a gift. Jude did, but shit, I didn't think things like that were overly common. Our family had a long line of healers, a gift that was passed down to the men of each generation. What my family didn't know was that I had a bit of a gift too. Mine was more subtle than my brother's gift of healing, but it was there.

Me? I dreamed things that came true.

No, I hadn't known I'd run into the guy I dreamed of when

MacKenna begged me to get her into the club party. In my dream he didn't have a cut, but then again, in my dream he wasn't wearing anything but a shit-ton of tattoos. The second he'd spoken and I saw the ink on his arms, I knew. Looking into his eyes confirmed it. Those same rich brown eyes had been staring into my soul as he slid into my body in my dream.

Damn, it didn't compare to the reality, though. Too bad I could never be with him again. He may have been meant to be my first, but there was no way it could go any further. He'd *seen*.

Dear God, he'd seen Angel's secrets. What if he said something? Angel would be mortified. I wasn't supposed to know. He'd hidden me in the closet to protect me, but like the foolish child I was, I'd peeked.

"Jasmine!" was barked at me as a hand gripped my elbow, spinning me around. I cringed as I slowly raised my gaze to my brother. It was like I'd fucking manifested his overprotective ass.

"Um, hi?" I said with a weak smile. Though I'd only been there a few times, I knew I wasn't supposed to be in the back hallway where several of the guys had rooms.

"What the actual fuck are you doing back here?" His eyes widened as he took in what I was wearing. "And why the hell are you dressed like that here, of all places? Please tell me I'm imagining this."

"Jude. I just needed to go to the bathroom, and I decided to sit inside for a bit. I figured this door would take me out closer to where everyone was. It's not like I've never been to one of your parties before. I'm a grown-ass woman. I'm not a kid that needs protecting." A wince marred his handsome face briefly, making me feel like absolute shit. Especially after Nico had seen a little of what my brother had endured.

Truthfully, I'd only ever been to one party, and it had been pretty tame. Family days didn't count. Before I blurted out any more stupid things, I inhaled deeply and slowly exhaled. "If I want to go to a party dressed up, then I'll go to a party dressed up."

"Not at my club, you won't. The guys that are in my chapter would likely respect that you're my sister, but this one isn't just our chapter. We have members from all over, and I don't know them all. They don't need to see that much of you." He waved his hands wildly at my short skirt and sliced-up T-shirt, then frowned before scrubbing a hand over his mouth. He'd only been a patched member for a short time, so I supposed he didn't know them all. Then again, I had no clue how many members there were total.

"If the club is so bad, why are you a part of it?" I asked him with a raised brow and plenty of attitude. It had floored me when he told me he was joining a club called the Royal Bastards. We had been raised very upper-middle class. It had been a surprise to me when he joined the army with Ogun. But it was mind-blowing when they joined the same motorcycle club as Ogun's dad. Well, stepdad, but he never saw his biological father, and though I didn't know the story there, I knew there was one.

"I trust my chapter, sis. The rest of the chapters may be fine, but I don't know them. That's all. I'd also rather not have to beat the fuck out of one of my own brothers if they got handsy with you—or worse, hurt you. That's why I would just rather you not be around when other chapters are here," he said with a heavy-hearted sigh. I guessed that was why he hadn't extended the invite to me for the party that night. When MacKenna begged for us to go, I hoped we could avoid my brother and the guys I knew he was close to, but I was very wrong.

"I get it, Jude. But if you don't trust the guys in this world 100 percent, then you're an idiot to be around them." My comment was more to convince myself I needed to stay far, far away. Though I knew it had to be done, the thought of never seeing Nico again made my soul cry out at the loss. I told myself it was for the best.

"It's Angel—I'd rather not even think of myself as Jude." His jaw clenched, and a hardness hit his eyes. "Come on, I'll give you a ride home. Things are about to get pretty wild. Not so sure you wanna be around for all that. I have an extra helmet for you," my brother said, and I bit my lip as I shot him an apologetic wince.

"What?" he asked in resignation.

"MacKenna is with me. She was dancing with that guy named Ghost," I said with a toothy smile and a shrug.

"Jesus H. Christ. I'll get my truck."

As he made a path through the crowd, several guys I'd never seen before gave me a once-over, and he glared. "Don't even think about it. This is my baby sister," he told several of them. By the time we reached MacKenna, the info must've spread, because there were few glances in my direction.

"You're done. Say goodnight, MacKenna," my bossy brother told her as she peeled herself off Ghost, who frowned, then glanced at me. His gaze was calculating briefly before recognition dawned, and he cussed.

"Shit. You were the brunette with her?" I could see the wheels turning, and I didn't want him to piece together who he'd left me with and how long ago that had been. Granted, we'd only met a few times, but he knew me. That was why I'd hidden from him when he found us talking to Nico.

"Yeah, but I got tired of waiting and went inside. I was surfing social media, but my brother decided to be a party-pooper when I was heading back outside." I gave my brother a scowl, and Ghost laughed.

MacKenna pouted, and I could see she wanted to argue, but Ghost kissed her and whispered something in her ear. Whatever it was, it had her grinning with a deep blush. Then again, that was one helluva kiss.

We followed my brother to his truck. The entire time, I

expected Nico to come after me. Despite how I'd lost my shit and walked out on him, I kind of hoped he'd experienced the same connection. Surely it couldn't have only been me. No matter how much I knew it was a really bad idea, something that powerful couldn't be one-sided.

A desperate longing whispered maybe he had a secret fix for his gift. Like some kind of way to prevent him from seeing everything in my dang head.

Yet, with each step, I knew he wouldn't be coming after me. By the time Angel helped me climb into the cab of his truck, my heart was heavy. It would seem that he was meant to be the one who took my virginity, but that was it.

Except if that was true, why did it seem there was an invisible bond that stretched and reached for him the farther away I went from the clubhouse?

That night I dreamed of a wolf standing at the edge of the woods staring at me with glowing eyes.

Three days later, I was waiting for my brother to meet me for lunch. As I sat on a bench outside one of our favorite diners, I absently scrolled through my phone.

The sound of an approaching motorcycle had me smiling in anticipation. Yet that feeling dissipated when two bikes appeared, and I watched as they backed up to the curb. My head cocked in curiosity, since he'd told me it would just be the two of us.

When the second rider pulled off his helmet, my pulse raced. The prospect patch on his back barely registered as I looked at the ink on the arm that hung the helmet on his handlebar. He and Angel conversed for a second, then my brother looked up and flashed me a happy grin as he swooped in on me.

Angel embraced me tightly as I stared into Nico's nearly black eyes.

"Miss me?" my brother asked as he released me and stepped back, tearing my attention from Nico.

I gave him a contemplative look. "Hmmm, maybe just a little," I teased, drawing a laugh out of him.

The fact that Nico was with him and Angel didn't seem angry had me breathing a sigh of relief. It was unlikely Nico had said anything, which had me covertly studying him as he approached. The incredible ache between my legs had only gone away that morning, but I still felt like I'd ridden a horse for about a hundred miles.

"Prospect, this is my sister, Jasmine," Angel said when Nico stopped next to him.

"Nice to meet you," he said with a curt nod. Our eyes held for a brief moment before he looked away. Though I knew my brother would have had his ass, it hurt that he didn't give so much as a flicker of recognition.

"You too," I murmured. We all went inside and grabbed a table. Talk about awkward—my brother motioned for me to slide in, and he dropped next to me. That put me damn near straight across from Nico's dark gaze. Not that I needed to worry, since it was locked on the menu.

"How's the job going?" Angel asked as he looked over the options.

"Um, good," I replied. I'd landed a graphic design job after graduation, and I loved it, but my dream was still to work independently doing website design. *One day.*

"That guy still giving you issues?" Angel asked, still pressing the menu. Nico's eyes lifted to mine, and I caught a flicker of irritation before he again dropped his gaze.

"It's fine."

Having personal discussions in front of the man I'd recently given my virginity to—who was acting like he'd never met me—was uncomfortable at best. Floyd was one of my coworkers who had been hitting on me pretty insistently. He'd been very careful not to do it in front of any of our bosses though.

"He doesn't back the fuck off, and I'm gonna kick his ass. You feel me, Jazzy?" Angel set the menu down and stared at me.

"It's under control. I've told him I'm not interested in dating him."

"You telling him and him listening are two different things."

"I get it. Are you ready to order?"

"Nice way of changing the subject." My brother smirked and waved the waitress over. The entire time we were placing our orders, the waitress was incessantly flirting with Angel and Nico. Okay, it didn't matter that she was flirting with Angel, but she didn't know if one of them was with me. Not that she was rude to me, but inside, I wanted to claim Nico as mine.

Nico may not have been there with me, but I really hated the smile he gave her as he handed over his menu. I wanted that smile.

As Angel and I chatted, Nico reclined in the booth with one inked-up arm stretched across the back of the bench seat. The sexy asshole didn't join our conversation and stared out the window like there was something incredibly fascinating out there. It was distracting as hell.

"So who are you exactly?" I asked, tired of him ignoring me.

Slowly, his gaze found mine, and he gave me a smirk that screamed *Really? We're playing it like this?*

"He's our new prospect. Nico officially became a prospect a couple of days ago."

"He can't speak for himself?" I asked somewhat snidely.

Angel snorted. "He doesn't do a fucking thing unless I tell him to."

My mouth dropped open.

They both snickered.

"I'm teasing." Angel slapped his leg like it was the funniest thing ever.

"Sort of," Nico added with a snort. "For the next year, my life is gonna pretty much suck."

"I'll never understand why you guys want to live your life like that. Screw someone telling me what I can and can't do," I grumbled.

"It's not like that." Angel rolled his eyes.

"Then what exactly is it like? Tell me how that shit works," I dared.

"That's club business, sis," Angel said before taking a sip of his water.

It was my turn to roll my eyes. "Whatever. Have your little boys' club. I'm surprised you all don't have a little treehouse like we had when we were kids. Oh wait! You do, but you call it a club-house now."

Angel's jaw ticked and I could've kicked myself for bringing that up. The treehouse had belonged to Korrie, but we had all played in there for years. Korrie had ended up being my brother's high school sweetheart until she up and disappeared with her mother. He hadn't heard from her again. It hadn't been pretty for a while.

My hand gripped his under the table in apology and support.

Our food arrived, and we ate in relative silence while I sneaked peeks at Nico periodically. Maybe more than that, but it was hard not to—the man was beautiful in a dark, forbidden kind of way. A way that told me I needed to be scarce at the clubhouse if I wanted to keep the two of us out of trouble.

Because nearly every time I snuck a glance at him, he was doing the same to me.

That was the last time I saw Nico for a long freaking time.

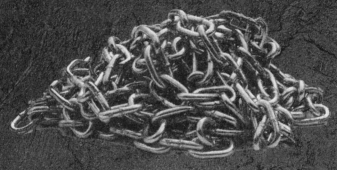

THREE

Chains

"LIGHTS GO OUT"—FOZZY

One year later.…

I t was my patch party, and the liquor had been flowing since they poured a bottle of Crown over my head to christen my shiny new patch. It was tradition in this chapter of the Royal Bastards. I mean… crown… royalty… Royal Bastards.

The Royal Bastards had become my family much earlier than my patch party. That had happened the night they rescued a terrified boy from an alleyway and prevented him from going to prison for murder—manslaughter at the least. Honestly, though? They were more than family. They were home, and I wouldn't do a fucking thing to jeopardize that.

I was halfway to shitfaced when she walked in.

Fuck. My. Life.

Legs for miles, and amber eyes haloed in chocolate that I wanted to melt into.

Jasmine.

The woman who'd happily handed her virginity to me on a silver freaking platter—little sister to one of my club brothers.

For the past year, I'd become fairly adept at staying away from her. For so many reasons, I knew it was a necessity. Thankfully, she didn't come by the clubhouse much. If she had, I couldn't say I'd have made it through the year without getting my ass kicked.

A year later, and I still wanted her, but I wasn't stupid. If I needed a release, I had my hand, or Cookie obliged me with a blowjob. I never fucked Cookie. I couldn't. Hell, I hadn't stuck my dick in a pussy since Jasmine.

Angel and I had become pretty close over the past year. He'd ended up being assigned as my sponsor in the club, and I couldn't have asked for a better one. The last thing I wanted to do was ruin that friendship by admitting I'd slept with his sister. Hell, I'd volunteered for as many runs as I could to keep me away from temptation. Not that I was nearly good enough for her, but it didn't stop me from craving her.

"Chains," she purred, and my back straightened as I steeled myself against her lure. The road name I'd been given only hours earlier seemed strange on her lips. Especially when I knew what she sounded like screaming my real one.

"Jasmine," I replied as I drank from the glass of Crown.

The party was in full swing, but everything faded away as I absorbed the changes in her. Gone was the young innocence of the night we met, and in its place was a woman confident in her skin. A heavy feeling hit my stomach when I wondered how many other men had touched what should've been mine.

"Congratulations," she murmured as her eyes trailed over my new cut.

"Thanks," I said trying my damnedest not to reach for her and brand her with my kiss.

"You never said anything to him," she said, and neither of us needed her to specify who she was talking about. Uncertainty broke through for a moment in the way she tugged her lower lip with her teeth. My eyes automatically found Angel, who was laughing with Voodoo and Phoenix across the common area. It was enough to remind me of why I couldn't toss her back on the pool table, flip up her skirt, and fuck the shit out of her.

Fucking hell.

"I said I wouldn't," I muttered, then became incredibly interested in my drink. Except the rich honey-color of the whiskey was the same damn color as her eyes. *Oh my God.*

My hand palmed my face before I scrubbed it up, then down. When I was done, I stepped back, hoping to get out of range of her subtle perfume. No way could I look in her eyes.

"If you'll excuse me," I said, needing to get away from her. Grappling for sanity, I turned and walked down the hall to my room. The glass hit my dresser with a clunk, and I went in the bathroom to take a piss. As I washed my hands, I stared at myself in the mirror.

The past year had been busy with prospecting, but I'd found time between runs to apprentice as a tattoo artist. Recently, I'd gotten a job at the club's tattoo shop, and I'd added a shit-ton of ink to myself over the past year. It was ironic that a man who was unable to touch people for fear of knowing way too much about them was a tattoo artist. Thing was, I excelled at it, and I had to wear gloves when I did my job, so it worked. I loved what I did.

With a sigh, I pulled on the thin leather gloves I was rarely without, flipped off the light, and left the bathroom. I stopped short when I saw her leaning against my closed door.

"What are you doing in here?" I asked warily. Fuck, she looked good. Deep red, off-the-shoulder sweater, loose black skirt that was too goddamn short, matching red Chucks, and a gold chain belt that rested over her hips. That dark hair rippled over her shoulders, making my fingers curl, and I wanted to fist it something fierce.

"Do I need to spell it out?" she asked bravely, but the nervous way she nibbled on her lower lip again gave away her uncertainty. It was her tell, whether she realized it or not.

"Jazzy, I can't." I gave up pretense and dropped my head in defeat. I fell against the wall for support.

"Why not? Can't you leave those gloves on? I overheard Angel talking to Hawk, and they said something about as long as you don't actually touch me with your hands?" The tiny bit of hope in her tone before she wet her lips was weakening my resolve.

"You know it's more than that. Your brother," I started.

"He doesn't need to know everything I do," she said in exasperation as she took a step closer.

"No, but he's now *my* brother. I can't lie to my brothers."

"Then just don't let him find out until we find a good way to tell him," she said as she stopped in front of me.

"Shit, Jazzy," I groaned as she cupped my length through my jeans. I'd been hard since I laid eyes on her; with her stroking me, I was fucking ready to explode. Precum was leaking out and soaking my boxer briefs, but I had no control.

"I'm not good enough for you, baby." I tried again.

Still trying to maintain my stoic resolve, I kept my eyes screwed shut. The heat of her breath caressed my neck before her lips teased the skin, and I weakened.

"Fuck me, Nico," she whispered against my lips before she teased the seam with her tongue.

At that, I was done. My hands gripped her ass, pulling her body in close to grind against her. My mouth ravished hers in a kiss that was more a battle. A mimicry of what I wanted to do to her pussy.

Soft moans and pants filled the room as I lifted her and she wrapped her legs around my hips. Still we stroked and swirled our tongues until I set her on the edge of the bed and broke loose to nuzzle against her neck. Her head fell to the side, granting me open access to pull her skin into my mouth, leaving it marked.

This time I wasn't just lifting her skirt. I stood upright as I shrugged out of my cut.

"Take it off." I motioned to her clothes as I hung the cut on a peg. As she slowly raised the sweater, I gripped my T-shirt at the back and ripped it over my head. Her rapid inhale as I dropped it to the floor had me casting her a glance.

Her appreciative perusal of my body as I dropped my jeans had me smirking. In one move, I kicked off my boots and shed the last few items of my clothes.

"Nico," she said in awe, and my abdomen rippled at her touch. She fingered the stone carving on the silver chain that rested on my chest. For a brief moment, I tensed. Then she released it, and her soft fingertips skimmed over my overheated skin. I relaxed.

"This is new," she whispered as she traced over the tattoo on my side. "A lot of this is new, huh?"

I gave a noncommittal grunt and opened my drawer to pull out a condom that I dropped on the bed. "Move up," I said shortly and watched appreciatively as she scooted her now nude body up the bed and rested her head on my pillow.

"Goddamn, you're more beautiful than I could've imagined," I murmured as I trailed a gloved hand up her calf. Then I climbed up between her legs and kneeled as if I was worshipping at the altar of her body.

Reverently, I trailed my hands up the outside of her golden tanned legs. Then I traced the tan line at her groin, comparing the lighter skin where her bikini must've been. Oh, to have been the sunlight that warmed her skin... damn.

Slowly, I explored every inch as she squirmed and panted,

wishing I could feel the softness with my fingertips. When I returned to the apex of her legs, I circled my gloved thumb over her clit. The corner of my mouth kicked up at her whimper.

Unable to wait another second, I dropped my mouth to her pussy, slipping my tongue through the folds to gather the dewy arousal that had begun to coat her inner thighs. A year hadn't diminished my memory of her taste. She was perfect—so sweet.

"Oh God," she whimpered as she tried to pull away from my mouth but then pushed back into me. I ignored the hazy visions that flickered at the back of my consciousness as I laved her slit and circled her clit. My shoulders supported her legs, and I gripped her thighs to keep her in place as I continued eating her like a man starved as she came.

"Not God," I said as I pressed a kiss to her inner thigh. "Chains."

"And you said you weren't good enough for me?" she breathlessly asked.

"Honey, I'll never be good enough for you, but I'll be bad all night long," I murmured against her warm skin. Laughter burst from her beautiful lips.

Teasingly slow, I worked my way up, trailing kisses as I went. I paused only long enough to roll the condom down my length. Then resting on my elbows, I notched myself at her entrance.

"Show me how bad," she said as she dug her nails into my ass and rose up to meet me.

One tilt of my hips, and I was seated deep inside her tight heat. Her nails dug into my skin, and she gasped. Fuck, no one had ever felt like they were made for me the way she was. Only the second time I'd been balls deep in her, and I knew there'd never be another like her.

With a whimper, she wiggled under me, begging me to move. Happily, I obliged. Each stroke into her tight sheath had me unraveling a little more. Afraid I'd blow my load like a teenage boy, I flipped her legs over my shoulders and circled that tight bundle of nerves. The faster I worked her over, the faster her soft little noises came.

Fingers clawing into the bedding, she began to pant and her muscles went rigid. Still, I moved at a steady pace as I fought this ending too soon.

When she whined and panted as her body went taut, I pulled out and fused my mouth to her pulsing pussy. I sucked on her clit and slipped my tongue in her sopping wet cunt to keep working her until she thrashed at the sensation overload and yanked at my hair.

Once the pulsing subsided, I gave her no mercy. I flipped her over, ass in the air, and pushed her chest into the pillows. "Hang on," I whispered in her ear in warning, and she whimpered.

Her pretty pink pussy glistened in the dim light of the room, and I trailed two fingers through her slippery slit, then rubbed her arousal into the leather. Unable to wait any longer, I drove my cock hard into her core and commenced fucking our brains out.

I smacked the perfect globe of her ass with my hand, reveling in the sound of the leather hitting her flesh.

"Harder," she urged. Surprised, my rhythm faltered for a moment before I grinned wickedly. My hand met her ass cheek again, and she tightened around my thick cock with a gasp. The red it left on her golden flesh had me so turned on, I knew I'd be coming soon.

"I'm going to come in this pussy," I ground out as I rammed my cock deep and held her hips in a bruising grip.

"Yes," she hissed as I continued to thrust—only faltering as that familiar feeling crept up my spine. "Don't stop."

"Not on your life," I said through gritted teeth as my balls tightened and I blew so hard in the condom, it wouldn't have surprised me if it broke. To amplify the utter goddamn bliss, she came again. Between my dick pulsing and her pussy squeezing, my eyes fucking crossed.

We both fell to the bed, me rolling off to the side so I didn't crush her. The room echoed with our heavy breathing as we fought to come back to earth. I honest-to-God didn't know what to say. My mind was completely scrambled.

"Holy shit," she whispered between gasps.

An incredulous laugh escaped me, and I pulled her closer. "You can say that again," I murmured into her sweaty neck before running my tongue up the side to taste her salty skin. Knowing I'd made her that way had my chest expanding.

"Now what?" she asked, still out of breath.

"Now we get cleaned up and get out there before anyone realizes we're gone." I intentionally misunderstood her question, because I wasn't ready to analyze the magnitude of my feelings for her. For the past year, I'd avoided her the best I could, but now all bets were off, and I wasn't sure how to handle that. Especially being newly patched and her brother being one of my patched brothers.

I crawled out of bed and walked to the bathroom on shaking legs. Once the water heated, I brought her a warm washcloth. She wiped her face and then the rest of her perfect body as I pulled my clothes on. My cut was last on, and I gave it a proud once-over, then slipped my arms through and shrugged it up to settle it on my shoulders.

"I'll go out first. You wait a bit, then make sure the coast is clear before you step out of here."

She nodded, but I could see the worry shadowing her honey-and-chocolate gaze. I leaned down and pressed a kiss to her lips that was slow but sensual before breaking apart.

"Thanks, babe. That was amazing," I said with a grin before drinking her in one last time.

42

She gave a half-smile and cocked a brow. "You're damn straight it was."

With one last glance at her beautiful profile as she dressed, I quietly stepped into the hall. I needed to find a way to talk to Angel ASAP.

As I got to the end of the hall, a firm hand dropped on my shoulder and pulled me around. Instantly, I drew back, ready to deck whoever had grabbed me.

"Easy!" Ghost demanded. I sighed in relief but gave him a glare.

"What the fuck, Ghost? You need to quit doing that. One of these days, a brother is gonna deck you, and it won't be their fault," I said with a chuckle.

Except he didn't laugh.

My smile faltered, and I looked at him in confusion.

"What the fuck are you doing?" he asked with his nostrils flaring.

I gave him a wary smile. "Celebrating. What are you doing?"

Out of nowhere, he double-fisted me into the wall, knocking the goddamn wind out of me. "This isn't funny! Are you trying to lose your patch the first day? Or do you have a death wish maybe?"

"What are you talking about?" I asked as I gasped for breath. I was getting frustrated, but at the back of my mind, I knew.

"Look, I know about last year when you first got home. I never said anything because it seemed like a one and done. You were one helluva prospect and kept your nose out of trouble, but you get patched and you're back at it like that patch on your back makes you invincible?" He looked incredulous as he gave me one last push into the wall and stepped back.

"Are you talking about Jasmine? Because—" I started, but he cut me off.

"Angel will *kill* you. And that's after Venom strips you of that patch you worked so hard for. You do *not* fuck with ol' ladies, sisters—or mothers, for that matter. Especially Angel's sister, fuck! He's so goddamn protective of her, it's not funny. If you know what's good for you and you want to remain a Royal Bastard, I suggest you never touch her again," he said as he raked a hand through his hair.

"But I—"

"No. No buts. I'm serious, brother."

Frustrated, I planned to try to talk to Angel, but then I worried. What if Ghost was right and he wouldn't hear me out? I'd lose Jasmine *and* my family, because if what Ghost said was true, Angel would make sure I never saw her again. Not that I was such a pussy that I wouldn't survive, but I wouldn't want to. Unless someone had grown up like I had, then been a part of something like the Royal Bastards, they wouldn't understand.

Ghost slapped a hand to my shoulder and steered me out into the common area. Cheers went up from my brothers and the brothers from visiting chapters. The alcohol had really been flowing, and it was evident by the laughter, noise level, and behavior of everyone there.

Unbidden, a grin lifted my lips. I'd straighten everything out later. Tonight was a night to celebrate.

"Chains! Our newest brother!" Phoenix shouted with a huge grin as he raised his glass to me.

They shoved me into a chair at the center of the room as I laughed. They all started chanting, and I gazed around the room with a confused laugh. Then it dawned on me they were chanting "Bastards" broken into two beats. Laughing, they ran in a drunken circle around me, wrapping me to the chair with ribbon I could easily break out of but didn't because I figured it was part of my initiation. If they wanted to "tie me up" and pour more alcohol on me, so be it. I'd survived the initiation line, so I'd survive one more liquor bath.

Then Cookie came sauntering through the crowd as it parted for her. Everyone was whooping. She gave me a saucy grin, and mine faltered a little when I saw she wore nothing but a skimpy thong. "What's going on?" I asked, unease settling over me.

After dancing around me to a sultry tune someone popped on over the speakers, she dropped to her knees. To hoots of encouragement, she made a production of removing my belt and unzipping my jeans. I tried to pull away, but the ribbon I thought I could break didn't budge.

"Cookie, what are you doing? Don't do that," I stuttered as soon as I realized what she was up to. Everyone cheered and laughed as she pulled out my cock and started stroking it. I jerked on the binding again.

Shit.

"Damn, boy, didn't know you carried a cannon in your pants," Kicker chortled. Any other time I would've been proud and joked with him. Hell, if it wasn't for Jasmine, I might've humored them and let Cookie suck my cock in front of them. Except things were different now—because of Jasmine.

Despite my protests, everyone kept cheering and chanting.

Ghost wasn't cheering, and I soon learned why. Evidently Jasmine had been making her way along the wall to get around everyone but had frozen when she hit a break in the crowd. That's when our eyes met. Her whiskey gaze darkened to mocha as her eyes became glossy, and I struggled against the stupid fucking ribbons.

Angel must've noticed his sister's horror at what she was seeing, because he pushed his way to her, blocking her from my view, and guided her out of the building. As I pulled at the bindings, what Ghost said kept poking at me. Jasmine deserving better than me. Losing my patch. Losing my family. Losing Jasmine anyway. I swallowed hard and closed my eyes.

"Enough!" I roared and the laughter fizzled out. Cookie backed off. "Take this shit off. Y'all are fucked up. You wanna drown me in whiskey, go ahead, but this is too fucking far," I said. Someone sliced through the ribbon, and it fell. As I stood and straightened myself, the ribbon fluttered to my feet.

"Sorry, brother, we were just having fun, and well, we uh…" Kicker muttered.

"Cookie's done that for you before, we just figured it would be funny," E said as he shoved his hands in his pocket.

"Yeah, well that's on my terms, fuckers," I grumbled as I stormed off to my room.

My chest burned and ached as if someone had stabbed me in the heart, but I blocked everything out. Wishing it had been Jasmine kneeling at my feet, I knew the rest of my life would be spent pretending it was her.

And a piece of me died.

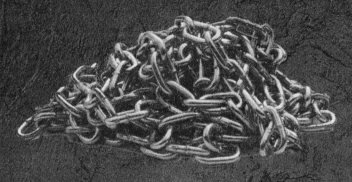

FOUR

Chains

"WOLF TOTEM"—THE HU (FEAT. PAPA ROACH)

Two years later…

"**J**asmine, just put on some boots, grab your jacket, and let's go," I said as everyone filed out of the clubhouse.

Everyone was preparing to head to the hospital to see Voodoo's new kid. It was a beautiful day, which was unusual for Iowa in the winter, so we were riding. Jasmine refused to go when Angel told her she wasn't driving herself.

"I'm not riding on the back of your damn bike. Why don't you have Cookie go with you?" she snidely replied. That comment sent my temper flaring, but I deserved it. Little did she know, chicks *never* rode on the back of my bike.

Since the day I'd been patched and she saw me tied to that fucking chair, she hadn't come to the clubhouse unless she absolutely had to—like now. She was staying with us because her father was a piece of shit and put her in danger because of his fucking gambling debt.

Like a coward, I'd used that night and what Ghost had said as my excuse to stay away from her for the last couple of years. Every fucking day I told myself I was doing the right thing. The truth was, I knew goddamn good and well she deserved better than me. Didn't mean I liked it.

"So now you're telling me you don't want to see the baby when five minutes ago, you were prepared to drive there. Do I have that right?" My arms folded over my chest as I cocked a brow, calling her on her shit.

"If it means I have to ride with you, then that's exactly what I'm saying." Her jaw ticked, and anger blazed in her eyes.

She hated me, and I shouldn't be hurt, because I'd cultivated that hatred to keep her at arm's length. Yet, her contempt for me cut me to the bone. Being without her was like severing one of my own limbs.

"Fine. Suit yourself," I said before I stormed out of her room and down the hall. She could stay with her nephew and Lynda. The prospects were there to watch over her, and Kicker was watching TV on the couch. He wasn't feeling good and didn't want to be around the baby. So he was staying behind to watch over Lynda and Trace.

Shit quickly went downhill. At the hospital, Voodoo's grandmother, who had come up with Jameson and Sadie, had a vision that had us all worried.

When Angel couldn't get Lynda to answer, Angel, Korrie, Raptor, Goob, Ghost, and I headed back to the clubhouse to find Angel's son, Jasmine, and Lynda gone. One prospect was dead, the other unconscious behind the bar.

As Angel slammed through the clubhouse, I went straight to Jasmine's room. In my mind, Angel had to have missed her. She had to have hidden herself and the others.

"Jasmine?" I called as I peeked in the room and the bathroom.

When I realized she wasn't there, panic began to set in—I was a mess.

Angel passed me in the hall after he checked all the rooms. At that moment, the only room that had mattered to me was the empty one Jasmine had been using. In shock, I fell back against the wall.

Kicker walked in on utter turmoil. "What the fuck is going on?"

"They're gone," I said, my reply hollow.

The events that transpired after that day would scar Jasmine so deeply, I feared she'd never recover.

If it was the last thing I did, I would avenge her.

PART II

FIVE

Jasmine

"WHERE ANGELS FEAR TO TREAD"—BRYAN ADAMS

Two months later…

"**J**asmine!"

I startled, and my laptop fell to the couch beside me. Blinking rapidly to clear the horrible memories that played through my mind on repeat, I finally focused on my brother. Crouched in front of me, he pleaded with his worry-filled eyes for something I couldn't grasp.

"I think we need to get you to a therapist," he softly said.

Panic welled up within until it was nearly choking me. "No!"

"Jazzy, what you went through was—"

"Stop!" I cut him off. The trembling started at my head and worked down my body. It was bad enough that the memories wouldn't get out of my head. The thought of having to voice what happened to me to a total stranger made nausea churn in my stomach.

Defeat made his shoulders slump, but on that I couldn't give in. Somehow, I'd find a way to work through it myself.

Or I'd die trying.

SIX

Chains

"UNDER YOUR SCARS"—GODSMACK

December…

Without flinching, I pulled the trigger, and the scumbag dropped to the dirty floor of the gas station bathroom. Blood immediately began to pool around his crumpled form. I wanted to empty my clip into his worthless body, but I needed to leave.

"Fuck you," I muttered over him. If I didn't care about leaving DNA behind, I would've spat on his corpse. Maybe even shit on his crappy ass scorpion patch.

Not a soul saw me walk out of the bathroom, get on my bike, light a cigarette, and pull out of the isolated lot. The attendant had been too busy watching porn on his phone, cameras were non-functioning, and there hadn't been a car for miles.

If I'd been in a cage, I might've run over the asshole's bike too.

The winter wind whipped at my leather jacket and bit at the exposed skin of my head, but I barely noticed it. There wasn't much

I cared about anymore. The one person I cared about more than anything was broken and wanted nothing to do with me.

After we found out some of the shitbags responsible for kidnapping Trace, Jasmine, and Lynda were still alive, I made it my personal mission to take them all out. It was the least I could do for her.

The two-hour ride home was black and cold—like my heart. When I parked my bike, I could barely feel my fingers.

I went to my room through the back door so I didn't need to socialize. Then I dropped to my bed and stared at the white ceiling.

There was a knock, and I sighed.

"Yeah?" I said with absolutely no emotion.

The door opened enough for Raptor to stick his head in. "Venom wants to know if there were any issues."

"Nope."

"Cool." He moved to leave, then paused. "Bro, you okay?"

"Peachy."

If I couldn't hear his breathing, I might've thought he left. Finally, he sighed. "If you need to talk, you know I'm here."

"Yep."

"Venom has the prospect taking the ol' ladies to the mall to go shopping tomorrow morning. He wants one of us to go along. You available?"

"Who all's going?"

"Loralei, Korrie, Kira, and Jasmine, far as I know," he replied. At her name, I inwardly flinched.

"Can't. Sorry."

He studied me for a moment. When I gave him nothing, he nodded. "No problem. Jigsaw is here, and he said he'd go."

I grunted, and he left.

Did I want to go? Yeah, because everything in me screamed to protect Jasmine from the world. If only I had demanded she go to the hospital with me on my bike. Maybe if I'd risked more, she wouldn't have been taken. Except I couldn't live by "if only."

Being in close proximity with Jasmine had been torture. Now it was worse. More than I could handle, because I wanted to hold her, and that was dangerous. She didn't want anything to do with me, and I told myself that was for the best.

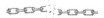

"Here you go," the prospect said as he placed the third beer in front of me. Not in a mood to talk, I gave him a lift of my chin in thanks. Catching on quickly, he moved down the bar to wipe it off and inventory the booze.

"What the fuck has been up your ass?" Angel asked as he took the seat next to me. He signaled the prospect to bring him what I was drinking.

No way could I tell anyone what was going on with me. Especially not him, though I suspected he had an idea. He'd cornered me after the rescue, but I remained tight-lipped.

He had initially brought Jasmine to stay at the clubhouse when we found out she was in danger due to their father's gambling problem. Their father was dying of cancer, and his bookies told him dying wouldn't forgive his debt, that they'd take Jasmine as payment. We figured they thought it would be incentive for him to pay the money. Except they underestimated the cold stone he had for a heart.

Hell, for all we know, he offered her up. Fucker. If I could get away with taking his ass out, I would. Because in my opinion he was as responsible as the Bloody Scorpions. If he hadn't been such a dickwad, Jasmine would've been safe at her house and not staying at the clubhouse. Though I knew she'd done her best to protect Angel's son.

If my brothers thought Angel wanted to kill his father and

the fuckers he owed money to, they would be shocked at the train of my thoughts. Torture wouldn't be nearly enough. I wanted to peel their skin off and rip their hearts out while they were alive to squeeze the last beat from the bloody organ.

"I'm good," I lied. Seeing it for what it was, he snorted.

Since Jasmine had come to stay at the clubhouse, I'd been crawling out of my skin. After what had happened to her, I'd been in agony. Helpless to do a damn thing, I kept my distance, though my body fought it with every molecule in my makeup.

The need to claim her burned in my veins. No matter how pussy-whipped it made me sound, I knew she was the half I needed to be whole. Without her I was a shell—a broken man. Yet, her brother was one of my best friends. A friend whose secrets I'd seen. Secrets that would probably horrify him if he found out I knew.

Not that I'd tell anyone—they weren't my stories to tell. I kept everything to myself. I may be a lot of things, but I was a goddamn loyal brother.

When Jasmine had been abducted along with Angel's son and Lynda, I wanted to kill the people responsible with my bare hands. I'd been robbed of the satisfaction that night. It left me feeling like a junkyard dog at the end of its chain, snapping its teeth in frustration. The things she had endured I could only imagine.

I wasn't sure which was worse, the things I imagined or what actually happened.

Though he'd never admit it, I think that's why Venom took pity on me and assigned me to their assassination.

Watching Jasmine decline was fucking killing me. Anger seeped from my pores, mixing with the helplessness I was drowning in. Fury burned within me every fucking minute of every fucking day. It was barely after lunchtime, and I was halfway to drunk because I couldn't function most of the time. I'd need to sober up by Monday afternoon for work, and that's all that mattered.

"Angel!" Venom yelled as he hauled ass into the common area and headed to the door. "Jigsaw's coming in, and we need you! It's Roscoe. Prospect! Get the gate!"

The prospect was over the bar and out the door before I could blink. Angel immediately left his beer sitting and raced after our president.

My heart stopped. Roscoe and Jigsaw had taken the women shopping. Jasmine had gone along at Korrie's urging. If Roscoe was hurt, how were the women?

Jerking on a pair of thin leather gloves, I scrambled off my seat and ran after them. I burst outside with my brothers. The prospect was rolling the gate open. Jigsaw came flying in and screeched to a halt.

"Sorry about the mess, bossman," Jigsaw said to Venom with a smirk, and I swear to fuck my jaw almost hit the ground. Loralei had bailed out of the back seat and into Venom's arms. Blood was splattered on the leg of her jeans. Stunned silence briefly ensued before Venom demanded to know who the fuck was in the back seat with Loralei. Whoever the guy was, he was fucking eviscerated—I'm talking guts lying on the floor of the SUV.

Jigsaw was nuts. Certifiably insane, if a man's innards splattered all over the floor was "a mess."

The rest of what he said was mere background noise as I ripped the door open and carefully lifted Jasmine out of the front seat. I brought her to the front of the vehicle, set her on her feet, and cradled her pale face in my gloved hands.

"Jazz, look at me." My words were spoken softly and as calmly as I could manage. She didn't respond well to chaos and yelling. Hell, she didn't respond well to anything anymore, and it was shredding my soul.

Reluctantly, her haunted amber eyes rose to lock with mine. The lighter gold furrow around her pupil had almost disappeared, while the brown ring around the outside seemed near black. The fiery burst of striations seemed to glow as tears filled them.

"Oh, baby," I whispered before I wrapped my arms around her and pressed her cheek to my chest. Her body shuddered as her hands desperately clutched the side of my shirt under my cut.

For the last three years, Jasmine and I had foolishly danced around each other, both of us denying the fact that we felt like half our soul was missing. I'd tried to drown the pain in booze, drugs, work, and women, but it didn't work. It stopped doing jack shit for me and left me a vacant husk of myself.

Every time Angel had bitched about some asshole she was dating, I wanted to go berserk and destroy anything in my path. The thought of another man's hands on what was mine made me insanely violent and full of rage. Yet, I couldn't have her.

With Jasmine living under the same roof as me, I tried my best to avoid her. But I was a moth, and she was the flame. Yet, my sad truth was that I'd willingly burn for her if she'd let me.

"I'm so tired of being scared, Nico," she said with a sad tremor to her melodic voice. "I can barely function. I want my life back." She cried into my chest. Not having a good response, my eyes fell shut as I held her in silence.

When I opened them, I found Venom's gaze locked on me. Shit.

But that wasn't the worst of it. Angel was staring at me with the muscle in his jaw jumping.

Fucking hell.

I carefully got Jasmine situated with the women when Venom called for all hands on deck with Roscoe.

Roscoe "woke up" a few hours later, but he refused to tell anyone exactly how he'd healed himself or what his story was. Voodoo hadn't

gotten anything from throwing his bones, and I wasn't touching the guy again. Whatever the fuck he was, had some serious energy. So much so that it damn near blinded me to see it. That was more than some guy with a gift.

When I left the infirmary, I sensed Angel right as he spun me around and pinned me to the wall.

Shit, shit, shit.

"Stay the fuck away from my sister," he ground out through clenched teeth.

Tired of everything, I shoved him off. I had a good couple inches and maybe fifty pounds on him. Didn't mean I wanted to fight him, but I was tired of him calling all the shots.

"Fuck off. I was only getting her out of the SUV that had a dead guy right behind her. No one else had made a move to get her out and make sure she was okay. Maybe you should be grateful that I was looking out for your sister," I snarled before walking away.

I went straight to my room and fell facedown on the bed with a groan. It didn't matter how many times I experienced my "gift," it always shook me and gave me a headache. This time it had made my head pound like it was going to explode. The run-in with Angel hadn't helped.

My mind wandered, and I must've dozed off, because I was dreaming of my mother. I was a little boy, and we were sitting by a fire in the woods as she chanted and sang. The language was a mystery to me, but it spoke to my soul. Guttural and yet melodic, she sang a song that I didn't understand, yet I was mesmerized.

"Nico," she said once she'd finished.

"Yes, Momma?" I asked.

Her soft hand caressed my cheek. "When you get older, there will be things you don't understand. Things will happen that might scare you, but you must remember what you have is a gift. Your father had this gift, and it has been passed down to you."

"Where is my father?" I asked her.

Pained, her gaze held mine. "He is with Tengri in the Eternal Blue Heaven," she said with a sad smile.

My mother was half Mongolian, and she had taught me some of her beliefs, so I knew Tengri was the god of the sky. She fingered the howling wolf-shaped stone around her neck, then she raised it to her lips and pressed a reverent kiss to the obsidian stone. Slowly, she lifted it from around her neck and draped it around mine.

The chain was long, and the pendant hit down to my belly. The metal was warm against my skin, and I lifted the stone to look at the intricately carved wolf. When my mother spoke, I lifted my gaze to hers.

"I have to make one of the hardest decisions of my life, but if it means you live, I would do it a hundred times over. I love you so much, Nico. You are my heart." A fat tear escaped her eye and trailed down her cheek.

"Momma? Don't cry. I'm going to grow up big and strong. I'll protect you, and you'll never have to make choices that make you sad," I bravely stated. My words brought out a laugh carried on a choked sob. She glanced over her shoulder, and I peeked around her to see what she was looking at.

In the dark shadows outside of the light of the fire, glowing spots dotted the darkness. A frown wrinkled my brow. "It's time." A growling voice echoed from the inky night. My heart started to race, but I tried to seem brave as I stood.

"Go away!" I yelled. My mother gripped my arm as a growl rose from the shadows followed by a snapping sound.

"Nico!" she whispered in admonishment, and I didn't like the fear in her eyes.

She stood, and I followed, but she placed a hand on my shoulder. "Stay near the safety of the fire. When morning comes, take your backpack and walk toward the sun. Don't forget your bag, and don't stop until you reach the town."

Confusion marred my brow. "But I want to stay with you," I argued.

Her bottom lip trembled, and the corners of her mouth turned down. "I know," she said with a sigh. "Wait here. Promise me. Until the sun rises."

"But—" I started.

"Promise me, Nico!" she interrupted. The urgency of her tone made me want to please her, so I nodded. Relief softened her face, and she pressed a kiss to my brow.

"You can't help you weren't born a wolf but like your father. It was my choice to disobey the laws of my people. If I have to do this to keep you alive, I will do it. I love you to the moon and back. When you hear the wolf's lonely cry at night, know that I'm watching over you," she said before she wrapped me in a tight embrace. Then she reluctantly dropped her arms and turned away.

As she stepped into the shadows, I thought I saw her shed her dress, but as soon as I blinked, she was gone—swallowed up by the shadows.

"Momma?" I called as I made a full circle, searching the dark night for where she went. "Momma!" I shouted until I was hoarse and my tears had dried on my face. Then I curled up on the sleeping bag my mother had laid out when I thought we were having an adventure.

As I drifted off to sleep, a wolf howled. Instead of being frightened, peace settled within me, and I slept.

With a jolt, I awoke. Still wanting to shout for my mother twenty years later, I bit my tongue and sat up. Hand shaking, I speared it through the longer dark hair on the top of my head. Then I rasped over the shorn sides several times to shake off the dream that was really a memory.

When I joined the army and became special forces, I used the technology at my disposal to look up my mother. I knew she'd been half Mongolian, because she'd told me, but I hadn't known she traced back to Genghis Khan. I'd never seen my mother again, and there was no record of her death. She'd simply dropped off the face of the earth that night.

Often over the years, I would think I saw a wolf hidden in the trees or at the edge of the park. Always, before I could search for it, the thing would be gone when I blinked.

I would dream of the wolf with a notch in its ear. At first, I was afraid. I'd been placed in foster care in a small town outside of Des Moines, Iowa, and there were wooded areas everywhere. I'd told my first foster mother about the wolf, and she'd laughed at me, telling me there were no wolves in Iowa.

When I'd gotten older, I had researched. There were wolves in Minnesota and people had claimed to have spotted them on rare occasion in Iowa. One had been shot in Northwestern Iowa, or so people believed. Nothing definitive though, because I couldn't find anything that said the wolf's body was found afterward.

It was another thing I'd never gotten an answer to—along with how I could see people's memories if I touched them. Occasionally, I was able to get readings from objects as well, but those visions were usually muted and not as mind-blowing as they were when I touched a human.

Never in a million years had I imagined finding a woman that was my soulmate.

Yet, because of my "gift" I was damned—never able to have her. Never good enough for her.

SEVEN

Jasmine

"LET ME HEAL"—SEETHER

Four Months Later....

Locked in my head, I sat in a dark corner of the clubhouse. Happy to be invisible, I placed my AirPods in my ears, closed my eyes, and tried to get lost in my head. If I didn't have something to occupy my mind, I relived every blow, each violation.

The website I was supposed to be working on sat untouched on the computer screen in front of me. Freelance graphic design and website management was the only thing keeping me from getting my car repossessed. Though I rarely drove it, so I didn't know why I bothered.

The week my father went to Angel with the news I'd been threatened, Angel and his brothers brought me to the clubhouse. I'd been furious. My vacation to warmer climates had been cancelled. The Royal Bastards were afraid I wouldn't be safe traveling on my own. God forbid someone go with me on my vacation so I could still get away.

If I hadn't been here… but I couldn't go there. That led me down a rabbit hole of mental torture that I'd rather forget about.

Since moving into the clubhouse completely, I hadn't really worked. I'd been fired when I didn't show up for work the week after my vacation was supposed to have ended.

Not like I could tell them I'd been abducted. My brother's club was shrouded in secrets and what I believed was some bad shit. I probably could've fought my termination, but that would've meant admitting something horrible had happened to me—and I wasn't ready for people to know that. This was bad enough.

The table rocked, and my eyes popped open.

"Hey, Jazz," Korrie said as she slipped into the booth across from me.

Pulling one headphone from my ear, I pasted a fake smile on my face. "What's up?"

Over the last several months, I'd gotten pretty good at acting normal. It was better than seeing the pity in everyone's eyes when they looked at me. If I pretended I was better, no one dug any deeper, and they took my smiles at face value. Sometimes I thought that was easier for them than addressing the uncomfortable subject of what had happened to me.

I was okay with that because it wasn't something I wanted to talk about either.

"The girls convinced the guys to finally let us get out on the town. We're all heading out to go dancing in Des Moines. I was hoping you'd come with," she said with a pleading gaze as she chewed on her bottom lip. The thought of leaving the safety of the clubhouse compound had me breaking out in a cold sweat.

"Brought you this to butter you up," she said as she slid what appeared to be my favorite drink across the table. A huge grin split her face, and I couldn't help but laugh. What she didn't know was that I'd already had one.

With a shake of my head, I reached for the glass and took a sip. "I don't know," I hedged before taking another drink. The vodka burned a little, telling me the prospect had made it strong.

"What do you say? I think it would be good for you to get out," she said. Slowly, she reached across the table and gave my hand a firm squeeze. "I miss hanging out with you."

Another drink, and the alcohol started to do its job. A warmth that left me slightly numb washed over me. That was what I attributed my bravery to—alcohol.

"Okay," I reluctantly agreed.

Dammit.

I was drunk off my ass, but it was fucking amazing. Nothing fazed me. No bad thoughts broke through the alcohol-induced cloud I was floating on. Laughter bubbled up as I danced on the crowded dance floor with a pregnant Korrie, Kira, and Loralei.

Sweating from being out there through a good five songs, I raised my thick hair up off my neck as we moved to the beat.

Firm hands encircled my hips, and panic hit for a split second before I wobbled slightly as I looked over my shoulder. The guy gave a me a white-toothed smile. My gaze appraised him, taking in his pressed, button-up short-sleeved shirt, expensive jeans, and Vans. He was the complete opposite of the bikers I was living with and the ones that had—Nope. Not going there.

"Hey. Mind if I join you ladies?" he said in my ear to be heard over the heavy bass pouring from the speakers.

"It's a free country," I said with a silly grin, ignoring the girls trying to get my attention. I twisted to face the guy with perfectly messy sandy-blond hair and blue-green eyes. He was exactly the opposite of the one I couldn't get out of my head. My arms looped around his neck as the song switched to a slower one.

The guy held my waist as we moved slowly around the dance floor. As we swayed to the sensuous tune, we passed Angel and Korrie. I ignored my brother, who watched me like a hawk. Then Voodoo and Kira danced close to us, and they both gave me a questioning gaze. I appreciated everyone wanting to make sure I was okay, but for one night I simply wanted to forget.

The song was drawing to an end when we passed by the area where the remainder of our group was gathered. My gaze locked on the dark eyes that owned me.

Nico.

Anger flashed in his dark depths, and a shudder ran through me. The song ended, and I thanked the guy. To his disappointment, I left him on the dance floor and walked toward the table where my friends and family sat.

Nico's jaw ticked, but I intentionally ignored him as I reached for my glass. After I emptied it, I shook it. "I'm getting another. Anyone else want one?"

They all declined.

Pushing my way to the bar, I got a refill and shoved the tip in the jar. As I spun to return, the guy from the dance floor was there. "You ran off before I could get your name," he said.

A sultry smile curled my lips. "Jay," I said with a laugh, thinking of the night three years ago.

"Jay," he repeated with a cocky grin. "Nice to meet you."

Before I could reply, my brother was at my side. "Beat it," he said. The guy's eyes widened comically before he gave me a sad smile and left.

Irritated, I rounded on my brother with anger burning bright within me. "That was fucked-up."

"We're leaving. Korrie's had enough." My brother had a protective arm curled around Korrie.

I quickly looked to my sister-in-law and saw that she was indeed pale. The thing was, I didn't want to leave yet. For the first time in forever, I wasn't thinking about the dark shit.

"Is it okay if I stay with the others? I won't try to lose them or leave with anyone else," I said, though it was with mentally crossed fingers.

Angel ran a frustrated hand through his dark hair, but Korrie grabbed his other arm. A silent exchange ensued, and he finally looked at me. I could tell he wasn't happy about it, but he nodded. "Just make sure you stay with the group."

Brightly, I nodded. "You got it," I said with a jaunty salute that had him fighting a grin as he shook his head at me.

"Be careful, sis. I love you."

"Love you too," I said, then pressed a kiss to his short beard and shooed him off. "Now go take care of my sister-in-law."

Korrie hugged me. They walked me to the group, where they said their goodbyes again and left.

As I drank from my glass, Loralei, Kira, and I danced at the edge of our table, happily singing along with the song. The guys watched us with tolerant expressions. I didn't miss the deadly glares they sent toward any guy dumb enough to look at their women in a lascivious way.

From the corner of my eye, I saw another guy bravely approach. He leaned in to be heard.

"Would you like to dance?" This one was dark-haired and reminded me a little too much of the broody asshole at the table.

Defiantly, I set my glass down and wobbled slightly as I turned back to the guy.

But before I could take a step toward the dance floor, a hand gripped my upper arm. The tingle of awareness that jolted through to my toes told me who it was without looking. Butter-soft leather against my skin made my breath catch.

With a frown, I flashed a glare behind me, trying to seem brave and more sober than I really was. Too bad it had nothing on the anger simmering in the dark-brown eyes that held mine.

The words I intended to spit at him turned to ash on my tongue.

"No" was all he said.

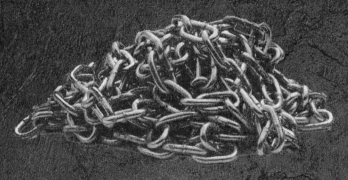

EIGHT

Chains

"NOT MEANT TO BE"—THEORY OF A DEADMAN

Man, *fuck this shit*.

"Jazz, you've had enough. Let's go." If I had to watch another man put his hands on her, I was going to lose my ever-loving mind. The second she started to walk off with the douche, I told Venom I was taking her home for Angel. He cocked a brow but didn't call me on the bullshit excuse.

We both knew Angel wouldn't have asked me to take his sister home. Venom sent Ghost and Blade with me, since we were the three who had ridden down. I wondered if he also figured Jasmine was safer with witnesses. Or was it me he was worried about? There was no way our perceptive president didn't know there was something off with me and Angel's sister.

"Who are you to tell me what to do?" she snapped as I dragged her to the exit. Thankfully, she didn't fight me too hard, because if I had to, I would've thrown her over my shoulder. We broke out into the cool spring air, and I brought her over to where the bikes were parked.

"Because you're drunk and your brother isn't here to do it. Now get on the bike."

Ghost and Blade remained silent as they sat on their bikes and pulled on their helmets and gloves.

"You're such a bastard!" she spat, and I gave her a wicked grin. The hissing kitten was better than the zombie with the fake smile she'd been for months.

"You say that like it's a bad thing."

She huffed and growled in frustration. When I handed her my helmet, she snatched it and shoved it over her hair. "I can't believe you expect me to ride your bike in this dress. Why can't I just wait and ride home with Voodoo and Kira? Or Venom and Loralei?"

My gaze traveled over the figure-hugging black dress with little threads of gold that reminded me of her eyes. I raked my teeth over my bottom lip. The anger was dissipating now that we were in the clear night air and away from the assholes that had been panting around her all night. The problem was, it was being replaced with something more dangerous.

"I'm not letting you go back in there without me. So unless you want me getting arrested for assault tonight, I suggest you hitch up that skirt and get your sweet ass on the fucking bike." I'd leaned in close so I could keep the conversation between the two of us. "You got me?"

Her lips parted in surprise, and I could see the pulse in her neck pounding as she speechlessly blinked up at me. Satisfied that I'd gotten through to her, I mounted up and shot her an expectant glance.

The kitten was spitting mad, but she was smart and did as I said. My brothers started their bikes, and I followed suit. Kickstands up, we were ready. Before we pulled out, I reached back and gripped her ass to pull her tight to my back.

"Hang on," I told her as we rolled out. She huffed against the back of my neck but did as she was told. When she pressed her long legs around my hips, I momentarily regretted my decision.

The ride back to the compound was damn near perfect. Cool, but not cold. The rumble of the three bikes and warmth of her body wrapped around me was damn near heaven—or as close as I'd probably ever get. If she was back there under other circumstances, it would've been better, but beggars couldn't be choosers.

Without thinking, I rested my hand on the side of her thigh as we cruised and the miles slipped away in the wind. At first she tensed at my touch, then she melted against my back and her legs hugged me tighter. My grip tightened before I slid my palm down to curl around her calf. I rode like that until we slowed down as we approached the compound.

Once we were parked and the bike ticked as it cooled, I reached back to help her off. She stumbled a bit when her feet hit the ground, and I steadied her as I got off my bike. Ghost and Blade shot me a concerned and warning glance but went inside.

Gloved hand at her elbow, I guided her around the building, punched in the code, and we entered the side door. A sense of déjà vu hit me, as it was the same entrance we'd used the night we met. I shook it off and opened her door before walking her inside.

She spun, and I expected her to lash out at me again, but she pressed her lips together as her eyes raked hungrily over me. My cock cheered, and her pause at my crotch told me she noticed.

I watched as her pink tongue wet her lower lip and she moved into my space.

Defensively, I stiffened when her hands splayed on my chest over my cut. Her fingertips traced the edges of my patches. Then those whiskey-colored eyes lifted to mine.

"You should fuck me, *Chains*," she whispered in a sultry plea as her pupils dilated and she inhaled the leather under her hands.

Temptation like I'd never experienced pulled at me, but the

still glazed and slightly unfocused condition of her beautiful eyes stopped me. Sober, she wouldn't let me touch her. With her still being drunk, I knew she'd regret it in the morning.

"No."

Her gaze dropped, and her shoulders drooped. She stepped back, and I turned to go.

"Chains?" she called, and I longed to hear her say my real name again. Squeezing my eyes shut, I paused, hand reaching for the knob.

"Yeah?"

"Um, can you help me?"

Fuck. I almost made it.

Slowly, I turned to see her pointing to the zipper at the back of her dress. She refused to meet my searching gaze.

"Sure," I bit out.

Lifting her dark hair, she exposed the back of the dress to me. As my fingers gripped the zipper, I longed to trail my lips along the bared skin of her shoulder and up her neck. The faint scent of her perfume seemed to twist through me, pulling me closer.

With supreme willpower that I didn't know I was capable of, I lowered the zipper and stepped back. If I was a lesser man, I would've taken what she offered and damn the consequences, but I couldn't do that to her.

"I should've known you wouldn't want me again," she muttered.

"What?" I asked incredulous.

"Oh come on." She held the front of her dress up as she faced me. "Don't act like that's not the case. If I can't forget what happened, I can't very well expect you to."

"Jazz, this isn't the time to discuss this. You've been drinking, my head is less than clear, and my brothers are down the hall," I said as I dragged my hands down my face.

"When is the time, *Chains?*" she asked, sneering as she spoke my road name.

"I'm not sure if I'm the one that you should discuss your—" I swallowed hard. "—ordeal with."

"Ordeal? *Ordeal?* I was beaten and raped, Chains! Over and over. My brother may have been able to erase the physical damage, but he can't erase the fucking memories! I'll never forget that man's dirty hands on me—his smell, the degradation, the fear, the helplessness. That doesn't go away! Since your gift is your ability to see everything in someone's head, I can't very well expect you to want to touch me, now can I? Can I, *Chains?*" She was shrieking like a banshee by the end of it, and her hands trembled violently as her teeth chattered.

Pain ripped through me, but I didn't know what to say or do.

She nearly went to her knees, but I grabbed her and helped her to the bed. She rolled away from me and was still. Unable to leave, but not knowing what the right thing to do was, I laced my fingers at the back of my neck.

When she didn't make any attempt to finish undressing, I moved to her dresser and pulled out an old T-shirt for her to change into. My chest caved when I realized it was one of my old shirts. I had no idea how she'd ended up with it, but I imagined she grabbed it from the laundry room.

Gently, I set it in front of her.

"I don't blame you for hating me," she whispered as I crossed to the door.

My head hung, then I looked back at her, still curled up on the bed.

"I don't hate you, Jasmine. Hate's the farthest emotion from my feelings for you."

As quietly as I could, I left her room.

It was one of the worst nights' sleep I'd had in a long damn time.

The next morning, there was a knock at my door.

"Yeah?" I called out, not in the mood to talk to anyone.

"Can I come in?"

Fuck.

It was Jasmine.

NINE

Jasmine

"I GET OFF"—HALESTORM

Insanity was my plea. Logically, it could be the only reason I was actively seeking Nico out.

After I announced myself, there wasn't a peep from behind the scarred wood. It would seem he was going to ignore me. Shoulders slumped, I turned away but spun back when I heard the door open.

"What do you want?" he asked. The door was open, but his body blocked it—a nonverbal cue that I wasn't welcome in his room. It hurt, but we'd made our choice years ago.

"I wanted to know if we could talk," I said, trying my best to control the quiver in my voice.

He pulled his lips flat between his teeth before he released them on a sigh and stepped back.

Tentatively, in case he changed his mind, I walked in after a quick glance to see that I wasn't observed. Though I was a grown-ass woman, my brother was ridiculously protective. As if I was helpless. I hated it.

He closed the door and leaned against it with his muscular, inked-up arms crossed over his chest.

Hungry, my gaze trailed over him, taking in all the changes a few years had made. It didn't matter how many times I'd seen him since being forced to move into the clubhouse for my safety. Each time my hungry gaze swept over him, I noticed something new. When he wasn't looking, I devoured every detail.

Gone was the close-cropped military haircut. In its place, his inky dark hair was long on top though still shaved on the sides. Tattoos covered nearly every visible inch of him except his handsome face. It made me wonder where all that ink traveled. Where before, he'd been lean muscle, he was now bulkier. Still chiseled and beautiful though.

One thing that hadn't changed was that he was sexy as sin and my body screamed for his touch every time I was near him. Despite the hell I'd endured to keep my nephew and Lynda safe, I still wanted him. The fact that he'd never want me again cut deep.

"Well?" he asked, making me aware of how lost in him I'd gotten.

My gaze dropped, and I bit my lip. In a defensive move, I wrapped my arms protectively around myself.

"I hate my life," I admitted, unable to look him in the eye. "I hate myself." My chest ached, and I wanted to crumble to the ground and fall apart.

"What?" His arms dropped, and he moved off the door. Yet, he still kept his distance.

"There isn't a day that goes by that I don't wish he had killed me," I admitted in a whisper, barely holding on. My throat burned with the suppressed tears. Despair rained down, nearly suffocating me.

"Jazz," he said, sounding shocked. The next thing I knew, he held me in his arms, my cheek pressed to his chest.

Anger had surged so many times, mixed with the despair. I had a stupid gift that did me no good. Not that anyone knew, but sometimes I dreamed things. Things that came true.

I'd dream of buying a purse on clearance, or maybe of a friend getting a promotion, that a traffic accident would happen in front of me, meeting the man I would give my virginity to, getting my website business up and running, but did I get a heads-up that my life was about to be destroyed? No. The universe didn't see that as pertinent information I needed.

Tears ran unchecked down my face as silent sobs shook my frame. I'd been unable to sleep last night, ruminating over what he must think of me. He might not hate me, but I hated myself. Couldn't look at myself in the mirror. Had come up with a hundred different ways to end my life. Yet every time I went through the motions to stop the torment, I saw Nico's face.

Not my brother.

Not my nephew.

"I don't want to live like this anymore. I'd rather die," I cried.

"Goddamn it, Jasmine, don't you dare say that." His arms tightened around me until I was afraid he might snap my bones. His heart was pounding under my ear, and I drew strength from its rapid but steady beat. It was crazy, but with his arms around me, I was stronger.

Needy, I slipped my hands around his back and my fingers clutched that back of his shirt. Feeling grounded for the first time in weeks, I held on for dear life.

"I hated you. For what you let that girl do after you'd just been with me. But you didn't want to, did you? That was you pushing me away because you think you know what's best for both of us instead of letting me choose too. Now I'm all fucked-up, and it's a moot point, huh?"

"Jazz, let me talk to Angel. We need to get you help. You need to talk to someone about this. Let me find a way for us. Fuck, let me be there for you. These last years have been hell but losing you would kill me. You're mine, and I can't deal with this anymore. Let me be your shoulder."

Shaking my head, I pushed out of his embrace. I was so damn fucked-up. Despite needing him, I knew he deserved better than me. He thought it was the other way around, but he was so very wrong. The fucked-up shit in my head would destroy anything we tried to build. Knowing he would always see me as broken gutted me. Knowing if he touched my skin, he'd see everything that happened killed me. It was bad enough he'd seen Angel's secrets.

"It was a mistake to come here. I don't know what I was thinking," I stammered as I backed toward the door. Except I did. I knew exactly why I'd crossed the hall. My soul cried for him—needed him in a way we could never be.

"Wait, baby, don't go." His eyes pleaded with mine.

My mind warred with my soul. My heart screamed at my body. Though I knew I needed to walk out the door and stay as far away from him as possible, that part of me that was tied to him won out.

I stopped.

Like he was approaching a wounded animal, and maybe that's exactly what I was, he cautiously moved closer. With each step, my resolve melted. When he stopped in front of me, I sucked in a sharp breath.

He wet his lips and tentatively brought his hands up to touch me, then he paused. My heart crashed.

"I have an idea," he said, then went to his bathroom, and I heard a drawer open.

My brow furrowed in confusion, wondering what he was doing. When he came back, he had something black clutched in his hands.

"They're what I wear when I tattoo my customers," he

explained as he pulled on black disposable gloves. He gave me an apologetic shrug, and hope blossomed in my chest.

He cradled my face in his gloved hands, and I ignored the smooth feeling of the plastic separating us. Instead, I reveled in the fact that he was touching me. My lids fell when his thumbs circled up the sides of my nose to smooth my brows. Tenderly, his fingertips traced over my face like a blind man trying to visualize what he was feeling.

Then he wrapped his arms around me and pulled me into his warm, strong body. For several moments we simply held each other. Our souls rejoiced at being together, and my heart raced in time with his.

"I need you," I whispered.

"I'm here," he said as his lips pressed to my crown.

Knowing he misunderstood, I leaned my head back to look at him. "No. I need you. I need you to make me forget."

"But you said...." He trailed off.

"As long as you keep the gloves on, you can't read me, right?" I questioned as I searched his face.

He sighed. "Mostly. When my mouth touches you I get faint ripples of foggy memories, but nothing I can see clearly."

"Something you can handle?" I asked, hopefully.

"Yeah," he reluctantly admitted.

"Then give me memories to overshadow the ones I can't shake. Let me remember us together instead of that... time," I begged. Desperate, I clutched his wrinkled T-shirt and stood on my tiptoes to reach him.

When my lips brushed over his, I paused to gauge his reaction.

His answer was to swoop in and deepen the kiss. Diving in, he acted like he needed to coax me—he didn't. I wanted this. I wanted *him*.

No. I needed him.

Desperate, I tasted him. I stroked my tongue along his and catalogued what pushed him over the edge. Hands on my ass, he lifted me, and I hooked my ankles behind him. He proceeded to fuck my mouth the way I was desperate for him to take my body. Consuming, desperate, bold, our tongues dueled and curled around the other until we were forced to break for air.

"Please," I begged, needing him more than the breath I'd greedily brought into my lungs. Nico would never hurt me. He wasn't like the asshole who'd hurt me. He was safe.

A few steps and we were against his bed. Lips fused to my neck, he laid me down and crawled up over me as he worked his shirt off. He kissed, licked, and bit every inch of uncovered skin, then he began to undress me to reach the rest.

My hands pushed at his sleep pants, and my feet took over when they got down too far for me to reach. Hungry for him, I kicked them to the foot of the bed once they cleared his feet. The heat of his erection burned into my thigh where it rested.

Unable to control my baser instincts, I sank my teeth into his shoulder as my panties were the last casualty of this war we fought to have nothing between us.

A groan escaped him as I licked over the tender spot I'd left. He reached between us and separated my folds with his gloved hands. One finger, then two slid through my wet lips before he slowly pushed them into my core.

"Nico, God, Nico. I need more than your fingers. I need you," I gasped as I clutched him to my breast where he was flicking my nipple with his tongue before he pulled it into his mouth and sucked. When he repeated the action on the other, I wiggled my hips, searching for what I wanted.

Except, he kept his fingers stroking and scissoring inside my wet pussy.

"Dammit, Nico," I whispered, because despite how good his

fingers worked me over, I needed him inside me. In that moment, he was all I could think about. My only memories were the first time we were together. The way he'd owned my body that night and by doing so, stole my soul.

His fingers left me, and I whimpered. Lifting my hips, I desperately tried to line him up, but he pulled back and slid his length through my wet slit but not inside. The friction of his cock stroking over my clit had me rubbing against him, blindly seeking.

Slow and steady, he continued to slide along me as he buried his face in my neck. His hot breath fanned my throat, and I tilted my head, silently begging him to put his lips to my flesh. Gloved hands caressed everywhere he could reach.

As he moved his hips, I dropped my hips on his backward stroke, quickly shifting the angle of my pelvis to capture the head of his cock. Then I used my heels to press into his ass as I drove upward and impaled myself on his thick shaft.

"Yes," I sighed in satisfaction.

"Oh fuck. God fucking damn." He gasped. "That feels so good."

He canted his hips, then drove hard into my heat. The warm, smooth feel of his cock stroking the walls of my pussy was sheer perfection. I'd never had anyone feel the way he did. In the past few years I tried to find that feeling with other people, but no one ever measured up.

This. This right here was the best—and proof we were made for each other.

He pushed up to brace his weight on his arms as his hips worked harder and faster. Dark brown eyes locked on mine and seemed to say all the things his words didn't.

"Harder," I demanded.

His eyes flared before they became intense, and he pounded into me in a relentless rhythm. The slap of flesh was rapid and punishing but wasn't hard enough. It was in that moment that I realized I'd never get enough of him. He could never fuck me hard enough, or deep enough, or long enough. I'd always be greedy and want more of his cock in me. I wanted him everywhere. I wanted him to erase everything but how he filled me.

Yet, each bruising thrust drove me closer to something I hadn't experienced since that first night—an undeniable soul-deep connection. With Nico, it was more than sex. This was something all-consuming and perfect.

Relentless, he fucked me as the ripples intensified and my muscles began to quiver. Suddenly it was there—an explosion of utter bliss. My body curled in on itself as I sought to wrap myself around that feeling and hold it as long as I could.

As my pussy clutched his shaft and spasmed violently, he slowed, drawing out that amazing ecstasy. Only when I collapsed back on the bed did he pause. Panting, he started down at me with passion burning in the windows to his soul.

Sweat left a sheen on his skin as he hovered over me. My fingertips trailed over the designs inked into his chest. Then my body shook with one last ripple of euphoria.

He slowly moved again, and I gasped. A wicked grin tilted his lips before he flipped us over so I straddled his hips. My hands slapped to his chest to balance me, and I let out a surprised "oh!" when he snapped his hips up and his cock drove so deep, I saw stars.

"Ride me," he demanded as he gripped my thighs.

And I did. With each downward movement, he rose and his cock went so deep my face tingled as my eyes rolled.

"That's it," he coaxed. "Fuck me. Come for me, baby."

My next orgasm built slower but was no less explosive as I felt the gush soak us both. My head hung as my chin pressed into my chest and my shoulders folded in. Nails digging into him, I shuddered with the force of my climax.

But we weren't done. The man was a beast. He lifted me off, causing me to whimper at the loss, but it wasn't for long.

Before I knew it, he had my face down, ass in the air, and he was plowing into my pussy. Nothing mattered but how good he made me feel. With each thrust, he drove out the bad and filled me with his light. As his rhythm faltered, I knew he was close.

His breathing became ragged, and his fingers dug into my flesh until suddenly he withdrew. I protested, but the hot splash of his cum as it hit my back and my ass reminded me we'd been foolish.

Too bad I couldn't find it in me to care.

He rolled us to the side and wiped his release off me with what I assumed was his T-shirt. Then he cradled me in his arms. My fingers laced with his glove-clad ones, and I felt true peace for the first time in years.

As I snugged into his body, I saw what looked like a sketchbook on his side table. Curious, I leaned forward and grabbed it.

"You draw?" I asked, surprised.

"Hey, give me that," he said as he reached to pluck it from my hands. "Of course I draw. I'm a tattoo artist," he said with a huff.

I sat up to keep it out of his reach while I opened it. He sighed and fell back to the bed as he threw an arm over his eyes.

Flipping through page after page of my likeness, I was stunned by what I saw. Every so often there was a drawing of a wolf. I knew it was the same wolf because in each one there was a notch in one ear. Seeing those drawings reminded me of the dream I had of the wolf. That quickly faded when I realized he'd drawn me from memory and with incredible recall of those memories.

"These are me! What the hell, Chains? Does my brother know you have this?" The dates started after our first time together.

"I'm still alive. What do you think?" Extracting the sketchbook from my hands, he tucked it away in the drawer of the nightstand. His face remained frustratingly neutral.

"You've been drawing me since that first night?" I asked as I leaned on an elbow and looked down at him. A warm, protected feeling blossomed in my chest at the thought. He'd been thinking about me for years. It wasn't only me that hadn't been able to forget.

"Can we talk about this another time?" he grumbled, and a soft smile kicked the corner of my mouth up.

"You're an amazing artist, Nico."

"Thank you," he mumbled. His arm tightened around me as I settled into his shoulder and curled around his side. In his arms, nothing could get to me.

Right as I slipped to the in-between of waking and sleep, I knew one thing with certainty.

He owned me body and soul.

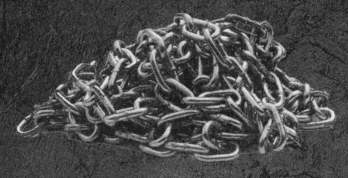

TEN

Chains

"BULLETPROOF LOVE"—PIERCE THE VEIL

That morning started the first of many clandestine couplings. We knew we needed to tell Angel, but each time she wanted one more time before reality crashed down. Part of me worried that Jasmine was using sex with me to bury what had happened to her, and not in a healthy way. I prayed the sex wasn't the only thing she wanted from me.

But goddamn, we were insatiable. Each time was better than the last, and I knew it was what addiction must be like. The high of my orgasms with Jasmine was better than the best quality weed, better than a bump of pure coke, and more addictive than straight opium. She was my drug of choice, and I never wanted to go to rehab.

Except I knew we were up against a ticking clock. Each time we were together, I said we needed to tell Angel, and each time she found a reason to wait.

"Chains!" I jumped at the sound of my name and blinked away

my distracting thoughts. I looked at Venom, who was staring at me with exasperation.

"Sorry," I muttered.

"As I was saying," Venom said sarcastically. "We still haven't uncovered who's behind the trafficking ring we stumbled upon the night we rescued Trace, Lynda, and Jasmine."

At her name, my chest clenched and my cock came to life. Shit. I scooted uncomfortably in my seat.

"The Bloody Scorpions were definitely the middlemen, not the ringleaders like we first thought," Facet explained, though we already knew all that. I fought rolling my eyes because this was all redundant and a waste of time. Especially since they all knew I was picking off the few remaining Bloody Scorpions one at a time. There were still three unaccounted for, but they'd gone to ground, and we were trying to ferret them out.

As soon as we figured out who was calling the shots, I'd take them out too.

Facet sighed as he gave Angel an uncomfortable glance. "One thing I also found was that it seems the people Angel's father owed money to are involved. That's likely why they told him they'd take Jasmine as payment if he didn't come up with the money. They likely would've gotten more for her than he owed."

Angel's fist clenched. "The only reason my father came here seeking my help was because he thought I'd cure him. He still wouldn't have found a way to pay the money back, and Jasmine still would've been in danger."

"No but they found out that you would do a lot to keep your sister safe," Venom murmured to Angel.

Angel's teeth ground.

"Did we ever find out who that number belonged to? The one Korrie's mom was texting?" Kicker asked.

"Nope. Burner, and it went cold after that night," Facet replied.

"You think it was Senator Damon?"

"Yeah, I do, but the guy is good. No one has been able to tie him to any of the shit that Korrie's mom accused him of. They're painting her as a nutcase with a grudge," Facet said with a heavy sigh.

"Dirty fuck. Maybe we need to dig into him more. Facet, I want you to see what you find out. Pull out all the stops," Venom said.

"Gotcha, bossman. Oh, and I was finally able to hack into the files from Santiago's report," he smugly announced. That had everyone sitting up a little taller.

"Go on," Venom prompted.

Facet began tapping away at his keyboard.

"According to one of the victims, there was another group before them. She had initially been a part of that group but had gotten sick and held back. She mentioned overhearing the men saying something about moving them to the transfer station, then to the 'sale barn' after getting them cleaned up for 'Mr. Black.'" Facet paused as he typed again.

"Everything else isn't very helpful. All of them were taken off the street, some in broad daylight. None saw their abductor's faces. What's disturbing is that they weren't local. With the exception of one homeless woman who was new to the area, they were all from out of state. Most from the West Coast." He shrugged. "That's all I've got."

"So someone brought them here to our area from around the country?" Raptor asked as he strummed his fingers on the table.

"From the Western states, yes," Facet concurred.

"But why? Why the middle of Iowa, for fuck sake? It's not

like we have any big cities that compare with the rest of the US," Kicker questioned.

"Maybe that's exactly why," Voodoo said as he stared at the table with a frown.

"What do you mean?" Venom asked.

Voodoo looked up. "We aren't equipped for serious investigations here. I mean, we're not backwoods, but we don't have big police forces—big fancy crime labs. Ankeny isn't exactly a hopping metropolis, you know. This is also the last place people would think a trafficking operation would be based. Then again, it's possible this wasn't the hub. It seems more like they were taking the women from the West Coast, holding them here, then shipping them on. Remember the brothers in Alaska broke up the transfer point there. Those women were bound for out of the country."

"So you think we were just a stopping-off point?" Angel asked, propping his elbows on the dark wood of the table and resting his clasped hands over his mouth. Periodically, his narrow-eyed gaze hit me.

"It's likely," Facet agreed. "Highly likely."

"We aren't going to be able to stop an organization like that." Raptor spoke up as he motioned to the fourteen of us sitting at the table. "There's no way our single chapter could hope to take on a massive human trafficking ring head-on. It's not feasible."

"No, but we can pass on what we know to the other chapters and keep those scumbag traffickers from doing it anywhere near our homes," Ghost piped in.

"You don't think we're trying to do that?" I asked. After all, we'd taken out all the involved Bloody Scorpions, including Voodoo's half brother. Then we torched the house. Of course, I was assigned to the elimination of the rest.

"Yes, but do you think that's really going to be the end of them?" Phoenix murmured.

"Honestly? No, I don't," Venom answered. "Des Moines is centrally located, and I-80 goes all the way from New York City to San Francisco. Not to mention, that house can't be the only run-down shithole they have at their disposal."

"It's not," Facet said and pressed his lips in a flat line.

"So now what?" I asked.

"We keep working this, and if it means we keep taking them out little by little, that's what we do," Venom said.

I shook my head. Venom gave me an exasperated look. "You got a better idea, genius?"

"If we keep picking off the lower levels, they'll only replace them. Over three hundred million people in this country, and you don't think they can find replacement bottom feeders to do their dirty work? We need to cut the head off the monster," I adamantly insisted. Picking off the one connected to hurting Jasmine was a personal vendetta. Stopping the organization was for the greater good.

No matter how bad the things we did may seem, we tried to work for the greater good. Most of the time, anyway.

"How do you propose we do that? Everything I'm finding is a dead end," Facet said as he slapped the laptop closed and fell back in his chair to glare.

"Korrie's mother knows more than she admitted during her trial. Way more. We need to find a way to talk to her," I replied.

"Oh surrrrre… because we're at the top of her accepted visitors list," Angel sarcastically said with a snort of disgust.

"Let me try to see her," I offered. Silence met my reply. They knew what I was offering. There was no guarantee that I'd see what we needed. I might see a lot of ugly shit and get hit with a shit ton of evil emotions before I saw a damn thing that helped.

"I'll look into it," Venom quietly replied. It wasn't a yes, but it was as close as I would likely get at that time. One by one, we nodded.

Tension rippled off the walls as we sat there, stuck in our heads.

ELEVEN

Jasmine

"BROKEN"—SEETHER

"Jazz, we can't keep doing this," he said as he drove hard into me, fingers entwined with mine as he pressed my palms to the wall. The contrast between the black gloves over his hands and the soft tan of mine was mesmerizing.

"Just fuck me, Nico," I demanded to get his mind off his worries and back to the task at hand.

We couldn't tell my brother yet. There was no way Jude would believe I was in the right frame of mind to make a decision like that. Especially after he told me his club brothers were off-limits—that he didn't want them "sniffing around me." After the night Nico had been patched, I let him believe I didn't approve of the club. It made it easier to not have anything to do with them. If I suddenly wanted a relationship with one of his brothers, he'd think I was off my rocker.

Savagely, Nico pounded into me. My tits that he'd pulled out of the cups of my bra bounced with each movement. The elastic of my leggings cut into my thighs as they spread to make room for him. All the memories receded, and nothing remained in my head but the floating numbness and the pleasure centered where we were joined.

Guilt curdled in my stomach, rising like bile in my throat. That I was using what we had to keep the awful memories at bay was downright sacrilege. But it was the only time I felt human. It seemed only when Nico was fucking me did the flashbacks fade to the shadows and I could feel again. The harder the better.

Because of that, he'd become my addiction. If I had my way, he'd be buried deep in my body twenty-four hours a day, seven days a week. I'd remain constantly high from his touch.

One hand released mine as he grabbed my hair and pulled my head back until the curve of my neck was so tight, I could barely swallow. "Fuck you?" he ground out as his lips brushed against my ear. "That's what you want?"

"Yesss," I hissed, pushing my thoughts away.

His breath fluttered over the column of my neck, hot and sensuous as his lips branded the skin. With each violent thrust, it huffed harder before he pushed me over the edge by biting that sensitive spot at the base where it met my shoulder.

Stars flashed behind my eyelids as I fought the hold on my hair. As my orgasm crashed over and over like waves on the jagged rocks in a storm, my body struggled to curl inward to savor the sweet ecstasy pulsing through me.

"Fuck, Jazz, you're killing me. So fucking tight. Goddamn," he mumbled between hot kisses to my exposed nape, but he didn't stop. He didn't let up until his cock swelled thicker in my core and his hips gave one last thrust before he tensed at my back. The throbbing of his length against my walls set off another orgasm.

I had to bite my tongue and hold my breath to stop myself from screaming.

He released my hair and rested his head at the top of my back. Breathing labored and ragged, he didn't move.

"Holy shit," I muttered as little ripples of pleasure continued.

"You can say that again," he agreed as he heaved a heavy sigh and withdrew. The emptiness I experienced when he vacated my pussy went deeper than just his cock stretching me. The moment he pulled out, I became hollow.

As he tied the condom, I righted my clothes and smoothed my hair.

Despite the incredible magic we'd just made, his jaw popped and clenched as he ripped off one glove over the evidence of what we'd done. Then he held it in the other hand and pulled off that one, leaving everything inside it. Angrily, he tossed the black ball of gloves in the trash.

Uncertain of his mood, I chewed on my lip as I watched him.

Then he began cleaning up the ink pots and everything he'd used to finish the tattoo on my shoulder. As I pulled my shirt over my head, the plastic he'd covered it with before we fucked like animals crinkled.

"Is it okay?" he asked in an emotionless tone, refusing to look at me.

I nodded, and there was a quick knock on the door before it popped open. "Goddamn, it smells like straight sex... in... here," Ghost said, trailing off as he realized I was in the room. His eyes widened as his gaze bounced from me to Nico and back. With each movement I watched the pieces click. Resignation registered in his eyes.

"Uh, Faith said you didn't have anyone on the schedule. I wouldn't have barged in if I'd known you were, uh, working," Ghost said as he uncomfortably gripped the back of his neck.

My heart was slamming into my ribcage as I realized we'd been caught and wondered what Ghost was going to do. Fear that he would tell someone made my hands tremble. He'd warned me off before, and I was afraid he'd feel obligated to say something now.

"I cleared my schedule so I could finish Jazz's ink," Nico said with absolute lack of emotion as he washed his hands. When he turned back around as he dried them, his lashes lifted, and he met my gaze but quickly looked away.

"Ohhhh-kay," Ghost said, sensing the tension thick in the air. "I'll just wait out in the waiting room."

Thankfully, he didn't say anymore, but he gave me an uncomfortable smile and about-faced his ass out of the room.

"I'm sorry," I whispered, conscious of the now open door.

"Why? You got what you wanted, right?" His words were snide, and my mouth dropped open in surprise.

"What?"

He snorted in disgust. "Well, you got your ink and got serviced by your stud horse. Two-for-one service," he rasped, full of harsh anger as he sprayed down his work surface with alcohol.

"Nico," I pleaded, hating that he was feeling that way but knowing deep in my heart there was some truth to it.

"Just don't. I think I'm beginning to get the picture. I'm okay to use to get your rocks off, but not good enough to be public with—right? I get to be your dirty little secret, and you get fucked the way you like it. Therapy via sex, I guess."

"That's not true, and you know it!" I whisper-yelled.

"From where I'm standing, that's exactly what this is. You refuse to go to counseling. Instead, you're using sex like a drug to numb the pain. Am I pretty accurate? That's what this is for you."

"It's not!"

"Then prove it."

"How?"

"Tell Angel!"

"Tell me what?" I froze at my brother's voice from the doorway.

If I thought my heart went into overdrive when Ghost barged in, it was nothing on what that voice did. I couldn't get my lungs to pull in enough air.

God, how much did he hear?

"That she had me put ink on her," Nico immediately rattled off.

Angel glanced suspiciously between us before he cocked his head at me. "You had him ink you?" he questioned slowly. I knew he was surprised because I hadn't said a word to him about getting a tattoo.

Turning my back to my brother, I tugged the neck of my shirt over to show him my new tattoo.

A relieved sigh left his lips at the obviously new ink. At least that part wasn't a lie.

"Looks good, sis." My brother's voice softened, and I knew he was looking at the tiger lily I'd had Nico put on my skin. It had been our mother's favorite flower. The design incorporated her name written below in her handwriting.

Nico cleared his throat, breaking the sad silence.

"You joining me and Ghost for lunch?" he asked my brother.

"Of course. That's why I'm here."

"Cool. Let me wipe everything down and I'll be ready." He wouldn't look at me, and his face remained cold.

"How much do I owe you?" I asked, unable to simply walk out.

"You're good. Just keep it clean. Follow the instructions I gave you."

"Are you sure?"

"Yep. You don't owe me a thing for my services. That's what I'm here for." Flashing a startled look at my brother to see what he made of Nico's reply, I winced at the double meaning.

"Well, um, thanks," I mumbled before I grabbed my purse off the counter and rushed out of the room. I didn't bother with a goodbye to my brother, because I didn't trust myself not to show my hand.

Not until I reached the safety of my car did my tears fall. I was fucking up. If I didn't get my head straight, I was going to ruin what Nico and I had. My heart knew that it was more than sex. My mind knew I needed to come clean with my brother. My soul was merely basking in the perfect connection with its other half.

Nico was risking a lot by keeping us a secret, but he was doing it for me—because I begged him for more time.

When I pulled out of the parking lot of the club's tattoo shop, I caught a bike in my rearview mirror. When I took the first right, it did too. At first I chalked it up to coincidence, but when I pulled into a gas station to fill up my car, he followed and parked around the corner of the building. All I could see was that he was messing with his phone.

I didn't really need gas, but I topped off my tank as I cast a furtive glance the biker's way. When I got back in my car and on the road, he started his bike and pulled out as well. A frown furrowed my brow as I stopped at a red light.

Squinting into the mirror, I tried to see if I recognized him. It sucked because he had on a plain black helmet with a tinted visor, and a plain black cut with a single patch on his chest. I couldn't be sure, but it looked like it was the colors of the Royal Bastards. Which was what worried me—the fact that I couldn't be sure.

When we turned the next corner, I caught sight of a wing tattoo on his wrist, and my gaze narrowed. Before I could lose my nerve, I slammed on my brakes and swerved to the side of the road. He quickly swerved to miss me, and the PROSPECT patch on his back confirmed my suspicions. He pulled over and hung his head.

"Why are you following me, Roscoe?" I demanded as I flew out of the car and propped my hands on my hips.

"Dammit, Jasmine, I almost hit you!" he exclaimed as he ripped off his helmet.

"That doesn't answer my question!"

"I'm doing what Angel told me to do. Now I'm gonna get my ass chewed," he bitched.

"For what?"

"Because I wasn't supposed to let you know I was tailing you," he grumbled.

"Well, you suck at it."

"No shit," he muttered as I stomped back to my open door and dropped back inside.

My hands were shaking as my mind spun. I couldn't help but wonder how long Roscoe had been following me. Did my brother already know about me and Nico? Was he biding his time? And if so, why?

Yeah, I should probably be grateful that Angel was looking out for me, but I was more nervous than anything. Our father had been calling and texting me, trying to get me to meet him for lunch or coffee, but I'd been ignoring him. Nico and I had been carrying on in secret. My brother was having me followed.

Nahhh. Nothing to be nervous about.

My fingers nervously strummed the steering wheel the entire way back to the Royal Bastards compound.

Shit.

After the way we left things at the tattoo shop, I'd been going crazy. I hated that Nico believed I was using him, but I hated that there was some truth to it too.

Impatiently, I waited for him to come back to the clubhouse.

There was a party going on by the time I heard his door open and close across the hall. I forgot what that one was for, but then again, the Royal Bastards didn't really need a reason to party. My brother asked if I was joining them, and I told him maybe later after I finished updating a website I managed for a bestselling author.

Cautiously, I opened my door and peeked out. Looking both ways, I didn't see a soul in sight, so I quietly clicked the latch and went across the hall. Taking a chance he may kick me out, I knocked once and opened the door.

His gaze whipped to the door as he tossed the contents of his pockets to the dresser.

"Give me a minute and I'll whip my dick out for you," he said, and my temper exploded.

"Nico, please stop. I didn't come in here to fight with you," I argued.

"No, you came in here to *fuck*." His sneer hurt.

"I didn't. I came here to talk to you," I said as my anger quickly fizzled.

"About what, Jazz?" He suddenly sounded tired, defeated.

Though all I had to do was be in the same room with him and I was turned on, it wasn't all about sex. I simply loved the fact that while we were in the act, all the bullshit disappeared.

"Us."

"I don't think there is an us, Jazz. The more I've thought about it, the more I wonder—is it worth it? To you, I mean. Having a man that has to wear goddamn gloves to touch you? I want to be everything for you, but I don't know how I can."

I didn't get a chance to reply because the door crashed open, nearly hitting me. I shrieked.

"What the fuck is going on? Why are you in here, Jazzy? What did you do?" Angel's eyes flashed in fury as he directed the last question to Nico, who raised his chin but refused to answer.

"He didn't do anything," I tried to defend him. It was me being in Nico's room that had brought my brother down Nico's throat.

"Chains? You need a woman to speak for you?" Angel taunted.

"Angel, knock it off. You're being crazy right now," I begged.

"No. Why is she in your room, goddamn it?" my brother demanded. Sensing the escalating tension, a few of the other club members that were standing outside stepped into the room.

"Angel," I begged as I clutched his arm.

"I said stop trying to defend him!" he roared at me as he shook me off.

I froze. Then my body trembled head to toe. Locked in my mind, I couldn't focus. My breathing became ragged. I could hear what they were saying but I couldn't respond.

"Get the fuck out. Look what you've done," Nico lashed out at Angel in a subdued but obviously furious tone.

"Jazzy," my brother started as his eyes reflected his regret. "I didn't mean to yell at you. Look at me, sis," he said in a cajoling tone. Except, then his voice faded to nothingness. The room was hazy and the roaring in my ears was nearly deafening.

The next thing I knew, I was being scooped up by Venom. He carried me down the hall to my room, then gently set me on the bed. "Jasmine?" he said softly as he laid his hand against my cheek.

A warm wash of peace trickled through me, loosening up my tense muscles and bringing my focus to his face in front of mine.

"Are you with me now?" he asked with a half-smile.

Swallowing hard, I nodded. "I'm sorry."

"Nothing to be sorry about, doll. But I need to ask why Chains had you in his room? Did he make you go in there?" he asked as he stared into my eyes. I'd never gotten used to them calling him Chains. He'd forever be Nico to me.

The thought of Nico forcing me to do anything was such a foreign thought that my face contorted in horror.

"No. Never. I went to talk to him," I whispered as I ducked my head.

Using the edge of his finger, he lifted my chin to bring my gaze back to his.

"Unless he's going to claim you and you're on board with that, I can't have that in my clubhouse. It's pitting two of my brothers against each other. Is that what Chains wants? Is that what you want? You as his ol' lady? Because right now this shit is creating a divide in my club." His usually gruff demeanor was softened as he spoke to me.

"I can't," I finally admitted.

"Why not?" he asked.

"Because he would see everything. Every time he touched me, he would see how dirty I am—how broken. It would kill him. And that would kill me," I said with a quivering lower lip.

"Then you have to stay away from him. I see how he looks at you and I know Angel does too. That man would lay down his life for you. If you can't accept that, then you need to let him go."

He was probably right, but why did the mere thought leave me with my heart gaping open?

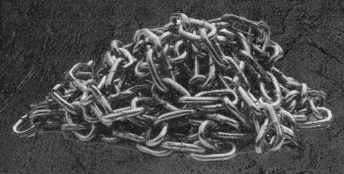

TWELVE

Chains

"REAR VIEW MIRROR"—DEADSET SOCIETY

When Ghost, Angel, and I had gone to lunch after I'd done Jasmine's ink, Angel had casually asked if things were okay between me and his sister. I played innocent, despite the betrayal that nearly choked me.

Except now he'd caught her in my room, and I thought I was likely a dead man.

"Goddamn, Angel. Chill the fuck out. She stopped by to have me look at her tattoo. The plastic came off and it was bleeding. She wanted to make sure it was okay." I pulled out a vape and hit it before I shoved it back in my pocket.

Pretty sure none of them believed my excuse, but I sure as fuck wasn't admitting I'd been banging Angel's sister every chance I got.

"You can all leave. Show's over," I said with a sneer to my brothers still warily observing.

They looked from me to Angel with disbelieving glances.

"It's all good," Angel said with a huff.

For a moment, the debate in their eyes was plain as day.

Once they decided we weren't gonna kill each other, they relaxed. Everyone but Ghost and Phoenix went back to the party.

"You think I'm stupid, Chains?" Angel asked me as he tipped his head back and stared down his nose at me.

"I've never once said I thought you were stupid, Angel. You're my friend. You were my sponsor, for fuck's sake. But more importantly, you're my brother."

"Then what's going on with you and Jasmine? It's more than a fucking tattoo," he said with a glare.

The thing about being in a club full of men with varying abilities was that we knew one another. Not a word crossed my lips, but Angel looked me in the eye, and he *knew*.

"Did you fuck my sister?" Eyes wide and teeth grinding, he watched me. The clenching of his fists didn't escape me, either. This was gonna hurt.

"It wasn't like that," I started, but I didn't get out another word before his fist met my face. Phoenix and Ghost were on him immediately, holding him back as he quietly struggled. He didn't want the rest of the brothers coming back, because I was sure he wanted to beat my ass without everyone intervening.

"Fuck!" I said as I worked my jaw back and forth.

"You don't do relationships, Chains. You *fuck*, and you don't care who sees. Sorry, bro, but that's not what I want for my sister." Deciding it was a good idea not to argue despite the fact that he was wrong, I again kept my mouth shut. The truth was, I'd had plenty of public blowjobs, but I sure as hell never fucked anyone in public. Because for the last couple of years, I didn't fuck at all.

The spring day was warm, and we were at his kid's birthday party. There was zero chance Jasmine and I would be alone there. Actually,

I was surprised I was still welcome. Then again, if he'd excluded me, he would've had to admit shit wasn't kosher with us.

Didn't stop me from clocking her every move.

Knowing I was risking a lot didn't help. Twice, I caught Angel glaring at me. He was standing with Venom as they spoke with the visiting members from the Flagstaff Chapter.

"I'll have to figure out when I can get in to have you finish up my back piece," Blade said, and I absently nodded.

"Sure," I said getting an uneasy feeling at the look Venom gave me as he spoke with Angel, Declan, and Wolfman. The Flagstaff brothers had a run that took them up north. They'd stopped on the way up and now on the way back.

My unease grew as Venom slapped Declan on the back with a grin and shook his hand, then he broke away to approach me. Determined steps brought him closer, and I realized Blade and Kicker had abandoned me.

"Chains," Venom said like I wasn't looking right at him.

"Yeah, bossman? What can I do for you?" Maybe I was overreacting and he only needed me to get more ice or something equally inane.

"Pack a bag." Nope. Not overreacting.

"Excuse me?" I had no idea where he was going with that.

"You're heading back with Declan and Wolfman to help them out."

"But they have Ink," I said, confused as to why I needed to go to fucking Arizona.

"Not sure what's going on with him, but they need you."

"But—" I started.

"Is there a problem?" He cocked a brow as he stared at me.

"No."

"Something I should know about?" He asked it, but the hard glint in his eye told me he knew the answer.

"No."

"Good. Then pack a bag. KSU in an hour. They want to get as far down the road as they can today."

"An *hour?*" I asked, incredulous. Kickstands up in an hour? Fucking hell.

"Did I stutter?" He shot me that stare that had cowed lesser men. My respect for him was the only thing that kept me from rolling my eyes.

"Absolutely not, P."

"Good." A sincere smile lifted his cheeks, and he gripped my shoulder in his meaty fist. "This is going to be good for you. All of you," he said as he pointedly held my gaze before glancing at Angel and Jasmine. The man did nothing by chance. He wanted me to see him look at each of us. It was his way of saying he knew exactly what was going on.

I inwardly cursed.

But I made myself a promise as my gaze briefly locked on Jasmine before she dropped her gaze and raked her teeth over her bottom lip.

When I got back, we were laying everything out on the table.

I just hoped she waited for me.

PART III

THIRTEEN

Jasmine

"I'LL BE OK" —NOTHING MORE

Funny how something so small can cause such profound changes.

"I'm very pleased with your progress over the last few months," my therapist Helen Thomas said with a kind smile.

"Thanks. I know it's going to be a work in progress for a long time. I just knew I needed to get my life on track now more than ever."

"Speaking of… how have things been going since our last visit?" she asked as she glanced down at her notebook.

"Really good. Thanks," I said with one of the first genuine smiles in a while. She looked up with a pleased but expectant expression as she waited for me to continue.

"Though I've been tired a lot lately."

My hand rested protectively over the barely noticeable bump. Yep. That tiny flashing YES+ was the catalyst I needed to get my shit straight. Besides being tired of feeling like that incident was all my life consisted of and allowing it to rule me, I needed to get myself in a better place for my baby.

"Have you told the father yet?" she asked with concern apparent in her gaze.

I sighed. "I just can't. Not yet. Not until I know I'm better."

"But you just told me you understand this is an ongoing process. There is never going to be an opportune time to tell him. Unless you're concerned for your safety if he takes it like an asshole?" Her brows rose as she waited to see if that was the case.

"No, not at all. But I know if I tell him, nothing will keep him from coming back, and he can't. He's out of town for his job, and I don't want him getting in trouble, so I'm taking advantage of this time to get myself where I need to be—or as close to it as I can get before he comes home. I want us to have a fighting chance." I also hadn't decided how I was going to tell my brother that Chains had knocked me up.

Not that us being together wasn't a hundred percent consensual, but after the way my brother had acted the day I was in Nico's room, I couldn't be sure. *Angel's club is so damn worried about what an inter-family relationship gone bad could do to the club? Wait 'til they found out about this. Shit is gonna hit the fan.*

"I'm sure there are ways he could come home briefly, but I understand. Just don't wait too long. He has a right to know and be involved too."

"I know, and I promise as soon as I'm able, I'll tell him." I prayed Nico would be happy about the baby.

My heart clenched at not knowing how much longer we'd be apart, but I tried to tell myself it was okay because that gave me more time to get myself straight. Then again, it also prolonged us not being able to do anything about our situation.

Which made me angry at myself for insisting he keep us a secret. Looking back, I could now see it was because I was fucked in the head, and he'd been right. I was using sex as my drug to self-medicate, my way of having control over my body. My therapist believed I'd been comfortable having sex with him because he was from the pre-rape part of my life and I trusted him. My actions had come back to bite me in the ass, but I was learning how to deal with that too.

But God, I missed him. Not just the sex either—that was simply a bonus. I missed his smile, I missed him holding me, I missed the sound of his voice, but most of all, I missed how when we were together, he always made me feel like I was important.

"I want you to continue to write in your journal. I also would like to see you find a way that works for you to tell the father. Maybe write out what you want to say to him," she said as she set her pen and notepad to the side. We both stood, and I grabbed my purse.

I made my follow-up appointment with the front desk and stepped out into the late August sun. Tilting my head back to capture it, I jumped when I heard a voice I'd hoped to never hear again.

"Jasmine," my father said. My heart skittered and raced as my eyes darted around to look for my ride.

"I don't have time to talk to you," I said as I tried to push past him. He gripped my arm, and I flinched at his touch. Panic began to sneak through me, and I had to force myself to breathe through it.

"Please, Jasmine. I need you to talk to Jude for me," he cajoled.

My indignation knew no bounds. "You seriously expect him to do anything for you? After everything you put him through? You're a disgustingly sick individual and I'm embarrassed to call you my father."

He stepped back as though I'd slapped him. The momentary shock was followed by a hard glint in his eyes. Thankfully, an orange Challenger pulled up, and he quickly walked off, disappearing into the crowded downtown street.

Ghost was around the vehicle and next to me in a flash. "Was that your father?"

"Yes," I ground out with a curl in my lip. I could see his indecision and rested a hand on his arm. "Not that I wouldn't have been okay by myself, but he's long gone. Don't bother."

"I don't fucking like it," he said, but I shook my head.

"He's harmless. Did you see him? He's like a walking skeleton," I said with false bravery, because that panic was feathering though the edges of my brain.

After a reluctant nod, we got in his car and left. As we drove, he tapped out the beat of the music on the steering wheel, but I could see he was holding something back.

"What?" I asked.

He shot me a quick glance. At first, I thought he was going to blow me off, then his face contorted in indecision and he turned down the music. "I feel torn right now. I'm in a very uncomfortable position."

My shoulders drooped. "Ghost, I just don't want everyone to know I'm going to counseling. My brother knows, and that's enough. It's embarrassing because they will all start looking at me with pity again. Do you know how sick I am of being the broken girl?"

"Jazz, no one looked at you like that," he tried to tell me.

"Bullshit. Maybe you didn't see it, but I did."

"That might be how you were seeing things, and we'll agree to disagree on the subject. But that wasn't what I was referring to."

"Then what were you referring to?"

He cast his gaze to my stomach, and my heart stopped. How had he figured it out? No one else had made mention of it, leading me to believe no one had a clue. Not confirming or denying a thing, I clamped my jaw shut and sat silently.

"It's Chains's, isn't it?" he asked, though the words were quiet.

The sudden lump in my throat not only caused difficulty swallowing, but I could barely breathe. My heart resumed at a ferocious pace, and I lifted a trembling hand to nervously cover my mouth.

"Why would you think that?" I finally asked, ignoring the slight catch in my voice.

"Because you've barely left the clubhouse for months, and one of us is always with you. When would you have hooked up with someone else? I'm not stupid. I know you two had something going on before he left. I'm not sure how everyone else didn't."

He was right. The few times I'd left the clubhouse on my own, Roscoe was my tail. Occasionally, I went to get hygiene items and food to contribute, but I usually went with someone.

"Unless you've been with someone else in the club that I don't know about," he offered.

"No," I adamantly insisted.

"That's what I thought. So how do you see this playing out?"

"What do you mean?"

"Well, it's not gonna be a secret forever. Eventually you won't be able to hide it with those legging things and loose shirts. Then what? I won't be the only one able to connect the dots. Do you know what kind of shitstorm that would create? You're setting Chains up for failure, and that's not fair to him. He has a right to know, but not only that, he also deserves not to be blindsided. Did you ever think that maybe the club would be supportive of the two of you together? Maybe you guys should've come clean and then this wouldn't be an issue," he said.

"Not an issue? We all know he got sent to Arizona because Angel didn't like the attention he was showing me. So the club you all love so much is willing to ship him off because he pissed them off, but they'd be okay with us being together?" I asked incredulously.

"They didn't send him to Flagstaff because he pissed them off.

Venom sent him to protect him because he knew Angel was on the verge of killing Chains. Initially, Angel was pissed at Chains because he got the impression you weren't interested and Chains was making you uncomfortable. Chains is a player. He's never had a serious woman in all the years we've known him. It's not a stretch for Angel to think he's using you."

I made a shocked noise.

"Hear me out," he continued. "I know that's not true, but because you two never made it public knowledge, no one knew that. Venom was only looking out for his club. He figured giving them both a chance to cool off would be for the best. Only you can clear everything up, since Chains isn't here right now."

"Well, I certainly can't announce to all his brothers that I'm pregnant with his child before I tell him!" I said in exasperation.

"I get that. But maybe you should at least tell him."

"How? You know him, Ghost. He will be on the next thing smoking to get back here and then his ass will be in a sling with the club. I can't do that to him."

"Maybe if you two worked things out, the club wouldn't have a problem with him coming home early. Family is important to us. If you and Chains are interested in a relationship, and you have feelings for each other, then that just makes our 'family' stronger. Right? Maybe you could go to him—kind of a trial run of you two together," he offered as a solution.

"I have my counseling. That's important to me, Ghost. Without my head being straight, I'm not going to be any good for Chains or our baby. But I promise you this. When he gets home, I will tell him immediately."

"What if they don't bring him home until after the baby is born? Did you think of that? The man deserves to be there for the birth of his child."

"That's if he even wants to be," I said with worry. Because part of my secret worries when he finds out is that he won't want the baby for the same reason he initially didn't want me. The thought of him being unable to feel the softness of our baby's skin on his fingertips broke my heart. Which got me thinking. Babies don't really have memories, so maybe it would be okay. I needed to ask him without giving it away.

"He will be," he insisted.

"Let me think about it, okay?" I pleaded.

"Fine. Just don't wait too long or you won't have a choice." That was the second warning I'd gotten in the same day not to wait too long, yet they needn't have bothered. My dream the night before had shown an angry Nico. He'd been furious with me and thought I wasn't planning to tell him. I knew what I needed to do.

"I promise."

"You know he asks me about you every time he calls," Ghost murmured as he turned a corner.

"What?" I whispered. My heart fluttered and tried to burst from my chest. I'd wanted to call him a million times, but I wasn't sure how to talk to him without slipping up and giving away my condition.

"Don't act surprised. The man is insane for you, but you should already know that if he knocked you up. That means the two of you were much more than friends. Honestly? I think your brother knows more than he's willing to admit, even to himself. To do what he did, he had to have been insane," Ghost said with a snort.

"Whatever," I said, trying to sound unaffected.

"Now what the hell did your father want?"

"Same thing as always. Wants Angel to talk to him. We all know he wants Angel to heal him, but that's never going to happen." Everyone in the club knew our father was responsible for our mother's death, but they didn't know all the reasons Angel hated him, and they went back farther than that.

I wasn't stupid. I knew that Angel asked the Royal Bastards to watch out for me when he left for the military. I was also pretty sure he threatened our father with them if he harmed me in any way. Which was why I didn't understand why he didn't think there was a possibility I could end up with one of them. Then again, I had put on a pretty good act for a couple of years.

He grunted as we stopped at the last light in town before taking the highway out to the clubhouse. I stared sightless out the window.

The light turned green, but we didn't move. With a frown, I glanced at him. He was staring in the rearview mirror. When I glanced back, the only thing back there were some people outside a restaurant.

"Ghost? The light's green."

It took him a full second to look at the light and shake himself out of whatever the hell had grabbed him. He blinked rapidly, and we left town behind us.

"What were you looking at? Was someone following us?" I asked him. With my father's surprise visit, it wasn't an impossibility.

"No. Just thought I saw someone I knew." His expression looked so lost, I wanted to comfort him, but I didn't know how. He could be a prankster, but he was tight-lipped about his personal life. I guessed something bad had happened in his past, but he would never say much. At least not to me.

When he parked outside of the clubhouse, I gripped his arm. "Thank you for the ride today. I really can't thank you enough."

"No problem. You know I don't mind."

It had been hell to evade the prospect for my first appointment. I had pretended I had an appointment in the massage clinic that was in the same building. He'd waited out front when I told him I didn't want him coming in the massage therapy place because it was weird.

I'd barely held my shit together on the way home. That first session had been rough.

Initially, I hadn't wanted anyone to know I was going to counseling. To me it had been embarrassing to admit everyone had been right and that I'd fought it so long. Then I was afraid that if it didn't work out, my brother would never let it lie again. He'd keep pestering me. I wanted to do this on my own before I told anyone.

Finally, I broke down and told Ghost, because my car hadn't wanted to start and I needed a ride. He was the only one around unless I rode with the prospect, and that seemed... wrong, I guess. To be on the back of anyone's bike but Nico's didn't seem right.

Anyway, Ghost had seen how emotional I was after my session, so he offered to take me each time because he was worried about me driving back like that.

"Can you do me another favor?" I asked him.

"Favors are racking up, doll. Not sure you're ever going to be able to pay me back," he said with a teasing grin.

Unable not to laugh, I playfully swatted his arm. "Knock it off. Can you see if you can find out when he's coming home?"

There was no need to specify who "he" was.

Ghost gave me a lopsided smile. "Yeah, I can do that. No guarantees, but I'll see what I can find out."

"Thanks," I said, and we both got out of the car.

After being in the sun, the dim lighting inside my brother's house was hard to adjust to. My brother was coming inside from the backyard, and Trace sat up on his shoulders.

"Aunt Jazzy!" Trace called when he caught sight of me. I grinned.

"Hey, buddy. Looks like you got a new ride."

"Dad said I'm almost too big for this, but I said he's got big shoulders so it would be fine," Trace reasoned, and we all laughed.

"Where's your mom and my new niece?"

"Mom is changing Angeline's diaper. Dad and I are gonna swim in the pool. Uncle Venom, Aunt Loralei, Uncle Voodoo, Aunt Kira, and baby Parker are on their way, too! You wanna come?" he asked with excitement.

The fact that my brother named his daughter after our mom almost made me cry every time I heard her name. In a good way, but it still really hit me in the heart.

"Maybe next time. Well, how about if I sit by the pool with you," I said with a smile. No way was I wearing a swimsuit in front of my brother, his club, and his family. Nothing said "hello, I'm pregnant" like a baby bump in a bikini.

"How did everything go today?" my brother asked. I'd finally decided to tell him I was going after about a month of sessions. Getting over my initial worries, I figured it would be good for him to know I had started doing something to get myself in a better place. Especially if I wanted him to accept that Nico and I were going to be a thing. Granted, I didn't need his permission, but it would make things a lot easier if everyone involved was cool with it.

Again, I prayed Nico wouldn't lose his shit about the baby. I prayed he was the man I thought he was; otherwise this could get really ugly.

"It went really good."

"I'm proud of you sis, and I'm happy for you. You deserve the best, and I only want to see you happy."

"Let's go get our swimsuits on!" Trace said as he waved his hands around. Angel clutched his thighs tighter.

"Easy there, cowboy!" My brother chuckled. "We'll see you out by the pool."

Since my leggings were a bit warm, I opted to put on a pair

of shorts, but kept the loose Boho-style off-the-shoulder top. Knowing the boys probably didn't, I grabbed towels from the hall closet and went out back.

"I was just going in to get those," Korrie said with a grin. Angeline was snoozing in her little baby swing under a huge umbrella. Absently setting the towels down on the glass-top table, I leaned over to fawn over my beautiful niece. It had me wondering if I was having a boy or girl.

"She's so beautiful," I murmured softly.

Korrie snorted. "No need to be quiet. That one would sleep through a tornado."

Angel jumped in the pool with a squealing Trace, followed by a big splash.

"See?" We both laughed.

"Aunt Jazzy! Come sit by us!" Trace called out as he swam toward the stairs.

I took one of the towels to the edge of the pool and laid it out as Trace climbed out of the pool. Before I could sit down, I heard the slap of wet feet on concrete. Trace flew past me and cannon-balled into the pool. Water exploded from the pool and soaked me.

Hair hanging in my face, I stood there sputtering. Trace surfaced, giggling his little ass off.

He was the only one, though. After I pushed the hair out of my face and dried my face off with the towel, I looked into my brother and sister-in-law's shocked faces.

"What?" I asked.

"Umm," Korrie said as she circled a pointer finger at my stomach.

Looking down, I saw the top that had once been flowing, was now stuck to me like a second skin. My four-month along baby bump was sticking out front and center. I'd never cursed being skinny more than at that moment.

"Oh!" I heard over my shoulder. I turned to find the whole troop was gawking at me as well. The women looked excited; the guys couldn't seem to pick their jaws up off the ground. Pulling my attention from the new arrivals with a sigh, I glanced back to my brother.

His once shocked face was steadily getting redder.

"Jude," I began, pulling out the real name card, then nervously chewed on my lip. "Remember how you said you just wanted me to be happy?"

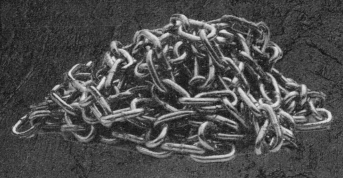

FOURTEEN

Chains

"HIGHWAY TUNE"—GRETA VAN FLEET

Two weeks later….

"Hey, Chains! Declan wants you in his office," Bones called. I set my beer down on the bar and made my way to his office.

I'd been sent to fucking Siberia—well, if Siberia were mountains in Arizona. Sure, the brothers there were cool as fuck, but it wasn't my home. Declan, Axel, Throttle, Bones, Brick, Doc, Kane, Wolfman, and the rest—I liked them all, but fuck, I was ready to go back to Ankeny.

And the worst part of being here—Jasmine wasn't. I couldn't protect her from the middle of Arizona, and it was driving me crazy.

Though that was exactly why I'd been exiled. No, I couldn't blame Angel for being pissed. Hell, I was one of his best friends. I'd shit where I ate.

In my defense, I hadn't known it that first night. I'd been young, dumb, fresh back from the military, and horny as fuck.

So I screwed up. Bad. I fucked my best friend's little sister. It might've been okay if I hadn't done it again. And again.

Okay... I'd probably want to kill me too.

But goddamn it, I missed her. Twenty times a day I picked up my phone wanting to call her or send a text. I'd been under explicit orders from Venom not to contact her, which was utter bullshit. Like we weren't both fucking grown-ass adults.

Yet I didn't. Mostly because I respected my prez, but also because she hadn't been speaking to me before I left. Call me an insecure fucker, but I was afraid I'd waited too long anyway. Why the hell would she want to talk to me by that time. Besides, I didn't know how we could possibly make things work if she wanted to keep everything a secret forever and I couldn't fucking touch her. Did I want to have to wear gloves with my own woman for the rest of my life?

Didn't mean I didn't ask Ghost about her every time we talked.

"Yeah, boss? You wanted to see me?" I asked as my gaze jumped from Declan, to Axel, to Throttle. Caution reared its head, making me shut my mouth as I waited to hear what they had to say.

"Pack your shit. You're heading home."

"Excuse me?" For four months I'd been in exile. Venom and a few of the brothers touched base with me a few times a week, but other than that, I hadn't seen any of them since early May. It was almost September.

"Raptor, Voodoo, Phoenix, and your new patch will be here tomorrow morning. You'll be riding back with them the next day. They're bringing something down for me, but they need to get back ASAP."

"What if I don't want to?" I did, but I was pissed that no one had given me a heads-up. Also, I was being treated like a kid and told what I was going to do. Again.

Not that being down in Flagstaff hadn't done me some good. I'd developed a great bond with the brothers there. Though I hadn't appreciated being forced to go, the past four months had also been productive. I'd been able to hire a couple of new artists for their shop, and business was booming.

It had also been good for me in other ways.

The day I was preparing to head down, Madame Laveaux had stopped in my room.

"Nico, it is imperative that you work on controlling when you read people and objects."

"With all due respect, Madame Laveaux, that's impossible. I've tried before," I said as I shoved clothes in my bag.

"You are being stubborn and lazy." She pointed a beringed finger at me. *"Work on it."*

Since I'd been down here, I'd tried. It was hit-or-miss, but I was chagrined to find that she was right. It was possible with serious concentration; I probably just needed more practice or tips from someone with my abilities. In the past when I tried to control it, I hadn't been successful, which had led me to believe it was impossible. Perhaps I gave up too quickly back then. It may never be something I could control completely, but it at least gave me some hope.

Declan leaned back in his chair as he strummed his fingers on the desktop. "You saying you want to make the jump to Flagstaff?"

The wind left my angry sails, and my shoulders slumped. "No," I said as I ran a gloved hand over my face.

"Didn't think so." Declan smirked. "But you'd be welcome any time if you changed your mind."

"Thanks, brother. I really appreciate that."

"It's been great having you here," Axel added. "I wouldn't

complain if you wanted to stay. I still want to have you do some ink on me one day."

"Any time, brother. Hell, if I have to hop a flight and come down to do it, I will."

"Nah, I'll be up there one of these days," he said.

We shook hands with the half embrace shit, then I did the same with Axel and Throttle, and I was excused.

Suddenly nervous, I battled the thoughts that swirled in my head as I went back to the room I'd been staying in at their clubhouse. Since I'd ridden down, I didn't have a lot to pack.

I pulled out a clean pair of jeans, a thermal, socks, and underwear and laid them neatly on the dresser top for tomorrow.

I was going home.

"You finally got patched, huh?" I asked Sabre as we stopped for gas. Honestly, I was surprised Venom hadn't voted to patch him early after he'd been stabbed in the parking lot the day he was a driver for Loralei.

"It's pretty unreal," he said as his silver eyes flashed my direction as he filled his tank.

"Well, congrats," I told him, and I meant every word. The Bastards were my family—well, the only family that counted. I appreciated any man who was welcomed into the fold as a member, because we were particular and only brought in the best of the best.

"Thanks," he said before finishing with the nozzle and replacing it on the pump. He looked a little uneasy, and I couldn't figure out why. Come to think of it, everyone had acted a little off, and I hadn't done a fucking thing.

Well… not lately.

"Let's get this show on the fucking road," Raptor called out. "Any of you girls need a potty break?"

We all flipped him off. He chuckled and mounted up.

The rest of us got on our bikes and hit the road. I left the mountains of Arizona in my rearview mirror and pointed my bike home.

The good and bad thing about riding is you have a lot of time to do one of two things. Clear your head—and think. I tried to clear my head, but all I could fucking do was think.

Each mile that rolled under my wheels brought me closer to the one woman I should've stayed away from. She was my kryptonite. An addiction that was likely to kill me, yet one I couldn't stay away from.

FIFTEEN

Jasmine

"NAME"—THE GOO GOO DOLLS

Well, so much for telling Nico first.

"Our babies are going to grow up together!" Korrie said, full of excitement and smiles once the shock wore off. The guys had all convened inside to grab beer while the women chattered out by the pool.

All the women were ready to plan a baby shower and gender reveal.

"Don't you do them together?" I asked.

"Psh!" Kira waved off my question. "If we break it up into two, then we can have cake and shit twice."

I laughed at her logic, despite my worry at what this would do to Chains. It made me feel like shit that everyone would know before him. That was one thing I zipped my lips on.

"So, umm, who's the father?" Korrie asked in a whisper with a slight wince.

My gaze dropped to my still wet top as I plucked at the embroidered hem. "Umm, well, I would rather not say yet."

Crickets.

"Uhhh, okay," Korrie warily replied, breaking the awkward silence.

"The dad doesn't know yet," I hedged, then regretted my words. What if they put two and two together? Everyone knew Chains had been gone a while.

"Oh," said Loralei.

"Are you okay with this? Did we make you uncomfortable being so excited?" Korrie asked, worry in her eyes.

I actually laughed.

"Yeah, I'm okay with it. At first, I was scared, but I'm happy. Is it crazy that I'm already in love?" I asked. My palms pressed protectively to the swell of my belly.

"Absolutely not! I was in love with little Parker before I knew if he was a he or she," Kira replied.

"Same, girl. Trace and Angeline owned my heart from the second I knew their tiny hearts were beating," Korrie added.

Loralei pressed a hand to her own rounded belly. "I'm completely in agreement."

Kira started to giggle, and Parker laughed in her lap.

"What's so funny?" asked Loralei as she cocked her head to the side, giving Kira a look as if she'd lost her damn mind.

When Kira had control of her laughter, she wiped the tears from under her eyes and kissed Parker's silky dark hair. "Look at us. We're a walking talking baby factory. Must be something in the water at the clubhouse."

My eyes went wide and I started to choke on my own damn spit. I grabbed my cup of water and gulped some down.

Korrie stared at me. My heart flipped and skipped as I watched the wheels in her head spinning. When her eyes bugged, I inwardly braced myself.

"It's Chains," she whispered.

"What?" I asked, pretending I had no clue what she was talking about. Another drink of water was in order to occupy my mouth.

"It's Chains. He's the dad, isn't he?" she asked in a dramatic whisper. Everyone froze, and three stunned gazes locked on me.

"I—Why would you even think that?" I stuttered.

Korrie scoffed. "Look, your brother may be blind, whether it's intentional or he's really that dense, but we've all seen the way you two looked at each other. That man was damn near eating you alive with his eyes before he left."

Inhaling deeply, I slowly let it out before casting a worried glance over my shoulder. "I don't want the guys to know until I have a chance to tell Chains," I said, tone heavy with worry.

"Hey, this is the girls' club. Mum's the word," said Korrie as she made a zipping motion over her lips. The others nodded in agreement.

"But don't be surprised if they don't figure it out, too." Loralei arched a brow as she looked at me.

"Do you think he's going to be anything but over the moon?" Kira asked rhetorically.

My shoulders lifted to my ears before dropping in a slump.

"How did Venom take it when you first told him?" I asked Loralei. Their pregnancy was an oopsie as well.

Her laughter pealed out. "You mean after he got mad and shit his pants?"

"That's what I'm afraid of," I said, staring down into my cup and rattling the ice cubes.

"Stop. Don't worry about the maybes and what-ifs. Because I can promise you, if he's a dick about it, I'll string him up by his balls my-damn-self." Korrie said before she pursed her lips and made a sassy snapping with her fingers.

"Damn straight. We've got your back either way, sister," Loralei said.

My gaze rose to stare across the yard. My cup dropped from my hands, water and ice splashing across the concrete.

"Oh shit!" I mumbled as I questioned what I'd seen.

"Jasmine!" they all called at once.

"Did you see that?" I asked with tremor in my voice as I stood. Blinking rapidly, I thought I must be crazy. That was the only explanation.

I rushed to the back of the yard that was enclosed with a wrought iron fence. Scanning the wooded area behind the houses and down behind the neighboring yards, I didn't see a thing. But there was no freaking way I'd imagined it.

"What the heck are you looking at?" my sister-in-law asked as she stopped next to me, holding my now wide-awake niece.

"Korrie, I swear to God there was a wolf at the fence staring at me."

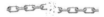

The guys searched the entire area. I hadn't lost my mind, because they found a single print in the dirt at the edge of the trees. Then absolutely nothing. No other sign of it. Which was crazy, because the trees open to CRP land and there was nowhere a freaking wolf could've hidden.

When I went to bed that night, I dreamed a large, gray wolf ripped Nico's throat out.

I woke up screaming and covered in sweat.

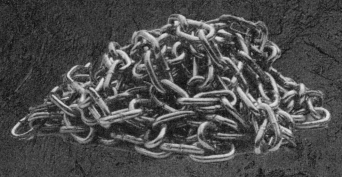

SIXTEEN

Chains

"TO BE ALONE"—FIVE FINGER DEATH PUNCH

When we walked through the door of the clubhouse, we were fucking tired and sore. Everyone welcomed us home, but again they seemed off. Fuck, I really hoped shit wasn't gonna stay like that. If so, I might as well have stayed in Flagstaff.

"Way to do an Iron Butt. I'll leave that shit to you youngsters," Kicker said with a chuckle.

"Not like we wanted to, but if we wanted to outrun the weather, there was no choice," grumbled Raptor. The prospect behind the bar handed him a cold beer as he dropped to a barstool.

"Goddamn, how can you do that?" Phoenix grumbled. "My ass hurts watching you do that!"

"Your ass hurts? What the fuck did you guys do on the way home?" Squirrel teased.

Raptor shot him a glare, I rolled my eyes, and Phoenix flipped him off. Sabre snorted as he sat next to me.

"Prospect, can I get a whiskey, neat?" I called across the bar, and he nodded as he pulled down the bottle of Crown and a glass.

"Where is everyone?" Raptor asked as he glanced around. It was a Friday night, and there would usually be more people around than there were.

"Few are out on a job, Blade is off doing God knows what, and Angel is at home with Jasmine since she wasn't feeling good," Squirrel said, and Ghost immediately pushed him in the arm and frowned. Squirrel held his arm.

"Damn, what did you do that for?" he asked Ghost with a pout.

"What's wrong with Jasmine?" I asked, and I swear to Christ you could've heard a pin drop.

"She caught a bug, and with the baby, it's done a number on her," Squirrel said and Ghost damn near kicked him off his stool.

My heart stuttered to a stop, and I couldn't breathe. Finally, I sucked in deep breath and looked at Ghost. "Baby?" I asked in a deceptively calm tone.

"Chains! A word," Venom called. My glass hit the bar with a loud clunk, and I followed my president to his office.

The world seemed to be spinning too fast. To the point where I had to reach a hand out to the wall to balance myself. My mind was reeling. I wasn't sure which way to take what I'd heard.

"Sit," Venom said as he motioned to the chair. He sat behind the desk, opened the drawer, and pulled out his bottle of Crown Royal XR. When he pulled out two shot glasses, one of my brows cocked up.

When both glasses were full of the golden alcohol the color of Jasmine's eyes, he slid one to me. For a second, I stared at it. Then my gaze lifted to his. Expression locked down, he raised the glass and motioned to mine.

Cautiously, I raised the shot glass. He held his out and we

clinked glasses, tapped the desktop with the glass, then downed the rich liquid. The perfect burn chased down my throat and warmed my stomach. Between that and what I'd drunk at the bar, my muscles loosened up, and I waited.

No way had he called me in his office just to do a shot.

"I have a job for you," he said as he poured a second glass for each of us and placed the bottle back in the drawer.

"Okay," I said. Not that a job would be unusual, but fuck, I had been back all of thirty minutes. It also didn't warrant sharing his good whiskey with me.

"Drink up," he said as he held his glass up again. Once we both finished, he stacked the glasses and leaned back in his chair. He stared at me over steepled fingers.

"Facet found the last of the Bloody Scorpions involved in the abduction."

I sat up straighter. Honestly, it had been months since I left, and before then, we hadn't had any luck.

"We need them alive."

"What?"

"We need to get all of the information we can out of them about the operation. Once we have what we need, Angel said he'll gladly help you with them, and so will Voodoo."

My brows rose, and I gave him a disbelieving stare. Angel was willing to work with me. Not willing to kick my ass? What the fuck had happened while I'd been gone?

"Uh yeah, okay. That's what you called me in here for?"

"Would it have been something else?"

"Well, you pulled out the good shit, and that's not your MO."

He raised his brows like he didn't know what I meant. Finally, I decided to just ask about Jasmine, because I was pretty sure this had something to do with that.

"Squirrel said something about Jasmine and a baby. What did he mean?" I studied the wood grain of his desk and held my breath for his reply.

"It would seem she's knocked up." At the tone of his voice, I looked up at him. "Won't say who the father is, either. Some of the brothers think it was some random dude and that's why she won't say."

My teeth ground together, and my blood began to boil at the visual of a "random dude" touching her.

"Know what I think?" he asked in a bored tone. At that moment, I really didn't. All I cared about was getting to Jasmine. I wanted answers.

I shrugged, and he leaned toward me with his forearms crossed and his intent gaze holding mine.

"I think it's yours," he dramatically whispered. My heart lodged in my chest, and so many emotions flooded me that I didn't know which end was up.

"What? But I didn't, I mean, I've been gone, I... uh." Unable to form coherent thought, I snapped my mouth shut.

"You trying to say it's impossible?" A sarcastic brow lifted as he studied me because he knew damn well it could possibly be mine. He was daring me to deny it, but I couldn't. Then I had to wonder why none of my fucking brothers thought to say anything to me. Especially Ghost, who I talked to most often.

Both hands covered my mouth before I dragged them down. "What if it *is* mine?"

"You're asking *me* that?" He pointed at his chest and gave me a look of mock surprise. Fuck.

"I mean what does that do to my standing in the club? How is Angel with this? Does he think it's mine?"

"You mean does he want to kick your ass? Probably. Is he handling all of this okay? That's debatable. He only found out a couple of weeks ago. But I can tell you that he and Ghost are the reason you're back so unexpectedly."

"How?"

"Because they both came to me separately and wanted to know when you were going to be home. Ghost went so far as to say he felt it was time you came back. Then Angel told me his sister was pregnant. I'm not an idiot, Chains. You think I never noticed the way you are with her? You think no one else did? Then she ends up in your room and Angel wants to string you up? When I took her to her room that day, I pretty much told her she needed to shit or get off the pot."

Disbelief screwed up my face.

"Don't look at me like that. I don't need high school drama in my fucking club. So either she was in the right headspace to be with you or you two needed to stay the fuck away from each other. I knew damn well there was no fucking way that was going to happen, regardless of what I had to say. That's why when the opportunity came up to send you to Flagstaff for a while to help with their tattoo shop, I jumped on it. I think you both needed time to figure out what you wanted without Angel going after you for your inability to keep it in your goddamn pants." And there was the Venom we all knew and loved. Stern, no bullshit, I-will-rip-off-your-head-and-shit-down-your-neck Venom.

I stood. No way was I going to question my president, but maybe he should've sent Angel's hot-headed self to Flagstaff instead of me.

"I'm going to see her."

He raised his chin. "She hasn't been staying here at the clubhouse for the last few days. She's been sick, so she's been at Angel's," he finally admitted in a gravelly voice.

Fuck.

Well, might as well get it over with.

"How are you going to handle this?" he asked me without so much as a flicker of emotion. His eyes seemed to ripple.

"What do you mean, how am I gonna handle this? I'm gonna find out if it's my kid, then go from there." After that, I honestly had no fucking clue.

"Better brace yourself."

"Yeah, I know." If it was mine, Angel was going to kick my ass.

And I was going to let him.

My gloved knuckles rapped on the glass of Angel's door. It wasn't long before I could see someone approaching through the rippled glass.

They already knew it was me. Angel had the highest tech security system known to man. The only question was who was going to answer.

The door swung wide, and I breathed a sigh of relief when it was Korrie. How I was lucky enough to get a brief reprieve, I didn't know.

For a beat she stared at me with pursed lips. Then she shook her head with a look that screamed she didn't wish she was me for a second.

"Come on in," she said as she stepped back for me to pass. I entered their house and swallowed hard. I'd been there before, but my gaze traveled around, seeing it with new eyes. It was more than a house; it was a home. Something I hadn't had most of my life.

"Is Jasmine awake?" It was only nine o'clock, but according to Squirrel, she'd been sick.

That was when Angel approached. His jaw clenched, but

other than that he remained impassive. His hand landed protectively on his wife's shoulder. Not that he thought I'd hurt her, but because she was his. That had my brain spinning too. It had me wondering if there was any hope of that with Jasmine.

And that thought nearly knocked me on my ass.

That thought spoke of a future.

"I'm here," she said from the stairs, and I looked up. My memories hadn't done her justice. It was possibly that mythical "glow" that I'd heard people talk about when Kira and Korrie had been pregnant, but whatever it was, she was stunning.

Her golden skin was radiant, and her whiskey eyes were smoky. I never would have guessed she'd been ill if it hadn't been for the slightly bruised look under her beautiful eyes that spoke of troubled or lack of sleep.

Taking her in, I noticed the small curve of her stomach, and my chest constricted. Not one time in my life had I thought I'd have a child. What kind of father would I be? Also, it wasn't often I could have sex that I could handle, let alone try to be in a relationship. Yet looking at her on the stairs as she nervously chewed on her lip, I wanted things I'd never hoped to have.

"Jasmine," I breathed.

As if suddenly realizing we had an audience, her cheeks flushed pink.

"We'll be in the den if you need us," Korrie said as she dragged a mumbling Angel behind her. He paused to shoot me a glare. I really wanted to flip him off, but I was too caught up in the woman on the stairs.

"Do you wanna go outside?" she nervously asked as she came down to the last step, putting us eye to eye. It killed me that I didn't know if her nervousness was because it was someone else's or mine.

"Sure." I followed her through the house and out back. She

took a seat at the patio table and crossed her arms in a defensive posture.

Catching a movement from the window, I glanced over to see Angel with his face damn near pressed to the glass, glaring at me. Korrie tugged him away, and I sighed.

Unable to sit, I stood with my fingers linked behind my neck. Though I wanted to wrap her in my arms and bury my face in her neck, I needed to know.

"Is it mine?" I asked, unable to wait another second.

The guilt on her face didn't answer my question.

The she nodded. Disbelief mixed with rage blasted through my veins. Though I might not have given the thought of having children much consideration, the mere thought that she might've considered keeping my child from me sent fury burning within my soul.

Not wanting to lash out but completely at a loss, I stood there panting, unable to draw a deep breath. It was as if I was suffocating. My mind was a jumble of disconnected thoughts.

"Did you even plan on telling me?" It came out as a pained whisper as I prayed she said yes. If not, my heart might shatter.

"Yes. Don't be an idiot," she snapped.

"When? Because I've been gone for four fucking months, Jazz. How long have you known? I'm sure it's been longer than the last few days." I was angry, but more than that, I was hurt and irrationally lashing out.

"Umm, hello? *You. Weren't. Here*, Nico!" She said as she gripped her hair in frustration.

"You couldn't call?" I asked, hating the way my voice broke at the end.

"Nico, please understand. I know you. If I had told you, there wouldn't have been anything that would have kept you away. I never wanted to be the reason you got in trouble with the club, or worse, got kicked out."

"Yet you refused to tell your brother about us when I begged you to!" I roared. Her logic infuriated me, but I took a deep breath before I continued. "How do you know they wouldn't have been supportive? Look at Loralei, Kira, Korrie—they were all welcomed in as family. And you're *already* family because of Angel."

Tears rolled down her cheeks, and I fought for composure, because I'd been a piece of shit. Too late, I remembered how she responded to anger and yelling. It gutted me to see her cry, no matter how pissed off I was. Gritting my teeth, I closed my eyes and tried to chill the fuck out.

"I'm sorry, Nico. I'm so, so sorry." She was all-out crying, and I hated it.

"Stop," I said as I dropped to my knees next to her. "I'm being an asshole and you don't deserve that." Her head swiveled slowly my direction, and I cradled her face in my hands. With gloved fingers, I wiped her tears and kissed over the wet trails.

"I wanted to be a better person by the time you got back. I didn't want to be the broken shell I was before. I hated that woman. I wanted you to know that when I was with you, it was because we needed to be connected, not because I needed control. I wanted you to be happy you were having a baby with me. I wanted to be *normal*," she cried, and my heart ached. This beautiful woman should never have to cry unless it was from happiness. She deserved everything good in the world—the best of everything. Though I knew that wasn't me, I remained there and selfishly kissed away her tears.

The sounds of the night wrapped us in their folds as I kneeled on the hard concrete and rested my forehead to hers. My gloved hands gripped her hair.

"You aren't broken, baby. You might be bent, but you're far from broken. You are the strongest woman I know. And you're right—if I'd known about the baby, come hell or high water, I'd have been home. But know this—I'm here now, and we're going to figure this shit out, because I'm not keeping my mouth shut anymore. You're mine, Jazzy. You hear me? *Mine.*"

She brushed the side of her nose against mine, and I nuzzled hers before brushing a kiss softly against her lips.

One way or another, I had to find a way to make this shit work, because I was never letting her go again.

SEVENTEEN

Jasmine

"HEAVEN"—KANE BROWN

My fingers were clinging to the leather of Nico's cut as he traced the seam of my lips, seeking entrance. Eager, I opened, and he plundered. We'd probably kissed hundreds of times, but something had shifted. This one was… more.

He slowly trailed his kisses along my jaw, then his lips grazed my neck, each touch soft and sensual. "God, I missed you, Jazz. You have no idea. You're so fucking beautiful and you're all mine," he murmured against the sensitive skin. Wetness pooled between my legs at his words, yet I held back. With my body changing daily, I was self-conscious and thought he wouldn't find me attractive anymore.

I needn't have worried.

He returned to my mouth and feathered kisses on the corners and a last chaste one to the center that lingered.

"So how bad does your brother hate me now?" he whispered against my lips when we separated.

I sighed. "He doesn't hate you. He's just angry with us." I paused and cringed. "Because we weren't honest with him."

He snorted in satisfaction because he'd been right. "So should I be expecting an ass whooping?"

My teeth raked over my bottom lip, and I winced as I shrugged. "I hope not, because I like this face," I said as I cupped his cheek. The bristle of his inky, short beard was coarse against my hand, and I tugged on the longer strands at his chin.

"You do, huh?" he said with a crooked smile, and my heart thumped madly. In the months he'd been gone, I had worked on a lot of things with my therapist, one of which was owning my feelings—both good and bad. When it came to Nico, there were things I regretted, but I had been working on accepting things I couldn't change.

Most of all, I realized one thing for certain—that I had fallen for him harder than I ever thought possible.

"Yeah. But more than that, I love what's in here," I said as I placed my spread hand under his cut and over his heart. The strong beat thrummed under my palm.

"Well, I love everything about you, Jasmine. There's so much goodness and light in you that I don't know how you'll handle my darkness, but I can't stay away."

A surprised inhale was all I could manage. He'd caught me so off-guard. If he noticed I didn't reply, he didn't say anything. Not that I didn't want to, but I didn't want him feeling like I was only saying it because he did.

His gaze fell to my small baby bump, and he dropped a hand to splay over it. "Fuck, I never thought I'd see this day. Do you know if it's a girl or a boy?" he asked with a hint of awe.

I shook my head. "I decided to wait until I could tell you. I was hoping you'd want to be there."

"Hell, yes." He nodded with the hint of a smile. Then he gave his head a slight shake as his brow furrowed. "Damn, I'm a little scared."

"You? I didn't know if I'd be raising a baby by myself," I said with a watery laugh. Then I sobered. "I also didn't want to tell you right away because I've been getting help. I have a therapist."

"That makes me so happy, but I would've been here for you. I would've supported you, Jazz." He gripped the hair at the base of skull again and tipped my head back to gain my full attention. I stared up into his dark mahogany eyes.

"I know, but at that time I wasn't in the right headspace. If it didn't help or I fucked it up, I didn't want you to see that. I didn't want you to know if I failed. It was important to me to work on myself before I tried to work on anything with us." My lids lowered, and I centered myself the best I could. Telling him all of that had been painful, yet cathartic.

"Well, I'm here now. I want to be here with you and the baby. I don't want to miss a thing if I can help it."

"Did you guys get your shit straight?" I heard my brother say from the patio door.

I gave Nico a questioning glance. He looked over his shoulder to Angel. "We're figuring it out."

"Good. Korrie needs your help, and I need to have a word with my *brother*."

With a glare, I cocked my head in warning at Angel. He'd made me several promises when I admitted who the father was. One of those was that he wouldn't beat the shit out of Nico. The other was that he wouldn't tell anyone Nico was the father of my baby until I could tell Nico. The last promise was that he would let us try to figure things out without losing his shit.

"I'll say goodbye before I go," Nico promised me as he drew his thumb over my lip.

One last parting glare at my brother, and I went inside. But I wasn't going far. If I needed to intervene, I would. Not that Nico would appreciate that, but Angel had given me his word.

"He's not going to kill him, I promise," Korrie said, and I jumped. Glancing over my shoulder, I saw her sitting on the chaise lounge in their sunken family room. A smirk curled her lips.

"I think I love him, Korrie," I admitted.

"I've no doubt. But you need to let them work shit out or it's always going to come between them. The club is a powerful thing with them. Not that our relationships with our men aren't as important, but they have a bond that is difficult to explain. Angel told me a little about Chains's past, and I can promise you, the club is vital to him. They *are* his family—the only one he knows. I just want you to understand that it's not fair to make him choose between you and the club." She took a sip of her water.

"I would never!" I said, upset at the mere thought of making him choose. But if they tried to make him stay away from me, I wouldn't go down without a fight.

Never again was someone else making my life choices.

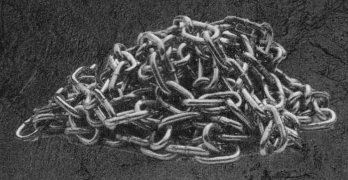

EIGHTEEN

Chains

"SAVIOR (GHOST NOTE SYMPHONIES)"—RISE AGAINST

It was late, and the clubhouse was subdued that night. E sat in the common area watching TV, but no one else was around except for the prospect at the bar. He went in the back to restock before going to bed for the night, and I lifted my drink to my lips as I held the ice pack over my eye.

"You look… like you could use a friend, young Nico," Madame Laveaux said, and I lifted my head from my hands.

"Jesus Christ, you scared the shit out of me!" Like her grandson, Voodoo, she had an innate ability to see things—know things. It had my anxiety creeping up—escalating. There were a lot of ugly things in my life I never wanted anyone to know.

"That looks terrible," she said, staring at my eye.

A snort escaped, but I didn't want to say *no shit*.

"My grandson cannot read you well. Did you know that?"

I shook my head, wondering where she was going with this.

"You need to speak to him. There is something he has seen, but he doesn't know it's about you."

"Then how do you know it is?"

She cocked an elegant brow and looked down her nose. "Because I know these things" was all the answer I got.

"Okay, sure. Talk to Voodoo. Got it." I gave her a mock salute, and she narrowed her eyes.

Belated fear coursed through me. My mood was overshadowing my common sense.

It was my turn to sigh. "Sorry. I'm in a shit mood, and it's not fair to take it out on you."

She harrumphed in acceptance.

"It's not hopeless, you know," she murmured as she stared deep in my eyes. She plucked my glass from my hands and took a drink. Surprised, I let her have it.

"How do you figure? I made a promise to a woman that I don't know if I can keep. I promised her we'd find a way to make this work, but I don't know how that's ever going to happen. I'm going to be a father that can't touch his own child unless he's wearing gloves. How would I explain to him or her why I can't touch them with my bare hands? Holy shit… what if they are like *me*?" Exasperated and worried, I dropped my face to my hands as my elbows rested on the bar top.

After a few long moments of silence, she sighed.

"There might be a way," she ominously announced. "That you could touch the woman you love and your children, I mean."

"Why don't I like the sound of that?" I warily questioned as I lowered my hands. Though we knew much of what she was capable of, the woman's full abilities were shrouded in mystery.

"It involves powerful magic, Nico. Therefore, I will only help you if she is willing. There must be true love." She poked the table with a finger as she punctuated her words. Her reply was dark and yet aloof. Eerily pale gray-blue eyes boldly stared me down.

"What magic?" Eyes narrowed, I questioned her suspiciously. A shiver hit me, sending chills through me.

"I had a vision about you and Jasmine. Afterward, I searched through volumes of old texts for a solution for you. I found something that I believe will work. It is a special potion that you each need to drink. If it works, it should have the ability to mute her thoughts in your head. If it's done before the baby is born, it will pass to your child. Voila! Your worries of family are solved." That didn't sound so bad. Maybe it tasted like shit. Oh, who was I kidding, this was Madame Laveaux; it was going to be more than some nasty-tasting drink.

"Pay attention!" she barked as she snapped her fingers in front of my face. Chagrined at letting my thoughts run away with me, I winced.

"These potions, they involve very different... um... recipes," she said as she tapped her lips thoughtfully. Unease settled in my guts.

"Like what?" I demanded. She rolled her eyes and huffed.

"So demanding. Maybe I won't help after all. Your manners are atrocious, boy."

My nostrils flared, and she chuckled.

"Teasing. You're lucky I'm a romantic. Be warned, it's likely not going to be pleasant." The baleful warning didn't sound good, neither did her wrinkled nose.

"How unpleasant?" This was beginning to sound like a child's fairytale.

"You will have to drink a potion that I would make for you. It must contain your blood in hers and her blood in yours." She shrugged as if this was no big deal.

"I'm not a fucking vampire! That's revolting," I snarled through gritted teeth.

"Aren't you?" A single brow rose, and she smirked. "You steal memories, thoughts, experiences from those you touch. Is that so very different?"

"You think I enjoy it?"

"Of course not," she scoffed. "But it is what it is."

"The point of my going away was supposedly to give me, Jasmine, and Angel time to cool off. You also instructed me to work on gaining control of my abilities—which I did, by the way. So why isn't that enough? I just need to make sure I keep them under control," I argued, my frustration building.

"Impossible. There is no way you would maintain control in moments of great emotion. Anger, terror, ecstasy; they all rob you of the ability to control yourself." She shook her head ruefully.

"So unless we do some crazy-ass ritual and drink each other's blood like vampires, we're doomed?" I asked as I shook my head in disbelief.

"Don't be dramatic. I didn't say that, but things will be as they are. Deal with it or try to change it. The choice is yours—well, and Jasmine's. You must talk to her because the clock is ticking. It must be done before she has the baby."

"Why?"

"Because it is the only way the baby will have immunity directly from its mother. Unless you changed your mind and you don't want to touch your child without gloves. It matters not to me, young Nico. I'm only an old woman trying to help." She took another swallow of my drink. The woman didn't so much as flinch at the straight whiskey. She had me in awe.

"What about if we have other children? Will we need to do this every fucking time?"

"Language! And in answer to your question, no. The transformation will be permanent once it has been done." She flicked a hand my direction, setting off the jingle of a wrist full of silver bangles.

"Sorry," I mumbled, properly chastised.

"You cannot force this on her. Though you are fated to be together, she has suffered damage to her soul. That can sometimes sever even the closest of bonds. Decker saw this, and that is why you were sent away. Not only to keep you and Jude from ripping each other apart and to learn to control your abilities." The woman rarely referred to any of us by our road names, yet when she came to visit, she stayed at the clubhouse in a guest room, not with Hawk and Julia or Voodoo and Kira. It was strange, but it was what she wanted, therefore she got it.

"If our bond has been that damaged, what's the point?"

"The point is, I believe this is fixable. She has made great strides, yet she still believes herself unworthy of you or any man. It will be up to you to prove she is, because she must be certain."

"How the hell am I supposed to do that?"

"That has not been revealed to me yet." She abruptly stood, the barstool scraping the floor. "You're a smart boy. Figure it out." Without a goodnight, goodbye, kiss my ass, nothing, she walked off. As she reached the entrance to the back hall, she turned. "Speak to Voodoo."

Then she soundlessly went to her room.

The next morning, I woke feeling as if I hadn't slept a wink. My sleep was plagued with nightmares of the wolf I always thought I saw when I was younger. In my dream, it killed Jasmine, then ate our baby. It was so horrific that I rushed to the bathroom and hurled until I thought my stomach would turn inside out.

When I was sure I was done, I stood on shaking legs and ran a trembling hand over my face before I rinsed my mouth, brushed my teeth, and used mouthwash twice. It took all that to remove the bitter taste of fear from my tongue.

Remembering Madame Laveaux's instructions, I dressed. My

eyes caught on the necklace I wore. It was such a part of me, I often forgot I wore it. I ran my fingertips over the smooth curves and realized my dreams might be because I'd always been obsessed with wolves. I laughed at my ridiculous mind for making me dream such stupid shit.

Once I had my keys, wallet, pistol, and had slipped on my cut, I went out to the common area. Not wanting to waste time, I went into the kitchen where several of the members were sitting at the long table. I grabbed a biscuit, loaded it with eggs, cheese, and bacon. As I passed the table, I swiped a piece of bacon off Ghost's plate.

"Hey! There's more right there!" He pointed to the buffet Reya was refilling. Her colored-contact enhanced green eyes looked over at me, and she gave me a once-over with a wanton gaze. It was no secret she thought she'd eventually become an ol' lady and didn't care who the patch was.

Not happening. She'd been with every brother here at one time or another, which was whatever, but that wasn't ol' lady material. She was also crazy as fuck, and I didn't have time for her bullshit.

"Yours is better," I said with a grin before I shoved the entire piece in my mouth and walked out to his grumbling.

Halfway to the door, I stopped when he called out to me. "Yeah?"

"I need to talk to you."

"Okay?" I drew out the word. "But I need to get going. I'm supposed to go see Jasmine."

He ran a hand through his shoulder-length dark blond hair. "Yeah, well, it's about that. I owe you an apology."

My teeth ground as I waited to see what he said. If he said he'd been with her, I might have to knock his teeth out. Especially after what he'd said to me all those years ago.

"I was wrong to steer you away from Jasmine." My shoulders relaxed, and I realized I'd tensed every muscle in my body.

"Brother, we can't change things that are in the past. It's more about acknowledging how we could've done things differently or better," I said. One corner of my mouth lifted.

"Yeah, well, I figured out she was pregnant several weeks ago. I didn't know it was yours at the time or I would've gotten her to talk to you. When I did confront her, I told her you needed to know. I wanted to apologize to you because I feel like I fucked with your life when I had no right to, but I was afraid of you getting kicked out after you'd only been patched a hot minute. You're a good brother, and I know the Royal Bastards are your family." He pressed his lips in a flat line.

"I know you were looking out for my best interests. Maybe you were right, though. I'm not sure I was ready to be the man I needed to be for her at that time. But I'm not fucking it up again. I'm going to do everything in my power to figure things out." I paused and wet my lip, because this was difficult for me. "This isn't just some chick having my kid, this is real. She's… she's important to me."

"I get it," he said with a haunted look that he quickly shook off. We embraced, and I shoved a bite of the sandwich in my mouth as I walked outside. The September sun was shining, and it was already shaping up to be a hot one as summer lingered.

Voodoo pulled in as I settled on my bike and slipped on my shades, so I waited as he backed in next to me. When he cut the motor, he pulled off his Ray-Bans and grinned at me. "Hey bro, where you headed?"

It was impossible to keep the grin from my face, but I looked away then back before I shook my head. "Going to see Jasmine."

He smirked. "Angel kick your ass yet?"

In answer, I pulled off my sunglasses. He whistled at the shiner I was sporting. "Damn, and he didn't take care of it afterward?"

A snort escaped me, and he laughed. "I had it coming. Didn't even put up a fight." I shrugged. Some people probably think the way we handle things is barbaric, but it's second nature in this world. You don't break the code without getting your ass beat. Truthfully, I got off lucky, and I damn well knew it.

He nodded, because he got it.

"Hey, before I go, your grandmother said I need to talk to you. That you had a vision that you didn't realize was for me."

Confused, he cocked his head, then understanding dawned. "Oh, yeah. I had a vision that didn't make sense, so I spoke to my grandmother about it, but I still didn't realize what it was about. She said it was you?"

"Yeah."

"Huh. You know how I've never been able to read you?"

I nodded as I waited for him to continue.

"It's the weirdest fucking thing. Anyway, yeah, I've had the same vision several times. Usually it's the same, sometimes there are slight variations."

While he spoke, I lit a cigarette and took a deep drag. I rarely smoked anymore, but something told me I needed it.

"Other than your necklace, what does a wolf mean to you? I keep getting this vision of a wolf with silver eyes and a damaged ear. You're never in the vision, so I didn't connect it with you." His brow furrowed in confusion.

My heart stuttered as he studied me.

Seriously, I damn near fell off my bike.

"Honestly, I have no clue, but I dream about that wolf a lot. For years of my childhood, I thought I was nuts because I often thought I saw a wolf. Last night was different though. It was fucked-up, man." My hand shook slightly as I took a long, deep drag.

"I'm gonna see what I can find out. Maybe Granmé can help me decipher some of it or can come up with a different idea."

At his mention of his grandmother and her ideas, a chill skated across my skin. It got me thinking about what she'd said to me the night before.

"I appreciate it," I said as I nodded and started my bike. He waved as he got off and turned to head inside.

Fuck, I needed to talk to Jasmine and hope she didn't think I'd lost my fucking mind.

NINETEEN

Jasmine

"SAY YOU WON'T LET GO"—JAMES ARTHUR

"You're going to wear a hole in my damn floor, Jazzy," my brother said as he sipped his coffee and read something on his phone.

"Don't even talk to me. I'm still mad at you for last night. You said you wouldn't hurt him."

"Hell, that was nothing. He was lucky that was all I did. And I said I wouldn't kill him. I never said I wouldn't blacken his eye." He gave a careless shrug, and I growled in frustration.

I'd slept like shit last night. No matter how many times I woke up, I fell back into the same dream on repeat. It was the same one I had occasionally over the years, but it was insane. It was of the wolf that watched me from the shadows. We were in the middle of freaking Iowa—there were no wolves here. So the odds of me encountering a wolf in the wild were less than slim.

"It was still fucked-up. He's your friend—your 'brother.'" I made air quotes.

My brother's expression went hard. "Yeah, he is. Which is

why he should've known what he was doing was wrong. What he did is against the club's code. The thing is? You're right, he is my friend, and I would've thought he'd at least have the nuts to come talk to me. Ask if it was okay. Tell me he wanted to be with my sister in more than a one-night way. Something. *Anything* but hiding it like you were his dirty little secret. That's what pissed me off more than anything."

A stabbing ache hit me in the chest like a shot. I sucked in a ragged breath because it was difficult and blew it out hard. "Jude. That wasn't his fault. He wanted to talk to you. He repeatedly said he wanted to tell you. But I wouldn't let him. If anyone was in the wrong, it was me. I shamelessly used him because I trusted him not to hurt me. And he let me," I said with a pleading gaze. I wanted my brother to understand it wasn't Nico's fault.

"Jasmine, I understand what you're saying, but regardless, as a man and a brother, he fucked up. We settled it. Drop it." Rarely, did my brother use such an authoritative tone with me. It wasn't harsh, but it was firm and brooked no argument.

"So you're good with him now?" I clarified as my hand rested protectively on my baby bump. His eyes softened. It was important that my brother and Nico be okay if he and I were going to make this insane relationship successful.

"I said it was settled, didn't I?"

"Just like that?" I asked, disbelieving.

"You want me to kick his ass again?"

"Hell no!"

"Well, that's good to know," the voice that I'd both missed and dreaded hearing for the last four months said from behind me. Butterflies let loose in my belly, and my heart damn near exploded as his deep tone poured through me like warm honey. Korrie must've let him in as she went upstairs with Angeline.

Slowly, I turned to face him and captured my lower lip in my teeth. God, the man was sexy. Tall, dark, and handsome barely covered it. Add in those tattoos that told a million stories, the dark hair that flopped over his forehead, and his mesmerizing eyes the color of the richest chocolate, and his beauty was damn near deadly. Muscles rippled with each movement, and damn did he fill out those jeans perfectly.

And he was mine.

"Hey," I said softly and way too breathlessly as his mouth kicked up on one side. Yeah, he'd caught me drooling. The shiner my brother had given him didn't detract from his good looks one bit, but it did make me want to smack my brother upside his head.

"You ready?" he asked. I nodded. Then he looked a little nervous as he cast a glance to my brother before locking on me. "Do you mind if we take your cage? I only have my bike, and I don't really want to risk it with you. I'll have to get a cage of my own soon," he said as his gaze dropped to where my hand still rested over the curve of my stomach.

"Look at you, already getting domestic and shit," my asshole brother said.

To my surprise, Nico flipped him off with a chuckle. Angel stood, and for a second I held my breath. I needn't have worried. They embraced, then my brother slipped on his cut that matched Nico's. Did it make me disloyal to my big brother that I thought Nico looked better in his? I grinned at the thought.

"What?" my brother asked as he caught my smile.

"Nothing," I said, my smile spreading wider.

He hugged me tightly. "God, sis, it's good to see you smile."

Pressing my nose into the soft leather of his cut, I nodded. "It *feels* good to smile," I agreed.

For a few moments, we quietly held each other and remembered simpler times. Then he stepped back and gave me a peck on the cheek.

"Take care of my sister," he demanded of Nico as he passed him. He gave him a squeeze on the shoulder and went upstairs to say goodbye to Korrie and his daughter.

Looping my arms around Nico's neck, I kissed his chin playfully.

"Are you sure you want me to go with to your therapy appointment?" Nico asked as we heard my brother's bike start, then the roar of his motor fading down the road.

After a deep breath, I nodded. "Yes, I am. I'd like you to meet Helen, and she wants to meet you."

We weren't going to have couples therapy, per se, but she did want to meet him and talk with us for a few minutes before I had my session. She and I had discussed it, and I wanted him to know what I'd been working on, the progress I'd made, and how he could help if I needed him to.

He stepped closer, and I backed up until he caged me in against the counter. "Then we're going to talk. Okay?"

"Yes. Talk." I literally had to repeat what he'd said because with him that close, my brain was scrambled.

He leaned in and trailed the tip of his nose along my jaw. The two piercings tickled, and I shivered. "Cold?" he asked, causing his breath to warm my neck.

"Uh-uh," I breathed out, nearly trembling at his proximity to my body. After everything I'd been through, I still wanted this man more than my next breath.

"Let's go," he whispered in my ear and placed a kiss on my temple.

He stood to his full height, which sent my senses into overdrive again and took my hand in his gloved one.

"What are we going to tell her about your gloves?" I asked with a thoughtful crinkle in my brow.

He shrugged, then grinned. "We'll say I have a skin condition and leave it at that."

"Okay."

Korrie still hadn't come downstairs, so I assumed she was napping with Angeline. Since Trace was in school, I set the alarm on the door as we left. He caught my hand and held it as we walked to my car.

"So what kind of vehicle are you gonna get? Jeep like Voodoo? Truck like my brother? Or are you more into muscle cars like Ghost?" I asked as he backed my car out of the driveway. He caught my eye as he shifted into drive.

"I was kinda thinking about a Range Rover or a BMW SUV," he said.

"Huh," I said in surprise. "I figured you'd want something cool."

"What's not cool about a Rover or a Beemer?" he asked as he turned the corner out of my brother's neighborhood.

Wide-eyed, I stared at him. "Those are like, umm… family trucksters," I said with my face screwed up in a scowl.

His laugh made me want to swoon. Then he glanced at my pregnant belly with an arched brow, and I did.

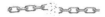

My counseling appointment went better than I thought. Nico was extremely supportive, and Helen approved.

Nico took me for a late lunch, then we went back to his room at the clubhouse. Since I'd let my apartment lease run out after my place had been ransacked thanks to my father, I didn't have a place. Neither did he. That would be one thing I needed to figure out, because I couldn't keep staying with my brother forever.

"I'm going to have to get a place soon," I said as I sat on the edge of his bed. He grabbed the chair from the desk and spun it around to straddle it. Resting his arms on the back, he propped his chin on his forearm and thoughtfully gazed at me.

"Me too," he said. "Can't have my kid here when I spend time with him."

"Or her," I added with a smirk, though his words sent a little pang through my heart. Did he not see us together later? I shoved my worries down for another day.

His eyes went wide. "Don't do that to me. Please don't do that to me."

My laugh was instantaneous and boisterous. "You're hilarious. You do understand that it's your sperm that determines whether it a boy or a girl, right?"

"Well, in that case, it's a boy. My sperm are badasses, and they wouldn't dare give me a girl." He seemed so certain and serious that I fell over onto the bed laughing.

Next thing I knew, he was sweeping my feet off the floor and depositing me in the center of the bed. As I continued to laugh, he crawled up and nestled his hips against mine. He kept his weight off me on his elbows.

"You think that's funny, do you?" he asked with a mischievous tilt of his lips. When he rubbed his beard on my neck and chest, I continued to giggle with an occasional snort. Breathless, I gasped as my laughter died down, but my smile remained.

"That was some of the funniest shit I've heard in a long while," I said, still grinning as I raised my hand to his cheek. The soft skin of his lower lip teased the pad of my thumb as I skimmed across it. Before I could pull it away, he playfully captured it in his teeth and flicked his tongue over the end.

He released me as he glanced down to the baby sandwiched between us. "This isn't hurting you, is it?"

I shook my head, and we both sobered as we stared in each other's eyes.

"I think you took what I said the wrong way," he murmured.

"What are you talking about?"

"When I mentioned needing a place, I saw the look in your eyes." He sighed. "It's not like I don't love the idea of coming home to you and my kid every night, but I didn't want you to feel like I was pressuring you to live with me. If you need to be independent and have your own place, I don't want to make you feel like I'm taking away your choices. I understand your need for control in your life right now."

"Thank you," I said, appreciating his thoughtfulness.

"Don't thank me too much. In any other circumstances, I'd be telling you that you're packing your shit and you and I are getting a place together because you're my fucking woman."

My heart thumped, and wetness pooled between my legs. Any other man that said that, I would've shot in the balls, but coming from Nico it was different.

"Am I?"

"What?"

"Your woman," I whispered.

His dark eyes burned into mine. "You have been since the night I took your virginity; I was just too scared and stupid to see it."

"But I've been with other—"

His hand stopped my words as he pressed it against my lips. "Please don't mention other men when I'm between your legs. You understand?"

My eyes widened at the feel of his hard length as he pressed it to my heated core, and I nodded.

"Good. This is what I propose."

My heart stuttered at the word "propose."

"We'll each get our own places. For the rest of the pregnancy, we date—yeah, I know it sounds corny. No pressure, no expectations other than really getting to know each other. Then if we decide this is something we want long-term, we let one of our places go and move in together. Yeah?" He waited as I digested what he said.

"Okay," I finally agreed.

A beautiful grin lit up his face, but then it dimmed. "There's one more thing."

"Why don't I like the sound of that?" I warily asked.

"I think I have a way for me to be able to touch you," he whispered with a furrowed brow.

"Then why don't you look happy or excited?"

"Because it's an odd solution, or fix, or whatever you want to call it," he said, then closed his eyes for a moment before staring deep into mine. "I'm not sure if I believe it will work, but I want to look into it more once we decide where this relationship is going."

"You're being extremely cryptic," I said with a wary squint. Despite my concerned curiosity, I trailed my fingertips over his face, as if memorizing every inch.

"I don't know whether to tell you now before we get more attached than we are and risk scaring you away or wait until I have you as addicted to me as I am you, first."

Despite the gravity of the conversation, the corners of my lips lifted and I bit my lip coyly. "You're addicted to me?"

"Baby, I already told you, if it was up to me and I didn't care what you thought, I'd tell you we're getting a place together because you're my woman. Period."

"Tell me how you really feel," I breathlessly replied.

"I want to protect you, worship you, and support your every need. But I also want to consume you, devour you, brand you with my mark, and *own you body and soul.*"

Holy fucking shit.

"Was that honest enough for you? Because I don't care about

who came after me, you were mine first. Everything will be right with the world as long as no man touches what's mine again." He punctuated his declaration with a slow, sensual thrust of his jean-clad cock against my needy core. I whimpered as my hips rose of their own volition to grind against him.

"I think I like the sound of that," I whispered in his ear.

With a growl, he rose to his knees and quickly divested me of my clothing. His gaze heated as he took in every change. Self-conscious, I tried to cover my breasts that had grown larger and reached for him.

"No," he said as he followed my curves, old and new, with the butter-soft leather of his gloves. Gently, he removed my arm from my chest. He sucked in a sharp breath before dropping his head to circle my already puckered nipple. A whimper escaped me as he moved to the other as he plucked at the first with his fingers.

"I need you, Nico," I begged.

Completely ignoring my request, he proceeded to slowly lick my most sensitive areas, ending with possessive nip of the tender flesh. He paused briefly to tenderly kiss the curve of my abdomen, but that wasn't what this was about, so he moved on. When he spread my thighs, his heated breath hit my core, and I clutched his hair tightly.

"Mmm, is this what my baby wanted?" he murmured between carnal kisses to my pussy. By the time he gave a swipe of his tongue through my wet slit and around my throbbing clit, I was writhing in desperation.

"Nico! Please!"

"Not until you come on my tongue. I need to taste you, Jasmine. Let me lick every drop of your honey," he said before he immediately went back to work. The man had mad skills with that mouth. My addled brain wondered if he was writing the alphabet or the words to his favorite song interspersed with thrusts into my core. Frankly, I didn't care what he was doing as long as he kept doing it.

It was heavenly. So much so that the second he sucked on my oversensitive clit, I detonated. Back arching off the bed, fingers tangled in his midnight-black hair, I screamed as I exploded all over his tongue. Then he worked every last spasm from my achingly empty sheath.

As I lay there gasping, I shamelessly begged him again. "Please, Nico, I need you inside me. Please."

One last swipe of his tongue sent a shudder through me before he climbed off the bed with a satisfied grin. Gaze hooded, I watched him slowly undress for me. Each section of inked skin he revealed literally had me salivating. He was a work of art, and I didn't mean only the tattoos. Every chiseled inch appeared carved by Michelangelo himself.

A thud signaled his boots getting kicked off. The clink of his buckle was followed by the sound of his zipper before his jeans hit the floor. Thick and long, his cock bobbed as he kicked off his socks.

As he towered above me, I dropped a hand between my legs and watched him stroking himself. When he reached the end, he gave his wrist a slight twist and shiny precum dripped from the tip. The sloppy wet sound of my fingers slipping through the arousal that drenched me had his breath hitching.

"I'm not wearing a condom. I haven't been with anyone but you since I left four months ago. I'm clean, and you're already pregnant. I want to feel your tight, wet cunt sliding over my cock—gripping it because it was made for me."

It wasn't a question, but I nodded. "Yes, please."

He gave me a wolfish smirk as he released his length and prowled up the bed to settle back between my legs. Those strong, inked hands lifted my calves and bent my knees as he spread my legs open. He gripped my wrist and removed my fingers from where they stroked my G-spot. Then he licked them clean, causing me to damn near orgasm again at the sight.

"Fuck, that's a pretty pussy," he said as he released my hand and let his shaft slide through the center of my soaked core. Then he gripped his length and slapped my clit with it a few times, making me whimper. My hips rose, intent on guiding him inside.

Finally, when I thought I would go insane with want, he lined himself up and drove as deep as he could go.

"God, yesss," I groaned as he withdrew and pushed in again. When he was fully seated, a tingle spread through me, and my eyes rolled. "So good," I drew out as I greedily clenched around him.

The feel of his smooth velvety skin against my pussy was incredible. Who would've thought a condom changed the feel of sex that much? But hell if it didn't. The heat of his cock burned against my walls, and every sensation was magnified.

Pushing my knees up and out, he changed the angle, and I damn near died from the overload of the way he stretched me with the hot silk-encased steel rod that he stroked in and out. The room was quiet but for our panting breath, the wet sound of skin against skin, and the slight squeak of the bed.

He released my legs to lean forward, and his lips captured mine as his hips continued to thrust. Relentless, he kept a steady pace as the pressure of my pending orgasm continued to build until I shattered once again.

As the bliss cleared from my haze, I gripped his corded arms. Staring into the dark depths of his dark chocolate eyes, I demanded, "Fuck me."

Instead of complying, he withdrew, and I whimpered. But before I could voice a complaint, he flipped me to my hands and knees and rammed his thick cock in to the hilt. A surprised squeak escaped me when he did it again.

"Can you handle it rough?" he asked as he paused.

I grunted in dissatisfaction at his stillness and heard him chuckle. "I'm fine," I said through clenched teeth. "Do it!"

"Oh baby..." he crooned. "I'm going to fuck you through the goddamn mattress. When I'm done with you, there won't be a single question as to whose pussy this is, because I'm gonna mark my territory all over you." He accentuated his promise with a smack to my ass that had my core clenching tightly around his cock. For a brief second, I saw the worry in his gaze as he wondered if he'd done something to trigger me.

What he didn't understand was that he was the only one I wanted. With him I was safe, cherished, and protected. If there was one thing I had worked out in therapy, it was that the horrifying memories had no place in our bed. I trusted him.

"Goddamn it, Nico, if you don't stop talking and fuck me...."

"Your wish is my command," he whispered.

That time when he did as I asked, I reveled in the give and take of our bodies. I didn't focus on the way he made me forget what had happened. I could only concentrate on how perfectly we fit together.

By the time he filled me with his hot cum, I was a rag doll collapsed in bliss.

And I knew I'd never be able to let him go again.

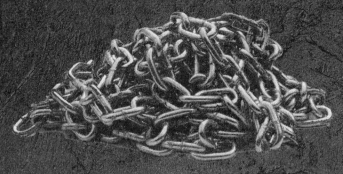

TWENTY

Chains

"GRAVEDIGGER" —DAVE MATTHEWS

A few months later....

Wiping the excess ink and blood from my work, I checked every bit with a practiced but critical eye. Then I set my equipment to the side. "What do you think?"

"Looks perfect," Venom said with a soft smile as he watched me finish cleaning the newest piece of his sleeve and cover it. It was his daughter's name and birth date written on the belly of a striking viper.

"You know the drill," I told him as he slipped his arms in his flannel and buttoned it.

"So how are things going with Jasmine?" he asked. Despite his nonchalant tone, his eyes studied me like a hawk.

Unable to hold back, I grinned. "Really good."

"Mmm," he said, then shrugged his cut over the shirt. "Madame Laveaux will be here tomorrow. She said something about you needing an answer for her by the time she got here. Does that make sense to you?"

My good mood plummeted.

I'd been procrastinating discussing the "treatment" with Jasmine. She'd asked me repeatedly if I was going to tell her what it was. Each time I put her off.

It would seem I'd run out of time.

"Yeah," I muttered before peeling off the black nitrile gloves and pitching them across the room into the trash. Not that I should be surprised. Voodoo's grandmother had called me several times to ask me what Jasmine had said. We both knew she was aware I hadn't given Jasmine the details yet, though I knew she was getting impatient.

"Thanks for taking that last-minute job in Texas with Voodoo for his brother-in-law's buddy," he said.

I shrugged. Though the things we'd stumbled upon with that job left me unsettled, I decided to keep my mouth shut for the moment. "No problem."

"You still gonna be able to do that job tonight?" he asked me.

"Yeah, I got it." Me, Voodoo, Raptor, and Angel were the best snipers in the chapter. That's why when we took on a job that required an anonymous assassination in a public place, it cycled through the four of us. This one was mine.

"You have all the details down?" he asked me.

I tapped my temple. "Yep. 2215 on the dot. The Station on Main Street, Kansas City."

Satisfied, he gave me a nod and walked toward the door. He knew better than to shake my hand when I wasn't wearing gloves, and I appreciated that.

"See you when you get back. We have church scheduled to discuss the shit that we found during the job for Dmitry,"

Venom said. I nodded and he left. Dmitry was Kira's brother. He'd called us in to help out with a situation one of his hockey buddies had gotten into.

A glance at the clock told me I had time to grab my shit, then swing by to check on Jasmine at her apartment before I had to hit the road.

I made quick work of cleaning up my station and said my goodbyes before I left the shop. Then I climbed on my bike, drove to the clubhouse, and went into the basement through the concealed door in the bar.

Knowing what I was taking with me, I went right for my new favorite. We had acquired several Remington Defense CSRs. The best of both worlds, it was a concealable sniper rifle that broke down into sections no longer than sixteen inches. It could be assembled in less than sixty seconds and broken down quicker. It was perfect for carrying in a saddlebag.

Methodically, I grabbed everything else I needed, shoved it in the small assault pack, and locked everything up again. Taking the stairs two at a time, I rushed out.

"Be back tonight," I called out to Raptor and Phoenix as they played a game of pool. Then I pulled out my phone and called Ghost.

"You about ready?" I asked him.

"Yeah," he said, sounding like he was running.

"Are you at the gym or fucking?" I asked without shame.

"You really wanna know?"

"Nope. 'Cause that's my answer."

"Meet you at your place in twenty," he said as I heard the pre-orgasmic mewls of a woman before the called ended. I shook my head and sped over to Jasmine's complex. I showed my ID to the gate guard, looked into the facial recognition camera, then entered the code to open the gate. The security of the place was the only reason I hadn't put up a fight when she decided to get separate places while we "dated."

On a tight schedule, I scanned my card at the door, then pressed my thumb to the reader, then bolted through the door and up the stairs. I let myself into her apartment and called out, "Jasmine!"

"In the office!" she replied. Her website design and management business had really taken off and I was so proud of her. It had been her dream that became her reality. Things were coming together beautifully for us too.

When I hit the doorway, she was already up and throwing her arms around my neck.

"I missed you," I said, and she giggled.

"You just saw me this morning before you left."

A grin stole across my face as I nuzzled her nose and pressed a chaste kiss to her bee-stung lips. It didn't matter how long I was away from her, it was always too long. When I had to fly to Texas to help Voodoo's brother-in-law and his friend, I'd only been home a week. The distance had me crawling out of my skin.

"And that was entirely too long ago," I said, then I stepped back to kneel at her feet. "Daddy loves you, and I'll be back later."

I kissed her very large belly as she sifted her fingers through the longer hair at the top of my head.

"What time do you think you'll be back?" she asked. "Or will you go to your place when you get back?"

"Don't wait up. It'll be late. But I'm coming back here so I can hold you."

An affectionate smile lifted the corners of her mouth, followed quickly by a concerned frown. "Please be careful," she begged. She had no idea where I was going or what I was doing, but she knew I had a mission.

"Scout's honor," I said, and she snorted.

"You weren't a Boy Scout," she scoffed with a smirk.

"No, but we can play like I'm one and you're a Brownie so I can eat you," I said.

Her laughter rang out, and my heart soared at the sound. "You are terrible."

Reluctantly, I stood. "Unfortunately, I gotta go."

One last kiss, and I rested my forehead to hers. It was on the tip of my tongue to tell her how I was feeling, but I couldn't. Not yet. She hadn't said it either, and I was loath to ruin the good thing we had going if she wasn't ready for it.

"I'll be back before you know it. Do you need anything before I go?"

"No, I have three more websites to update and I'm done for the day. My back is killing me, so I think I'll soak in the tub after I'm done."

"Grrr, now I'm thinking about you naked in the tub. I've got a chub from the mental image."

Again, she laughed. It was my favorite sound. One last kiss and I left, ensuring her door was locked.

I made it back to my place with five minutes to spare, but Ghost was sitting on his bike thumbing through shit on his phone.

"Damn, what did you do? Nut, smack her ass, and leave?" I joked with a chuckle.

He shrugged. "Pretty much."

My eyes rolled, and I went inside to change. While Jasmine had chosen an apartment, I had bought a house. It was in Angel and Korrie's gated neighborhood and was the perfect setup for a family. Jasmine had fallen in love with it, but she was being stubborn about moving in. I respected her choice, but it didn't mean I had to like it.

Dark jeans, black T-shirt, black boots, black hoodie, and an old black leather jacket was my uniform for the night. In less than ten minutes, Ghost and I were heading down I35 toward Kansas City.

The job was a sadistic, abusive husband who was cheating on his wife with his secretary. The last time he'd beat his wife so bad that he put her in the hospital for two weeks and had the authorities believing it was a mugging. While she was in the hospital, he was fucking his secretary in his office and in their bed.

Her brother found out and tried to get her to go to the authorities, but she was terrified.

That's where we stepped in. The brother was loaded and connected to Gabriel De Luca. Oh, and he also happened to be another of Voodoo's brothers-in-law. Storm Montgomery had married Voodoo's stepsister, Rose. We'd all been surprised as fuck when she had turned up, but we'd quickly taken her under our wing.

Ghost and I parked our bikes in a parking garage, then I slung the small backpack over my shoulder and we casually walked down the sidewalk.

"We made good time," Ghost said as we reached the building Facet had scouted out as our best location.

"Yep," I said as I grabbed the fire escape ladder with a gloved hand and pulled it down. When there was no response to the slight sound it had made, we climbed up to the roof.

The intel we had from one of the shitbag's men said the douche canoe was going to arrive at the popular nightclub around ten fifteen. Storm wanted the hit to be public. He wanted it to be known that he was cheating with the secretary when he died. Evidently, the dickwad's parents were real assholes too. Storm wanted it to make the papers that he was a lying, cheating fuck. Personally, I didn't give a shit. A job was a job, and the mark was a piece of crap. That's all I needed to know.

After we each pulled on a thin black balaclava, we got to work. It took no time at all to set up, and then we waited. Ghost kept me apprised of the time as I watched the comings and goings at the club through my scope. When the time came, I needed to ensure there was no collateral damage. It was a busy club, and there were a lot of people that would be standing in line to get in.

The guy had bodyguards that traveled with him because he had several enemies due to dirty business practices. That made it helpful for us too. There would be so many possible suspects, that they'd never figure anything out. Besides the fact that we were good at what we did.

"There he is," Ghost said barely above a whisper as the tool helped his mistress out of the fancy town car dropping them off.

From the second he said that to the moment the guy dropped dead on the sidewalk probably took less than a minute. Before he hit the ground, I was breaking down my weapon and packing up. Ghost and I ripped off the balaclavas, shoved them in the pack, and quickly made it back to the ground. We were walking back to the bikes as if it was another normal Saturday night.

We were turning into the garage entrance when I had a strange sensation and turned slightly right. I heard the pop, and my arm was on fire.

"Fuck!" I said as I stumbled and fell. Ghost disappeared, and I painfully got back to my feet, then hurried to my bike. Wincing, I stashed the bag in my saddlebag, locked it, and climbed on.

Ghost reappeared as I was starting it. "You okay?" he asked, and I nodded. "Guy disappeared into thin air, and I don't know how far behind him the other guys were or how the fuck they knew it was us."

We both looked at the other with concern, and I knew we were both wondering the same thing. Did the guy have the same ability Ghost did?

"Let's go!" I said, gritting my teeth against the burn. We raced out of the garage on the opposite side and didn't stop until we hit a small gas station right after crossing back into Iowa. We filled up, then moved into the shadows alongside the building.

"Take off your jacket," he ordered.

"I'm fine," I insisted, but I was feeling a little lightheaded.

"That wasn't a request, goddamn it!"

"Jesus fucking Christ," I muttered, then I flinched as I shrugged out of my jacket.

"Holy shit," he said under his breath as he realized my hoodie sleeve was soaked with blood. Using his knife, he sliced off the sleeve, wrapped it in a plastic bag, and shoved it in his saddlebag.

As Ghost assessed the damage, I breathed deeply to keep my head steady. I winced a few times but didn't make a peep as he wrapped my bicep and grumbled to himself.

"We need to get you home to Angel. We're about halfway. Think you can make it?"

I nodded, but shit started to spin when I did.

He whipped out his phone, and I heard him talking but half of it didn't register as he ran inside and came out with a Gatorade and clean hands.

"Drink this," he said as he held out the open bottle. I shot him a deadpan look but took the bottle with my left hand and chugged it.

"Let's go if we're gonna go," I said as I handed him the empty bottle that he stashed in his saddlebag with the bag holding my sleeve. I prayed he hadn't left any evidence behind when he went inside.

Ghost was bitching and cussing the entire time we got situated until we hit the road again. It was like I was driving drunk, but I forced myself to keep my eyes open and riding in a straight line. The rest of the trip was a blur. The next thing I remembered was awkwardly kicking the kickstand down, then falling off my bike.

I woke in the infirmary with Angel staring down at me. If thunder had a face, it would look like him at that moment.

"What the fuck are you talking about?" he asked me with his arms crossed.

Obviously, I'd said that out loud.

"Uh, yeah, you did." A dark brow arched as he blinked at me.

"Fuck, how long have I been out?" There was a slight twinge in my arm that hit me as I sat up.

"That will go away soon. You got back here about two hours ago."

"Shit, Jasmine," I said as I tried to get off the gurney.

"Sit your ass down. You know better than to pop up like that. Go slow. Just because I healed you doesn't mean you're good as new yet."

"I told her I'd be there," I argued.

"Well, I guess it's a good thing I had Phoenix go get her. They should be back here any minute now," he said with a shake of his head. I glanced at the time.

"Dammit, Angel. Why would you wake her up at four in the morning? You should've just let me go to her," I grumbled as I fell back to the pillow, not wanting to admit I was lightheaded.

"I didn't wake her up. She called me, worried about *you* because you weren't there yet."

"Shit," I muttered. Jasmine needed her sleep, and she didn't need the stress of worrying about me.

Venom, Raptor, Voodoo, Facet, Squirrel, and Blade came in. "Good to see you're doing okay," Venom said as he gave me a gruff but concerned look.

"Jesus, don't any of you sleep?" I asked as I sighed and closed my eyes.

"Someone ratted us out. Gabriel's men picked up the informant to see if he double-crossed us. No way did that guy just happen to know it was us to shoot at," I heard Ghost say and cracked an eye open.

"If they knew it was us, then who's to say they don't plan to come after us?" I asked, suddenly worried about the safety of our families, but mostly Jasmine and my unborn child.

"That's why we're bringing everyone in. We'll be on lockdown until we get some answers from Gabriel," Venom said. "Everyone is already here; we're just waiting on Jasmine and Phoenix."

Jasmine was going to be pissed. She loved having her freedom. The last thing she would want was to be confined to the clubhouse again.

A commotion in the hall had all of us on edge until I heard my woman's voice in the hall. "Ghost, if you don't let me in that room right fucking now, I'm going to rearrange that pretty face of yours!"

"And that's my sister," Angel said with proud grin. In truth, all of us were pretty happy to hear her sounding so spunky. She'd continued with her therapy every week and had made massive strides. Though she occasionally had a setback or two, I was proud as hell of her.

The door flew open, and my whiskey-eyed, sable-haired, pregnant as fuck avenging angel burst in. "Nico!"

"I'm fine, I promise," I said as she rushed to my side and wrapped her arms around my neck. Without thinking, I hugged her with my hands splayed over her soft long-sleeved T-shirt. The tips of my fingers brushed the skin at the neck of her shirt under her untamed hair. When ripples of memories started to surface, I quickly balled my fists and lifted them off her while keeping her in my embrace.

Her cold hands palmed my cheeks when she pulled back. "When you didn't show up, I figured it was okay because you said it would be late, but when you weren't home by three, I started to panic and called Angel. He sent Phoenix, who made me *pack a bag.*"

With a wry smile, I sighed. "Sorry, babe. We'll get shit sorted as soon as we can."

"As long as you're okay, I don't care. And I'm staying in his room," she firmly announced to her brother with a glare. He gave it right back to her, but quickly backed down when she snapped, "No! This is *my* life and *my* decision. For fuck's sake, Angel, how the hell do you think I got pregnant? Like I haven't seen the goods already." She rolled her eyes at her brother.

I couldn't help it, I laughed my ass off at Angel's expression. He flipped me off.

"Well, let's get this big oaf to his room so we can all get a little sleep," Venom instructed as he motioned to me.

Angel and Ghost helped me to my feet and kept me steady as I walked back to my room, where I promptly collapsed on the bed. Angel might've healed me, but afterward the "patient" was always a little weak and groggy. The amount of damage impacted how Angel fared. Then again, if I'd been out for over two hours, he already crashed and recuperated.

"Scoot over," I heard Jasmine say after she shooed everyone out of the room and locked the door.

Too tired to argue, I did as she asked and waited for her to climb in. She leaned over me and kissed my lips. "I'll be back in a sec, okay?"

I nodded, hating feeling so tired.

She went in the bathroom, and I heard her messing around, presumably getting ready for bed. Then she shut the light out and used her phone for light to get to the bed.

When her warm body curled up into mine, I wrapped an arm around her and held her close. My baby gave my arm a boot, and I smiled. I'd worry about what had happened later. For the moment, I was going to enjoy the feel of my woman cuddled up close, knowing she and my baby were safe.

For now.

TWENTY-ONE

Jasmine

"SOMEONE WHO CARES"—THREE DAYS GRACE

I woke with a start. Nico's arm reflexively tightened around me. With a sigh of relief, I relaxed when I realized it had only been a dream and I was safe in bed with the man I loved. Though I was having a hard time shaking off the dream of the wolf with silver eyes.

Holy shit. I love him. Not that I should be surprised. In the back of my mind, I knew I'd loved him for years. Stubbornness and fear had kept us apart, but no more.

It had shaken me to the core when I had that dream that Nico had been shot. When he didn't show up at my apartment, I called my brother. Imagine my surprise when he said he was sending Phoenix for me and to pack a bag for a few days. I'd never told a living soul about my dreams, so I didn't know how to tell my brother I'd known something was wrong.

There was a knock on the door, and Nico stirred behind me. "Who is it?" he called out in a voice rough from sleep.

"It is Madame Laveaux. Open the door. You must hurry!"

We both jolted out of the bed. Immediately, I missed the heat of his bare chest against my back.

Not bothering with a shirt, he padded barefoot to the door. With each step, I admired how his jeans sat low on his hips. He glanced over his shoulder as I was pulling one of his T-shirts out of the drawer and over my head. It fell nearly to my knees, and he smirked.

He'd barely gotten the door open before Madame Laveaux barged in and barked, "It's time."

"Time for what?" I asked in confusion as my gaze flickered from her to Nico and back.

"You must decide," she said to me as if I had any idea what she was talking about.

"Decide what?" I asked, baffled at the wizened woman glaring at Nico with her arms akimbo.

"You *still* haven't told her?" she questioned with a huff.

Imagine my surprise when I saw my big, burly man appear chagrined and drop his gaze. Then again, Madame Laveaux had always had that effect on people. No one wanted to cross her out of fear that she might curse them. Those of us who knew her well simply respected the hell out of her and, along with a tiny dose of fear, did our best not to piss her off.

"Told me what?" I said in exasperation as I threw my arms out.

Madame Laveaux sighed as she shook her head. "Leave it to a man. I should've spoken to you myself. I've known you since you were little, chasing after the Ogun and Jude in your little pigtails."

Nico had the balls to give me a playful grin at her mention of me in pigtails. I rolled my eyes, and he snickered.

"This is not a laughing matter!" She propped her fists on her hips and glared at Nico.

"Okay, look," I finally said. "I have no clue what's going on, so will someone please quit beating around the bush and tell me what you're talking about?"

"I have brought the ingredients with the exception of the two most important," she began. "Nico was supposed to talk to you to see if you were willing to commit to him."

I choked, and he helpfully patted my back.

"Commit?" I believed we were pretty damn committed to each other, but was she talking about us getting *married*? And what the hell did that have to do with the price of tea in China?

She sighed. "Jasmine. Do you love him? If so, I have a solution to the interference of his gift in your relationship. However, if you have not been able to heal your heart, it will be not only dangerous, but unadvisable."

"Madame Laveaux, you can't put that kind of pressure on her," Nico argued with a furrowed brow. His sleep-tousled hair flopped in sexy disarray over his forehead and covered one deep brown eye.

"No, Nico, it's okay. I should've told you before, because when I thought something had happened to you, I was beside myself with worry. When we went to bed, I was so thankful you were alive, but I realized I could've lost you without telling you how I feel. I do love you, Nico—more than words can say. Not that this was how I planned on telling you." The last bit I muttered.

Mouth hanging open, he stared at me blinking for a moment before his face lit up and a smile brightened the room. He pulled me to him until my massive baby bump was sandwiched between us.

"You love me?" he asked with that wicked, wicked gleam in his eyes that matched his naughty grin.

"Yes," I boldly admitted.

"Well, hot damn. Because guess what? I love you too."

We both stood their grinning at each other like fools until Madame Laveaux cleared her throat.

"If you two are done making googly eyes at each other, we don't have much time."

"Again, time for what?" I asked.

"This big oaf was supposed to talk to you about this," she muttered. "I found a solution in an old text. Nico wants to be able to freely touch his woman and his children—I can help with that. There is a special recipe that I must work with, however. It has certain ingredients that must be gathered a specific way. I brought everything with me except for what you must provide."

"And what might that be?" I asked, glancing from her to Nico. He didn't look happy.

"Blood from you both."

"Excuse me?" I deadpanned.

Nico let loose a heavy sigh. "Now do you see why I was reluctant to bring it up?" I wasn't sure if he was talking to me or Madame Laveaux, but it didn't really matter.

"What exactly will this magic elixir do?" I asked with a disbelieving gaze and making sarcastic quote motions when I said "magic elixir." If I didn't know half of what I knew, I might think the woman was off her rocker. The thing was, I knew a lot. The abilities my brother and many of his friends had were things most people believed were out of books and movies.

"It will subdue his ability to read you. He will no longer see your thoughts and memories. If it is done before the baby arrives, then it will pass from you to the unborn child and any further children you might have. It will be unpleasant, and there is some risk to you and the baby, which is why it's imperative you're certain this is what you want. If your heart is not one hundred percent onboard, the results could be disastrous. You can't force someone to love you, because the magic knows the truth." The ominous declaration made my stomach drop and my heart stutter.

"Hurt my baby?" I turned to face Voodoo's grandmother with

bugged eyes. The thought of anything happening to it had ice running through my veins, and I rested a protective hand over the now large bump.

"There is a slight chance, but if you truly love him, there will be no worries," Madame Laveaux said as she gently laid a hand to my shoulder and her silver bracelets jingled. "You must look deep in your heart and decide if the love you feel for him is a forever love and not a passing fancy."

For a moment I was nervous, but then a calm passed over me, and I knew my answer. "I love him more than my next breath. He and my baby are the two most important people in my life."

He stepped up behind me and pressed a kiss to the crown of my disheveled hair as his arm wrapped around me to rest over mine on my pregnant belly.

"I have no hesitations," he said in my ear, and my heart filled to bursting.

"Good. Then you must follow me to Voodoo's temple. Hurry get dressed."

"What's the rush?" I asked.

She paused with her hand on the knob. "It must be done before the baby arrives."

"But we have time," I argued with a laugh.

"The baby will be coming tomorrow." She stared at us with an expression that brooked no argument.

Nico and I glanced at each other in shock. I wasn't due for another two weeks. Madame Laveaux snapped her fingers, and we were clambering to get clothes on. Within minutes we were rushing out to the common area.

Voodoo was waiting, and he motioned for us to follow him.

The January wind was biting and numbing as I tugged my beanie down over my ears and clasped Nico's gloved hand in mine. Silently, we followed Voodoo down the snowy path that led to the farm across the field. The shed he used as a temple loomed ahead at the back of the property.

With each step, my heart pounded harder. There was no doubt of my feelings, but the abilities Voodoo and his grandmother had were unnerving at times.

The snow swirled around our legs as the wind picked up. By the time we reached the small building, it was whipping my hair in my face. Voodoo ushered us inside, and we were immediately enveloped in warmth and the cloying scent of incense. Candles were scattered around the room and were the only light source.

We stomped the snow off our boots on the mat.

"Come. Sit." Madame Laveaux said as she waved a hand to indicate we should sit on the other side of the short table. It barely sat two feet off the ground. There was a rug under it that I knelt on, then cast a glance at Nico. He gave my hand a reassuring squeeze.

The moment we both settled in across from her, she began to chant in a language I didn't recognize. My gaze took in the odd items laid out on the red fabric over the table. There were also two small glass bottles with the stoppers set to the side with an intricately decorated silver dagger.

When her chanting abruptly ended, the candle flames flickered, and a shiver skated over my skin.

She held out a delicate hand to me, and I placed mine in hers. Her skin was cool and soft as she turned my palm up.

Without a word, she picked up the silver dagger and brought it to my hand. Instinctively I pulled away, but she held me in a surprisingly strong grip. "Be still!"

I froze. "I'm sorry! This is a little freaky!"

Again, she brought the knife to my hand with a shake of her head and a sigh. She used the razor-sharp tip to pierce the end of my index finger, and I gasped. Blood immediately pooled, and she held my finger over one bottle. When seven drops had fallen in the bottle, she capped it, then used my bleeding finger to trail over Nico's bottom lip before she pushed my finger in his mouth. We both startled before the wet heat of his mouth wrapped around my injured finger stirred a primal need in my core.

Then she removed it and placed a small silk square over it and motioned for me to hold pressure on it.

"Control your senses, young Nico," she murmured, then repeated the process with him after removing his glove. But with him, she placed eleven drops in the bottle before corking it. When she raised his finger to paint his blood over my lower lip, my heart raced.

The second his blood hit my lip, a tingling sensation washed over me. The coppery tang hit my tongue when she pushed his fingertip into my mouth. Then my tongue began to tingle. My lips closed around him, and I realized he was touching me. His respirations were labored, and his eyes were closed tight.

He released a relieved breath when she removed his finger and placed a matching square of silk over his, which he held in place.

She chanted in a low murmur as she made motions and lowered her head as if in prayer. Then she abruptly lifted her head, and her silver-blue eyes hit us both.

"Now you go. I need peace for this work. One tiny miscalculation and it could have disastrous results." We froze and gave her mouth-gaping stares.

She rolled her eyes. "Kidding—I just need time to work. I will find you when the time is right. Do not go far."

Dual huffs of relief left us as we glanced at each other and shook our heads.

As if I'd go far when she told me I was having my baby tomorrow.

Jesus, what had we gotten ourselves into?

Voodoo stayed behind with his crazy-ass grandmother, and I

returned to the clubhouse with Nico. I'd always loved the woman, but damn she had a flare for drama.

While Nico had an impromptu meeting with Venom and Raptor, I made a sandwich, then went to his room. Exhausted, I rested in his bed, only waking when his heat pressed against my back and the weight of his arm wrapped around me.

Cocooned in the safety of his arms, I slept.

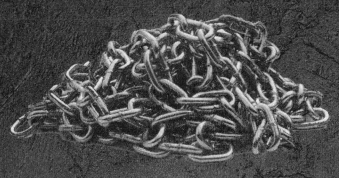

TWENTY-TWO

Chains

"YOU"—BREAKING BENJAMIN

"Y ou sure you're doing okay, Chains?" Venom asked as we all sat at the table for church that afternoon.

"Hell, yeah. Thanks to Angel," I said.

"We need to discuss what we stumbled into when we went down to Texas to help Voodoo's brother-in-law." Venom's fingers thrummed on the dark wood. Kristoffer Halvorson was an NHL hockey player who played for the Austin Amurs with Kira's brother Dmitry and her cousin Jericho. Kristoffer had run into some trouble when the father of his ol' lady's twins was killed and the assholes went after her—yeah, it was a crazy situation.

"I'm not so sure we need to get mixed up in that any more than we already did," Raptor muttered.

"So we just let those motherfuckers kill a brother in arms because he found out about what they were up to?" I asked. Though I never knew him, I was special forces the last few years of my time in the army. If you couldn't trust the guys in your team, who the fuck *could* you trust? Shit.

"I'm not opposed to ensuring that the men responsible for taking out one of our nation's elite like that are dealt with. Especially considering two of the guys are supposed to be people who had his back," Voodoo murmured.

A chorus of "amen" rounded the room. With many of us being veterans, it struck a chord with us that Adam had been a victim of such betrayal.

"Adam had all the details on that thumb drive. He should've gone to his superiors and turned the info in to them instead of shipping the drive back to his baby mama," Kicker said.

"Maybe, but he wasn't sure who all he could trust. I believe he was waiting until he got back so he could go through his trusted chain of command. That's only a guess, but it's clear in the notes on the drive that he wasn't sure who he could trust on that mission. He specifically said he was worried he might not make it back alive because he thought at least one of the guys knew he was onto them. That had to have been a shitty feeling," I argued.

"So do we pass the drive on to the appropriate channels, or do we deal with this on our own?" Voodoo asked the question we were all thinking.

"I say we pass it on. We aren't the world's police," muttered Squirrel.

"No, but we have taken it upon ourselves to ensure that the victims of the world get justice in situations where we don't think the system will do it," Angel added.

"True, but we're usually getting paid to do it," grumbled Squirrel.

"Then you don't need to be a part of it," I interjected as I shot to my feet.

"Easy, bro. This isn't personal, but you're making it that way," he volleyed back as he also stood.

"It *is* fucking personal. Adam didn't deserve to be killed

because some piece of shit motherfuckers were greedy. There isn't anyone to step up for him. As far as the US and his family is concerned, he was killed in the line of duty. We know that's utter bullshit. So how will the guilty parties be held accountable? Huh? If I have to do it on my own, I'll take leave and hunt them down myself," I ground out.

"Sit down!" Venom said as he banged his fist on the tabletop. Squirrel and I still glowered at one another, but we did as we were told.

"We'll put it to the vote. But first, I need a show of hands that would be willing to take the job on even if it meant it was pro bono." Venom looked each of us in the eye with a cocked brow. It was nearly imperceptible, but I could see his jaw ticking under his salt and pepper beard.

Voodoo, Angel, Raptor, Phoenix, Sabre, and I raised our hands. Following right behind us were Ghost and Blade.

"You know I'm in for all the tech help," Facet piped in.

"So do we even need to put it to a vote if the majority are in?" Ghost asked before he chuckled.

Venom sighed. "Probably not, but we need to set some parameters and deadlines. We'll need to narrow down the team. I want the plan ironed out in detail before anyone goes off half-cocked."

"That sounds fair," agreed Raptor. The rest of us nodded. Squirrel sighed as he shook his head. Fuck, he was pissing me off.

"Chains, I know you are one of the supporters of this, but you've been gone a lot, and we really need you at the ink shop." Venom's words irritated me a bit, because he was the one who sent me away for four goddamn months. Then he sent me on the mission to Texas for Voodoo's brother-in-law and his friends. Not that I begrudged them the help, but now he was worried about the time I'd missed at the shop?

"Whatever you need, boss."

We made tentative plans that would change depending on the intel Facet rounded up. Though I may not be hands-on with the mission, the tightness in my heart eased that we'd be serving up justice for Adam.

We were sitting at the large table in the kitchen having dinner when Madame Laveaux entered. All conversation ceased as everyone looked to her with curiosity in their gazes.

"It is done," she said as she looked at me and Jasmine.

Voodoo, Kira, Angel, Korrie, Ghost, Venom, and Raptor were the only ones who knew what we were doing. At first, Angel was not on board, until Madame Laveaux told him it wasn't his choice. I still wouldn't say he was convinced—more like resigned.

Voodoo's pale blue eyes shifted from us to his grandmother before he stood. Kira gave him a questioning look, and he gently squeezed the nape of her neck in reassurance.

"We will need Ghost, Sabre, and Phoenix as well," Voodoo's grandmother instructed. Her gaze hit Venom in silent request, and he nodded. The men she requested stood without question. Though Phoenix and Sabre had no clue what they were needed for, their actions were a testament to their loyalty.

Appetite gone, I scraped my food in the trash and left the plate in the sink. Jasmine did the same, and we were again trudging through the cold to Voodoo's temple, this time with a small entourage.

Madame Laveaux motioned us to take out seats as we had before. "Please remove your gloves," she said to me. Immediately, I complied.

A fire crackled in wood-burning stove in the corner. With the exception of a small lamp, candles lit the room.

With steady hands she set a bottle before each of us. Then she set two small silver cups next to the bottles. It might have been a trick of the flickering candlelight, but the contents of the bottles seemed to swirl and move. It was dark but with a lighter, almost marbleized appearance.

My heart hammered against my ribcage, and a buzzing rang in my ears.

She whispered things we couldn't decipher as she lifted the bottle in front of me and poured it into the cup. Next, she repeated the motion with Jasmine's.

"You must drink at the same time," she instructed, and I didn't question it. Everything about the ritual seemed surreal and odd, but that was the story of my life.

As one, we reached for the cup in front of us. The metal was oddly warm against my fingertips. We lifted them to our lips, then with a reassuring nod from Madame Laveaux, we tipped them back and swallowed.

The liquid was thick, hot, and vile. I gagged but managed to swallow.

At first, I didn't think it worked, and I opened my mouth to say so. But before I could utter a word, everything I looked at seemed to warp and distort. The faces of my brothers and Madame Laveaux seemed to twist and contort like they were liquid that had been stirred. Heat unlike anything I'd ever experienced burned in the pit of my stomach before it slowly consumed me like a slow burning fire.

A gasp next to me had my head slowly swiveling to look at Jasmine. Her face was white as a sheet, and her eyes were unfocused. Sweat beaded on her face, and I watched as it ran down her neck. The same warm trickle slid down my temple to drip off my chin.

I thought I heard Angel shout.

The murmur of voices rippled around us, but I couldn't focus, and the actual spoken words eluded me. It was the most bizarre trip I'd ever been on. Pressure squeezed my head, and my eyes burned as if hot pokers were being driven through them.

Words escaped me, though I tried to make my lips move. My arms were weighted, and I was unable to move them when I saw her waver. Before she hit the floor, Ghost caught her. Through it all, I was paralyzed—unable to lift a finger to help her.

My body began to feel like it was being ripped apart, molecule by molecule.

What happened after that, I couldn't say, because the room began to spin faster and faster until all the colors blended together and the blackness swallowed me.

⚬⚬⚬❬❭⚬⚬⚬

Images and a kaleidoscope of colors morphed and circled before they began to come in focus. Blinking away what seemed like sand in my eyes, I slowly shifted my gaze to search the room. I found I was lying on a thick fur pallet on the floor of Voodoo's temple. Candles flickered, casting eerie shadows on the surfaces of the room.

The small building had no windows, so it was unclear how much time had passed. Everything seemed to be moving in slow motion.

With difficulty, I rolled my head to the side to see Jasmine laid out next to me. Her eyes were closed, and panic rolled through me, as I was sure she was dead.

Willing my body to move, I tried to lift my arm. That's when I realized I was holding her hand.

No gloves.

Bare skin.

Fingers twined.

And in my head was blessed silence. No images bombarding my mind. No sounds drowning me.

My heart began to race.

"Jazz," I croaked in a raspy, coarse voice. Still she didn't move, and I damn near hyperventilated. What if the reason I was getting nothing from her was because she was dead? Pain like nothing I'd experienced through Madame Laveaux's ritual, or at any time in my life, ripped through my chest at the thought.

"Jasmine," I pleaded. "Baby, wake up."

A painful tingling spread through my body when I tried to move, much like when a limb falls asleep and the circulation is returning. As if waking from a thousand-year nap, my body gradually came to life. Yet, I was weak as a newborn colt.

"Jesus," I muttered.

Unwilling to release the hand I was holding for the first time, I weakly rolled toward her. I held a trembling finger to her neck and damn near shattered when I couldn't feel a pulse. I continued my way up, and a sob broke free when a barely there puff of breath escaped her nose.

"Jasmine," I said in relief as I cradled her cheek, reveling in the softness of her skin and my ability to freely touch her. Still clasping her fingers with one hand and cradling her cheek and neck with the other, I rested my head on her shoulder.

Time slipped away as I breathed her in, and tears fell from under my lids to drip on her shirt. Silently, I cried, unsure if they were happy tears or terrified ones.

When soft fingers sifted through my hair, I raised my head to stare into the golden gaze of the woman I loved. Tears freely rolled as I laughed and she smiled.

"It worked," she whispered.

I nodded. "Yeah baby, it sure did."

The words had no sooner left my lips than her face contorted in agony. Weakly, I pushed up to frantically search for a source to her pain.

"Nico!" she cried as her body tried to curl up from the mat. A feral scream was ripped from her lips, and anxiety seared through me, robbing me of breath.

My hands trailed over her body, searching for something, anything to tell me what to do. For the first time since my initial vision at sixteen, I wished I could see what was wrong through my touch.

"Fuck," I cried. "Help! Voodoo! Ghost! Someone!"

It seemed like a lifetime before the door slammed open, followed by the icy wind that shrieked outside. Snow blew in, and the door slammed shut. Afraid to look away from Jasmine, I heard the footsteps near.

"Ahhh, it's time," Madame Laveaux said in a matter-of-fact voice, and I peeled my eyes from Jasmine's contorted face to the serene one of Voodoo's grandmother. She barked orders, and Voodoo gathered items and set them next to Jasmine. I heard him on his phone before he ended the call and slipped it in his pocket.

"What are you doing?" I asked in a panic.

"What's does it look like, young Nico? I'm going to deliver a *bebé*." She gave me a bright smile, and I nearly hyperventilated.

"No, we need to get her to the hospital," I argued, cursing my continued weakness.

"Chains," Voodoo barked. "We won't make it. The blizzard has created near white-out conditions. The path from the clubhouse to here is barely passable on foot, let alone the roads."

Jasmine began to relax, but her brow was beaded in sweat. Wild eyes found mine and she whimpered, "I'm scared."

"Shh," Madame Laveaux soothed as she gripped Jasmine's free hand in hers. "You listen to me. Madame Laveaux has delivered more babies in the swamps than there are gators."

Voodoo chuckled. "That might be a bit of an exaggeration,"

he mumbled, and she flashed him a glare that only had him laughing harder.

"Ogun," she snapped. "The people of the swamps have come to me for more of their needs than you could fathom. I've delivered many a *bebé* without issue. So you keep that laughing trap shut and do as I say."

The cajun in her tone grew heavier the more she berated her grandson, but at her declaration, some of my fear subsided. Some, certainly not all. With great effort, I rose to kneel next to Jasmine.

Cold burst into the room when the door flew open again. "Shut the damn door!" Madame Laveaux snapped.

My fear nearly dissipated when I heard Angel's voice from behind me. "Damn, it's insane out there right now!"

He shed his outerwear and took over for Voodoo on Jasmine's other side. Besides his abilities to heal, he'd been a medic in the army. Whether or not he'd helped birth any babies, I had no clue, but I was glad he was there.

"I got here as fast as I could, sis," he said and gave Jasmine a grin.

When she returned it, my heart soared. Then she looked to me, and a tear escaped from the corner of her eye. "Our baby is coming," she whispered.

"Yeah." The ridiculous grin wouldn't leave my face as I held her hand in wonder. Both from the ability to actually hold her hand skin-to-skin and the pending arrival of our child.

The two of us had opted to wait to see the sex of the baby. She wanted to be surprised. She had also laughed at me when I insisted it was a boy. I was sure it was, though I hadn't touched her to find out.

"Not long now, Jazzy," Angel reassured her.

But he was wrong.

The process took hours.

We were thankful for all the candles, because the power went out.

Though I was slowly regaining my strength, Jasmine seemed to be weakening and tiring. Angel couldn't do a damn thing to help her yet for fear of causing harm to the baby. He wasn't sure if it would treat the placenta, and in turn the baby, as something that needed to be removed and healed.

Knowing if things went to shit, he could help her didn't ease my worry as I watched Jasmine on the verge of giving up. At the next contraction, she weakly cried, "I can't do it anymore."

"Yes, you can," I told her. "You are the strongest woman I know, remember?"

"Jasmine," Madame Laveaux said, "you will push and your baby will come."

My wide eyes shifted to her, and I prayed Jasmine didn't lose her shit on poor Madame Laveaux. Not that the older woman seemed fazed by any of Jasmine's shouting over the last several hours. She had simply given Jasmine a serene smile.

To my surprise, Jasmine nodded, and I gently brushed her wet hair off her face.

At Madame Laveaux's encouragement, Jasmine did indeed push, and our baby entered the world in a voodoo temple during the middle of a blizzard.

"It's a girl," Madame Laveaux announced as she gave her a cursory wipe down and laid her on Jasmine's chest. During the extensive labor, she had removed Jasmine's shirt and dropped a soft flannel blanket over her for modesty. Now I knew it was so she would be able to lay the baby skin to skin.

"It's a girl," Jasmine repeated in awe as she reverently checked her fingers and toes. Once she was content with our daughter's digits and that everything was as it should be, she beamed at me.

"Do you want to hold her?" she asked, and I froze.

"I don't…." I trailed off, unable to finish my sentence. The fear that the ritual didn't work for the baby had my hands trembling as I curled them into fists. The temptation to reach for her was so strong, but still, I was nervous.

"You'll never know if you don't try," she murmured as her hand cradled our baby's back and head.

Swallowing with difficulty, I stared at the tiny dark-haired human in Jasmine's arms. Finally, I nodded. Madame Laveaux finished up with the placenta and clamping the cord with a freaking cable tie she'd dipped in alcohol.

Jasmine wrapped the flannel around our crying baby and had Angel hand her over because her arms shook. With the flannel separating us, I grew more confident as I spoke softly to her. After a moment, her cries diminished to little shuddered breaths and she stared at me with dark, knowing eyes.

My fingers shook as I slowly reached out to stroke one tip along her balled-up fist. Nothing hit me except love unlike anything I'd experienced before. Yes, I loved Jasmine unconditionally, but the love I had for the tiny helpless human in my arms was otherworldly. In that moment, I knew I would do anything in my power to protect her and keep her safe.

"Fuck," I muttered when I realized not only had I been wrong about her being a boy, but that I'd be beating the boys off for years to come. Because I had a *daughter*.

Heaven help me.

TWENTY-THREE

Jasmine

"EVERY LIE"—MY DARKEST DAYS

Four months later….

Ehria Angeline may have entered the world in the middle of a blizzard, but she brought sunshine to my life.

We had decided to name her after Nico's mother and mine. The months flew by, and she grew more beautiful with each passing day.

"Where are my girls?" Nico called out as he got home from work.

"In here," I called out from my office where I was finishing up the last project for the day as Ehria played with her toys on the activity blanket. At the sound of her father's voice, she immediately stopped her movement and seemed to listen intently for his approach.

He stepped into the room, and she began to kick wildly as her chubby little arms windmilled in excitement.

"How's your ink doing, babe?" he asked.

I grinned. "It's good."

After Ehria was born, Chains insisted on me getting his brand, and I had no complaints. Wearing the brand of a Royal Bastard was a deeper commitment than a wedding band. He had done the work himself, and I loved it. It was a chain in the shape of a heart. In the center it read "Property of Chains."

To make it better, he had drawn a jasmine flower and had one of the other artists ink it over his heart. Then he had inked Erhia's name and birthdate on his forearm. Surprisingly, he was able to squeeze it in with all the work he already had on him.

"Where's Daddy's girl?" he asked with a brilliant smile as he crouched by our daughter. "How was her check-up? I'm sorry I couldn't make it," he said.

"The doctor said she's in the ninetieth percentile for height and the seventy-fifth percentile for weight. Hitting her milestones like she should, too. And no worries, it was only a check-up. Besides, I would've had to worry about the new nurse tripping over her tongue if you were there." I laughed because the nurses flirted shamelessly but harmlessly with Nico anytime he went with us. He rolled his eyes with a chuckle and a shake of his head.

With a fond smile, I watched her antics as she waited for him to pick her up. He reached for her, and she cooed. I laughed, but abruptly stopped and studied her with narrowed eyes.

"Did you see that?" he asked as lifted her into his arms. Unsure if he was referring to the same thing I thought I'd seen, I blinked and remained silent a moment.

"See what?" I asked, trying to sound normal because I was a little freaked out.

"Her eyes," he said as he held her up in front of his face. Completely unfazed by our disbelief, she batted at his face and grabbed for his nose and beard. "They looked like they had a silver ripple that ran through them for a second," he said, and I swallowed hard.

"What could that be?" I asked, suddenly uneasy.

"I have no clue. You haven't seen that before?"

"Not once. You?"

"Nope."

"Maybe you should call Ogun or Madame Laveaux," I said, my tone full of uncertainty.

"Maybe it was our imagination," he tried to rationalize. Uncertainty was heavy in his tone as he pulled his gaze from our daughter to me.

"Both of us?" I questioned with a cocked brow. We stared at each other but neither of us said a word. Then he pulled out his phone and made a call.

"Bro, are you busy?" he asked, then listened.

"Can you come over afterward?" I could hear the other party speaking but couldn't make out what they were saying. It sounded like Ogun, but I wasn't sure.

"Yeah, bring whatever you think you'll need. I want you to look at something for me."

He ended the call.

"Was that Ogun?" I asked.

"Yeah."

"Do you think she's okay?" I asked, worry nearly drowning me. There were a lot of things I'd learned to handle. The thought of something happening to my daughter was completely out of that realm.

"I mean, she seems okay, but that was strange. Voodoo is coming over, and he's going to try to do a reading." He handed our daughter back to me, and I cradled her close.

"You don't think it's that stuff we drank, do you? What if it messed with her and we didn't know? Nico, I'm a little scared." Ehria squirmed because I was holding her tighter than she liked.

A gasp escaped me when she pushed against me and growled. The moment I loosened my hold on her, she was babbling contentedly.

"What the hell?" Nico asked before he crouched down to look in Ehria's eyes. Oblivious of the concern she was raising in her parents, our daughter drooled as she smiled and reached for her father.

He played with her until Ogun arrived. When he went to the door, I followed.

"Thanks for coming so soon," Nico said as Ogun ran a hand through his dark hair. Before he came inside, he paused. With a furrowed brow, he cast a slow, sweeping glance around the neighborhood.

"Yeah, no problem," he said, shaking off whatever had made him pause. He came in, and Ehria got excited. She loved all her uncles.

A brilliant grin lifted his cheeks as he swooped up my daughter and raised her over his head. "Hey, pretty girl! Did you miss Uncle Voodoo?"

Of course, she giggled. Then swear to Christ, her eyes flickered silver again. Ogun's brows shot up, and I knew he'd seen it too.

"That's, uh, new?" he questioned as he cast a sidelong glance our direction. We both nodded.

"Huh," he said, then handed her back to me and went straight for my coffee table. He carefully unrolled a worn flannel cloth, then pulled several items from a small pouch that he arranged on the table. Next he lit several herbs that he let burn on a small dish.

He motioned for me to sit across from him with Ehria. I had to be extremely diligent because she kept trying to grab the items. Once he was set up, he swept his hand over the table, indicating I should cut the cards he'd set in the center.

"Hmm," he said with a frown as he laid out the cards. Then he emptied a small sack into his hand and gently tossed the contents to the table. With great concentration he studied the small bones, coins, stones, and shells.

Finally, he rested his hands over the cards and the items he'd thrown and closed his eyes. A low humming preceded a murmured chant, but still he didn't speak directly to me. Eyes closed, he appeared completely still.

Ehria used that moment to lean over. Her chubby hand swiped a small stone. Before I could remove the item from her fingers, Ogun's hand shot out and held hers. His eyes shot open, but they were unfocused. Though it looked like he was staring at Ehria, he was more staring *through* her.

Minutes ticked by, still we remained silent. Surprisingly, my daughter was quiet. Then he blinked several times, frowned at Ehria, and shook his head. She immediately dropped the stone and gave him a grumpy look.

He inhaled a long, deep, shuddering breath, then slowly exhaled.

"I saw the wolf again," he said with a confused glance to each of us. "It's not dangerous, yet it is. It's frustrated and impatient. Jasmine, maybe you and Ehria should go stay at the clubhouse for a bit. The feeling I got… it was off. Something is coming, but I don't know what."

"No, Ogun. Absolutely not. This is our home. It's secure. Nico and Facet installed the security system themselves. We're in a gated community. This is as safe as it gets. I'm not taking my daughter to stay at the clubhouse," I insisted.

"Babe, I still have to go to work. I'd feel better if you at least went to the clubhouse during the day. You can work in my room." Nico sent me a worried gaze. "For Erhia."

Irritated, I huffed. Though I hated the idea of hiding away

at that damn clubhouse again, there wasn't much I wouldn't do for Nico and Ehria. "Fine. If it makes you feel better, I'll go there when you leave for work."

Nico breathed a sigh of relief. "Thank you. I will absolutely feel better."

Ogun began packing his things and then stood. "I'm going to call my grandmother on the way home. Maybe see if she can give me more insight."

"Would you like to stay for dinner?" I asked. "Sabre, Raptor, and Ghost are coming."

He smiled. "Much as I'd love to stay for your cooking, Kira made her Stroganoff for me. I need to get home."

"Heck, if I'd known she was making that, I would've invited us over for dinner at your house." I gave him a cheeky grin, and he chuckled.

"I'm sure she made plenty," he offered, but I waved him off.

"I'm teasing. I have a casserole in the oven, and the guys are probably on their way. Not that I wouldn't love her Stroganoff, but I can't see wasting ours and standing the guys up."

He pressed a kiss to my head. "I'll see you at the clubhouse tomorrow."

I nodded.

Ehria pulled at my hair as I tried to make sense of everything that had transpired since Nico had arrived home from work. As I sat there, I could hear Nico and Ogun quietly conversing at the door, and I wondered if there was something they weren't telling me.

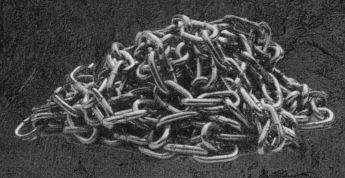

TWENTY-FOUR

Chains

"I AM MACHINE"—THREE DAYS GRACE

"I really believe the wolf is more symbolic than actual," Voodoo said as I walked him to his bike. I digested what he said as he stashed his things in his saddlebag.

"Then why would I think I'd seen wolves as I grew up, and why would I dream of a wolf long before I even knew Jasmine existed?" I asked, frustration lacing my words.

"I don't have a good answer for that. Unless it was something of a premonition. We don't have textbooks or rulebooks on how our abilities act, you know." Voodoo shrugged before he straddled his bike.

"Thanks again for coming over," I said.

"Anytime, brother, anytime." He grinned. His grin quickly faded, and the air seemed to crackle with something electric. With a frown, he glanced around, as did I.

"What the fuck is that?" I asked. The air seemed heavy, like before a raging storm, yet there wasn't a cloud in the sky. My hair stood up all over my body. We scanned the quiet neighborhood, but nothing seemed out of place.

It was a small gated community on the edge of town. Further down the road was the clubhouse and the farm. Several of us joked that eventually the club members would own every house in the development. As it was, Angel and I had houses here. Venom and Voodoo were both looking at houses on the next street over. There was a thick tree line behind the last street because it butted up to CRP (Conservation Reserve Program) land.

"You felt it too?" he asked with a frown.

"Yeah, but I don't know what the hell it was."

Nothing changed, and he started his bike. I waved, and after one last glance around, went back inside.

Jasmine had Ehria in her high chair as she tried to get her to eat some pureed shit that looked repulsive. "I don't blame you, sweetheart. I wouldn't eat that shit either," I whispered conspiratorially to my daughter, who smiled with a face covered in some messy goop.

"You are not helping," Jasmine sternly snapped as she tried not to smile. "What time are Ghost and Sabre coming? I thought they'd be here by now."

After I shrugged, I held my laughter as I pulled out enough plates for everyone and set them on the counter. We were eating in the kitchen since it was an informal dinner and the boys were coming. It was just family. Inside, I snickered a little.

Informal. Who would've thought someone like me would be thinking in terms of formal or informal? My second foster family I got yanked from was so abusive they made us kids eat on the floor like dogs "so we wouldn't make a mess at the table." Sometimes over the years, I was simply happy to have a meal. Period. Now I owned a house with an actual dining room.

"Thank you," she said with a soft smile when I sat next to her where she sat sideways feeding Ehria.

"Want me to take over?" I asked.

"Nah, she's pretty much done. At this stage, she's not super interested in baby food, but I wanted to start her on a little bit since her doctor said it was okay." She stood, placed the small bowl and spoon in the sink, then washed our daughter's face with a cloth. Once she was done, she handed her a teething ring and sat with me to wait for the boys.

She leaned over and kissed my cheek.

"What was that for?" I asked with a crooked grin.

"For being so sweet. Who would've known?" She laughed, and I shook my head with a smirk. The entire scene was so domestic and everything I'd ever wanted as a child but never really had after my mom disappeared.

"Knock, knock!"

"Honey, I'm home!" Ghost and Sabre said as they came in the front door.

"Don't make me regret giving you two the code," I grumbled as they burst into the kitchen, all smiles. "Where's Raptor?"

"Got hung up with something at the clubhouse. He said he'd have to take a rain check."

I nodded.

"My girl!" Ghost said before swooping Ehria out of her chair. He held her above his head like she was flying, and she giggled.

"Ghost, I wouldn't do—" was all Jasmine got out before the creamy, gooey shit flew out of my daughter's mouth and splatted on Ghost's cheek. His eyes slammed shut, and he froze.

Sabre took her from his hands before either Jasmine or I could move, wiped her chin with a napkin, and held her to his chest. "It's okay, Uncle Sabre won't let you get all shook up and lose your lunch."

Jasmine tossed Ghost the cloth that he caught with one eye open. He wiped his face, then gave Ehria a mock stern look. "Young lady, you're lucky I have a soft spot for you."

Sabre put her back in her chair and gave her back her toys and teething ring. She happily chewed on it as she seemed to watch us like a hawk.

Everyone dished up a plate and sat down at the table.

"Damn, this is good," Ghost said after his first bite.

"Hell yeah, it is," agreed Sabre.

Jasmine's cheeks flushed a pretty shade of pink. "It's nothing special, just something my mom used to make."

"Well, it beats my cooking or prison food any day," he said without thinking and shoved in another bite. Ghost never talked about his time in prison, though we all knew why he'd gone at eighteen. We also knew that was where he met Shank, then became part of the Royal Bastards after he got out. Other than that, it wasn't anything he wanted to talk about, and we respected the man's privacy.

The rest of the meal was eaten in comfortable silence as everyone enjoyed their food. Sabre and Ghost both got up for seconds, and Jasmine stood. She tried to take my plate, but I rested a hand on her forearm. When I experienced nothing but the warmth of her skin and the love that burned in my chest, I was amazed. Each and every time, I was utterly amazed.

"I've got it. Leave yours with mine. I'll take care of it."

Love shone in her eyes as she leaned down to press a soft kiss to my lips. Instinctually, my mouth parted and invited her in. She gave a light, slow swoop of her tongue against mine before she withdrew and gave a big sigh. "Thank you for being you," she murmured against my cheek.

"It's me who's been blessed," I said as my hand cupped her hip and I stared into her topaz-colored gaze.

Her lush lips curled into a soft smile. "I think it goes both ways. I'm going to give Ehria her bath."

I stole one last kiss, then released her.

Ehria got excited when Jasmine reached for her. My heart was full to bursting at the sight. Not that I didn't still worry, but I'd been so blessed with both of the females in my life. I'd do anything to keep them safe.

"Say goodnight to Daddy, Uncle Ghost, and Uncle Sabre," Jasmine said as she made Ehria wave at my brothers when they sat back at the table.

They each kissed her cheek. Ghost pointed a finger at her that she promptly curled her fingers around.

"Remember, no more of that puking business," he sternly said, then yelped when she bit his finger.

"She just cut her first tooth," Jasmine replied proudly. "Be careful!"

"Goddang, that thing was sharp!" Ghost said with eyes wide as he cradled his finger to his chest.

"Who are you telling?" Jasmine said as she unconsciously covered her nipple.

My lips pulled between my teeth, I tried not to laugh at the motion. I pushed back my chair and stood. Then I plucked my daughter from Jasmine's hands to give her some love before I handed her back to Jasmine. True to my word, I cleaned up after the meal, then sat at the table with the guys.

Once I heard the bath water running on the other side of the house, I ran a hand through my hair and sighed.

"Everything okay?" Ghost asked as he raised his glass to his mouth.

"I don't know."

"What do you mean, you don't know?" asked Sabre in confusion.

"Something weird happened today."

"Like?" Ghost prompted.

"Like something is up with Ehria. I don't know what it is yet, and Voodoo was just here but couldn't get anything off her either."

"Well, what happened, exactly? Is she okay? Does she need to go to the doctor?" Ghost asked as he and Sabre intently waited for my reply.

"It might be nothing, but her eyes…" I shook my head after I trailed off. "It was odd. They rippled a silver color."

"Well, maybe her eyes are changing color," Ghost said with a shrug.

"No. They both have brown eyes. Even if they carried the recessive gene for blue eyes, it would be unlikely that Ehria would have silver eyes or gray eyes—that's extremely rare. Also, simple eye color wouldn't 'ripple,'" Sabre replied, making air quotes.

Ghost cocked his head and frowned. "You think she has some kind of gift other than yours?"

After dragging my palms down my face, I rested my elbows on the table and crossed my arms. "I have no clue."

"Huh," Ghost grunted.

"She also, um, it sounded like she *growled*," I admitted.

Sabre's brow cocked as he shot me a disbelieving stare. "Come again?"

"I don't know."

"What do you know about your mother's family?" Sabre asked as he stared at me intently.

"Not much. I never knew any of them. As a kid, she told me her family was dead. We moved around a lot until she left me in the woods, so I never saw any family."

"Wait. She left you in the woods? How did I not know this?" Ghost asked, then sat there with his mouth hanging open.

I shrugged. "You never asked."

"Where did she leave you in the woods?" Sabre asked, ignoring Ghost. He watched me strangely as he waited for the answer.

"Northeastern Iowa. I moved to Des Moines when I aged out of the system. We moved around a lot though. I was young, but I can remember living in Michigan, Wisconsin, and Minnesota. The night she left me in the woods, we were on a camping adventure. Well, that's what she called it. We had been living in southern Minnesota, but we crossed into Iowa to camp. Then she left. She told me to walk toward the sun in the morning. I did because I thought she'd be waiting for me. Obviously, she wasn't." My gaze dropped. It was a little embarrassing to admit that my mother ditched me like an unwanted puppy.

"That necklace you wear. Did she give it to you?" Sabre had worked out with me in the past and had remarked on it, but I'd merely said thanks because he was a prospect at the time. He didn't need to know my private details.

"Yes," I warily replied.

"Have you ever been able to get anything off it?"

"You think I didn't try the minute I realized what was happening to me?"

"How old were you when you realized you had your gift?"

"I guess I had it all my life, just not noticeable until I was in my teens. Why the twenty questions?" I asked, getting a little frustrated.

"I have a theory. I've seen something like that before when I lived up in Michigan. But how the hell that could happen with you and Jasmine is weird. Let me look into something, and I'll get back to you." Sabre chewed on his lip as he looked lost in thought.

"Well, don't keep me in suspense. At least tell me what you're thinking?"

He looked to Ghost with an uncomfortable expression.

"Why you lookin' at me?" Ghost asked. "I have no clue what you're thinking."

Sabre sighed. "Okay, you know that I'm from New York?"

"Yeah," I said, and Ghost nodded.

"Well, I called that home, but I moved around a lot too." He got a strange expression, then shook it off. "When I was in Michigan, I ran into a group of people in the Upper Peninsula. They were a pretty closed-off community. One of the members was in front of me at a gas station. He remarked on my eye color when he turned to leave, but quickly ended the conversation after maybe a minute."

"Why?" I asked, not understanding what he was getting at.

"He, uh, seemed to sniff me, and his eyes rippled with a silver, but it was gone before I got a good look at it. He went out to the pumps and got into a truck with several other men. The gas station attendant told me to stay away from them because they were bad news. I was only in town for a few weeks on a job site, so I didn't care what they were as long as they left me alone. On one of the last days, I had gone hiking." He inhaled deeply before letting it out in a rush.

"And?" Ghost prompted.

"And I came across a naked kid caught in a trap."

"A what?" I demanded.

"Look, I know. There was this crying coming from in the trees and I went to see what it was. This kid was stuck in a trap and was trying to pry it off his leg. He looked terrified when I went to help and didn't say a word as I tried to release it. When I finally got it open, he backed away from me. I tried to calm him, because I wanted to take him to town for help. Though it was a rubber-jaw coil-spring trap, I was pretty sure it had broken his leg, but he fucking growled at me when I reached for him."

"Damn, that is weird," Ghost said.

"No. The weird part was when the kid's eyes shimmered silver, then he turned into a fucking wolf cub and limped away whimpering. Before I could follow, a huge black wolf broke through the trees, snarled at me, grabbed the kid/cub by the scruff of his neck, and ran off into the woods. I didn't stick around after that. I went back to my hotel and packed my shit. I collected my paycheck through then and left." He raked a hand through his dark hair.

"Wait. Are you trying to tell me you think my daughter is a fucking shifter?"

"What?" Jasmine said, and all three of our heads swiveled to look at my stricken woman.

"Aw, shit," Sabre muttered.

TWENTY-FIVE

Jasmine

"REMEDY"—SEETHER

I slept like shit that night. How the hell was I supposed to sleep when there was a possibility my daughter was a freaking wolf? I didn't understand how that could be possible. I wasn't a shifter; Nico wasn't a shifter. It was crazy, wasn't it?

My mother's family were Native American, and my father's half was part Native American, but part God only knew. I'd grown up knowing there were a lot of things in the world that couldn't be simply explained. But the thought that two humans—though gifted—could give birth to a shifter? Insane.

Half asleep, I was going around and gathering everything I needed to bring with me for the day. I hated having to drag it all to the clubhouse, but I made a promise. Now that they had put that worry in my head, I was more than happy to be somewhere with other people while Nico was at work.

"I put the playpen in the back of the SUV," Nico said as he stood in the doorway. His fingertips hooked the doorframe, and a sliver of his sexy inked abs peeked from under his shirt.

"Stop tempting me, or neither of us is going anywhere today," I said with a mischievous smirk.

He snorted but dropped his arms. "You about ready?"

"As ready as I will be. How long do you think this is going to be the norm?"

"Hopefully not long." He looked uncomfortable for a moment, and I narrowed my gaze at him.

"What aren't you telling me?" As if our daughter possibly being a shifter or having wolf traits wasn't enough.

At first, he looked like he was going to deny that he knew something I didn't. Then he sighed. "Voodoo thinks that maybe the wolf is symbolic of your father. With what Sabre said, I don't know what to think now."

A sharp inhale was followed by a shaky exhale as I shot him a worried gaze. "But how can that be? You drew a wolf innumerable times. It never seemed to be a threat."

"I'm not sure. Madame Laveaux is talking about coming for a visit to see Parker next week. Voodoo's going to see if she can get a better read. Until we know more, try not to worry."

A wry chuckle escaped my lips. "That's easier said than done. So how long do you think it will be before she moves up here? She's been up once a month since that baby was born."

With a smile, Nico shook his head. "No clue. She says she can't stand the cold here and that she would miss her home in the swamp, but I think it's a matter of time."

Nico grabbed the diaper bag and my laptop bag, and I followed him out the door with Ehria snuggled into me. He placed them in the SUV, and his hand wrapped around the back of my neck. Having him touch me never got old. The kiss he gave me was so full of promise that I was tempted to tell him he better cancel his appointments.

He broke away, and I leaned toward him with a sigh. He

chuckled and nipped my lower lip before giving me one last chaste kiss. Ehria was pulling at his cut the entire time.

"See you at the clubhouse tonight when I get off," he said as he kissed our daughter on the head and went to his bike parked next to the Range Rover he'd insisted on getting months ago. He was too handsome for his own good, and I sighed at the sight of him as he straddled the seat and slipped his sunglasses on. I wished he'd wear a helmet year-round.

Then I cleared my head and set Ehria in her car seat before I climbed behind the wheel. When I started the vehicle, Nico backed out and started down the road.

Before I could back out, I realized I'd forgotten Ehria's blanket. She'd never nap without it. "Shit," I murmured, putting the car in park again.

Not wanting to leave Ehria in the vehicle unattended, I quickly unbuckled her and rushed up to the house. I entered the code, went inside, and grabbed her blankie off the couch. She snuggled it as soon as I tossed it over my shoulder between me and her cheek.

"That's better, huh?" I said with a soft smile.

When I locked the door again and rushed toward the car, I stopped short with a shriek. "Oh my gosh! You scared me! Can I help you with something?" I asked the woman standing in my driveway.

For a moment, she simply stared at Ehria, then she met my gaze and pulled out a gun. My heart stopped, and I struggled to find a breath.

"Give her to me," she quietly demanded. Terrified, I hesitated. The metallic slide and click of the round being chambered got my attention really quick.

"You can't take my baby. Please," I begged as tears welled in my eyes and I stared at the gun. Ehria grabbed my hair as if she knew something wasn't right.

"I said, give her to me." Her hard dark eyes bored into me, and I shivered. Then they flashed silver, and I froze.

"What was that?" I whispered in shock, but she ignored me.

"You have no idea what you're doing. She must come with me. If you want her and her father to stay safe, give her to me," she demanded in a harsh whisper. My mind was spinning, trying to think of something to stall her until maybe Nico realized I wasn't behind him or someone drove past.

"Take me with you. She's only four months old, and she's still breastfeeding. She needs me. Once she's older, you can send me away, kill me, whatever, but please don't take her from me now," I pleaded. Anything to buy me time.

Indecision warred on her face. Finally, she glanced around and motioned for me to move. When I stopped at the SUV Nico had bought and insisted I drive, she snapped, "No! The car over there."

Fear shot through me as I glanced at the car parked the wrong way in front of my house. I thought if we took the SUV, we stood a chance of Nico finding us because I knew it had a location program on it. Now all I had was my phone, and if it died, we were well and truly fucked.

"Buckle her in, then you drive," she demanded. "Hurry."

With shaking hands I buckled Ehria into the car seat. Worried it didn't fit her properly, I hesitated.

"Get. In." The woman was losing patience, and I didn't want to give her a reason to change her mind, so I quickly got behind the wheel. She got in the back seat next to my daughter. It made my heart stutter. There was an apple core in the cup holder. Thinking quickly, I grabbed it with my right hand as I turned in the seat.

"Where are we going?" I asked as I switched it to my left hand.

"Turn around and drive!" she barked.

Doing as she said, I tossed the apple out the door and into

my yard by the driveway. I had no idea if Nico would see it or if an animal would run off with it first. I had to do something, though.

"How did you get into the neighborhood?" I asked as I pulled away from the curb. At one time, I might've been a trembling mess of panic and uselessness. Thanks to my ongoing counseling, my beautiful daughter, and Nico's support, I was stronger than the woman I'd been a year ago. That didn't mean I wasn't terrified; I was just better at holding my shit together.

She ignored me, and I cast a glance in the rearview mirror. What I saw stunned me. The woman was staring at my daughter with awe and tears shimmering in her dark brown eyes.

"Please don't hurt her," I whispered.

At my plea, the woman looked up, and our eyes met in the mirror. With an almost regretful expression, she sighed. "It's not me you need to worry about."

I was afraid of what she meant by that.

When we left the neighborhood, I noticed the car we were in had one of our neighborhood scanners that opened the gates for us. The woman either lived in the neighborhood, or she'd stolen the car. The strip was made to separate if removed, so she couldn't have stolen it from another vehicle.

Shit, what if the apple belonged to one of our neighbors because this was their car?

She instructed me on where to drive. My heart bottomed out as the miles slipped away. My phone vibrated in my back pocket over and over. Thankfully, with the sounds of the road, she didn't hear it. I prayed Nico and the club would be coming for us soon.

As the miles slipped away, I began to lose hope as each glance in the rearview mirror didn't show the cavalry coming to the rescue. My old anxiety and insecurities clawed at my throat. Then I thought of the sweet little girl in the back seat relying on me and took a deep, grounding inhale.

"How much further?" I asked when we'd been on the road for three hours and were closing in on Minneapolis.

"It doesn't matter," the woman murmured.

"Well, it does, because Ehria will be waking up soon to eat," I said as my breasts tingled and ached, signaling my milk coming down.

At the mention of my daughter's name, the woman gasped, and I noticed her eyes go wide in the mirror.

"E-Ehria?" she stammered.

Thinking I may have hit a sympathetic nerve by giving my daughter a name, hope bloomed in my chest. "Yes. Ehria Angeline. We named her after her father's mother and my mother."

A tear ran down her face, and she took a shuddering breath. A delicate hand covered her mouth as she looked out the window and sniffled.

"Ma'am?" I asked her when she didn't answer me about stopping.

"We'll be stopping soon," she said in a tone that sounded choked up.

Heart hammering, I continued to drive until she spoke up again.

"Take the next exit, then take a right."

Driving with an unknown destination was nerve-racking, but knowing we could be nearing the end of the journey with an unknown future might've been worse. I followed her directions until I stopped at a gas station. I thought we were gassing up, but she told me to pull around back.

"Get out," she told me. "You can come back here to feed her."

Glancing around, I didn't see a soul that could help. Resigned, I got in the back seat and unbuckled my daughter, who was waking up. When I lifted her from the seat, she arched her back, pulled her legs up, and stretched her arms by her head. Then she blinked her big green-gold eyes sleepily as she smiled.

"Hey, baby girl. Mommy's here," I said as I snuggled her close and inhaled her perfect scent. Trying to ignore the stranger sitting on the other side of the infant seat, I unbuttoned my shirt and lifted my sports bra with one hand to feed my suddenly ravenous daughter. When I didn't move fast enough, she growled as her fingers clasped my shirt. I jumped at the sound.

The woman chuckled.

"She's demanding, isn't she?"

"Who are you?" I asked. I'd been afraid to ask before, but she had let me go with and was letting me feed my daughter. Maybe she had a heart after all.

"It doesn't really matter," she murmured with the corners of her mouth downturned.

Ehria had barely finished burping when a silver Tahoe with dark tinted windows pulled up next to us. I rushed to situate myself.

"Stay here. Do not get out," she commanded as she opened the door and climbed out.

She rounded the car, and a man got out. They began speaking, and it was obvious from his expression and body language that he wasn't happy. A second man joined them, and I guessed he was the driver.

"What the fuck is she doing in there?" I could hear him demand through the glass.

The woman rapidly gestured to me, then to the other man, but she spoke quieter than the second man so I had no idea what was being said. Finally, the first man shook his head and rounded the car. He jerked open the door and unfastened the child seat. Protectively, I held Ehria close. The man glared at me but didn't speak.

My door opened, and I squeaked.

"Get in the SUV with your daughter, and do not speak or they *will* leave you behind—and you won't be breathing," the woman said to me with a brief flash of fear in her eyes.

Afraid, I did as she instructed and climbed in to buckle Ehria back in. The second man slammed my door shut, and I had to pull my leg quickly out of the way to avoid it being smashed. The woman climbed in the other side of the back seat. I watched as the men wiped down the vehicle we'd ridden in, telling me I was correct, and it had likely been stolen.

Neither of the men so much as looked at me when they got back in the vehicle. We got back on the road and continued North. After about an hour, I fell asleep with my hand resting protectively over the infant seat.

I jolted awake when the vehicle bounced on an uneven road. Confusion in my half-asleep state had me glancing around without comprehending what I was seeing. Finally, I realized we were deep in the woods. We pulled into a long metal building that had several other vehicles exactly like the one we were in and parked.

"We're here," she said as they shut off the motor.

"Where?" I asked.

"Shut up!" the driver demanded. "Do not speak unless spoken to. You do not question anything. You don't so much as whimper unless told to," he said with a sneer.

Asshole.

Grinding my teeth, I fought saying it out loud.

"Gather your daughter," the woman softly instructed.

Not needing to be told twice, I did as she said and got out of the vehicle on stiff legs. Ehria woke and rubbed her eyes before she looked at me with a smile. She was such a happy baby, and I'd been so blessed. I prayed I got to remain in her life as long as possible.

Oh Nico, where are you?

We exited the building, and a group of people approached us. The silver-haired man in the center seemed to be in charge as he stepped forward, and the rest stayed behind him. Some seemed surprised, others angry, and the rest wary as they stared at me and the woman.

"Ehria! What is the meaning of this?" the leader roared, and I frowned in confusion as I glanced down at my daughter. What the hell did he expect a four-month-old to fucking say?

"The infant is still feeding from her mother. She needs her until she can be weaned," the woman said. Time seemed to slow as the pieces clicked in place. The woman was named Ehria. The look on her face when I told her my daughter's name.

Holy shit. She was Nico's mother.

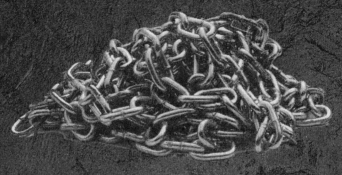

TWENTY-SIX

Chains

"STEP INSIDE, THE VIOLENCE"—RED

In the short distance to the clubhouse, I must've checked my rearview mirrors a hundred times. What was taking Jasmine so long?

I flipped my kickstand down with my foot and pulled out my phone. Her phone rang until it went to voicemail. Frowning, I called again. And again.

Ghost and Phoenix pulled in next to me as I was shoving my phone back in my pocket and kicking the kickstand back up. Angel walked out of the clubhouse.

"Where you going? You just got here," he asked.

"Jasmine!" was all I shouted before I tore out of the compound like the road was on fire behind me. It was mere seconds before the roar of bikes caught up to me, and Angel pulled up to ride next to me as Phoenix and Ghost fell in behind.

We entered the neighborhood, and for once I cursed the security that slowed me down. By the time we reached the house, my heart was in my throat. The SUV sat in the driveway with the driver door open.

I'd never un-assed my bike faster in my life. Seeing her purse in the passenger seat with the diaper bag had me damn near hyperventilating. My hands brushed over everything, but I got nothing. For the first time, I cursed the fact that I couldn't read my woman or my child.

"Jasmine!" I shouted as I raced to the house and barreled inside. "Jasmine!"

Silence.

"No. This cannot be happening again. No way."

"She's not answering her phone. I checked her stuff, and it wasn't in the vehicle, which means she has it with her. You have her location on your phone, right?" Angel calmly asked, pulling me out of my panic.

"Yeah. Yeah, I do." Fumbling, I pulled out my phone again and flipped through the screens until I found the app I needed. My stomach churned and my heart was about to blast through my chest wall. Her phone was north of here, and I busted out of the house with Angel on my heels.

Before I could get on my bike, I saw Ghost holding an apple core by the stem. "What the fuck are you doing?" I demanded. "We need to go!"

"This was on the edge of the driveway by the road. It seems weird that someone in this neighborhood would toss an apple core out on someone's lawn." He cocked a brow.

I approached him and snatched the apple core. What I saw had me dropping it like it was red-hot.

"No way," I said, stunned, as my head pounded.

"What was it?" Angel asked me.

Disbelief had me reeling.

"It was my mother," I whispered, aghast.

"I sent a message to Venom. He said to proceed with

caution, and he would send back-up to catch up to us. Let's go," said Angel.

Once I mounted my phone and left the location screen open, I started my bike. I was already on my bike and pulling out of the driveway and I heard Ghost cussing. "Goddamn it!"

They quickly caught up to me. We hauled ass up the road, but none of us had prepared for a high-speed chase, and we had to stop for gas before we could catch up.

As quickly as we could, we fueled up. As I was on one side of the pump, Angel was on the other. "Bro, we don't know who has her or if they're armed. We can't go racing up on them because we could put them in danger. I say we follow at a safe distance until they stop."

"That's my ol' lady and my baby!"

"I get it, Chains. And it's *my* sister and *my* niece—I don't want anything to happen to either of them either."

"Fine. But when they stop, we move in," I argued.

"If it's safe to do so, yes." Angel was much calmer than I was, and I had no idea how he was managing it. We took off our cuts and locked them in our saddlebags. No need to advertise who we were as we followed whoever had taken my family.

Fuck. My family.

The thought of losing them nearly brought me to my knees.

In no time, we were back on the road, but they'd gotten quite a lead on us. I cursed myself for not turning around the second I realized she wasn't behind me. Now between gas stops and traffic, they were a good thirty to forty-five minutes ahead of us.

As I watched the movement of Jasmine's phone, I prayed like I'd never prayed before. To a God I barely believed in and to the gods of my mother. The stone around my neck seemed to heat against my skin as I did, though I convinced myself it was my imagination.

When it stopped outside of Minneapolis, I experienced anticipation that we were nearly there. I motioned to Angel that they had stopped, and he nodded his understanding. The closer we got, the harder I prayed that we got there in time and the hotter the stone was against my chest. We pulled off the interstate and stopped a few blocks away at a fast-food restaurant.

"What do you want to do?" I asked Angel, antsy to reach them.

"I need to call Venom to give him a quick update, then I say we go up on foot. They'll hear our bikes if they haven't already," he said. Though I knew we needed to keep Venom in the loop, I was on edge at having to wait. Thankfully, the call was brief.

"We good?" I asked him as I grabbed my phone off the bracket on my bike.

"Yep, let's go," Angel took the lead, but we hadn't gotten a block when the phone started moving again.

"Shit! Fall back! They're moving again!" Not waiting, I raced back to my bike, shoving my phone back on the holder and starting the motor. The little blue beacon was coming back toward us.

As it passed where we were, there were two vehicles. A silver SUV with tinted windows, and a black Mercedes with the same. We waited until they were a block or so away where we could see them, but they were far enough ahead before we pulled out.

The car went straight, and the SUV got back on the interstate.

Anxiety like I'd never experienced hit me as I tried to decide which one to follow. At the last minute, I motioned for

Angel to go right, because the blue dot caught up and was merging onto the interstate.

Staying at a safe distance so as to not draw suspicion, we followed them for about an hour. Ghost and Phoenix got off the interstate to fuel up. It wasn't much later when they drew up behind us. Then Angel and I got off to do the same.

"Why don't we just try to stop them?" I demanded as I rushed to get the pump ready.

"You want to risk them hurting your girls?" Angel replied, and though I hated the helplessness, I knew he was right.

"Where the fuck do you think they're going?" I asked as the gas reached the top and I slammed the nozzle back in the pump.

"No clue. Let's go."

It seemed like the quickest pitstop known to man as we put the gas caps back on, hit the throttle, and roared out of the lot. We caught up to Ghost and Phoenix and rode behind them. Since we could see the silver SUV further up the road, tracking Jasmine's phone wasn't as important. Didn't mean I shut it off. As long as I could see that blue dot, I had faith that I'd catch up to that SUV and get my woman and my daughter back.

By the time the vehicle pulled off the interstate, we had been driving for about five and a half hours, had stopped to fill up one more time, and we were near Duluth, Minnesota. We skirted the city and continued north. My hands were cramping, and I released the handgrips one at a time to flex and stimulate the blood flow.

We had to drop much farther back and rely on my tracking app, because the traffic out that far was nearly non-existent. If we had kept the vehicle in our sights, they would've also spotted us.

After crossing over Island Lake, the blue dot left the main road. I signaled my brothers to slow down as we approached where they had turned. It had stopped and wasn't moving any longer. What we were met with blew my fucking mind.

"What the fuck?" I heard Ghost exclaim.

The road literally ended with a thick covering of bushes that seemed to grow right over the dirt drive.

"Shit. Let's go," Phoenix sad as he turned his bike around on the narrow road and left. Not too far down the road, he pulled off into a roadside rest area.

"What the fuck was that about? We needed to figure out how they got around those bushes!" I shouted at him.

"There were cameras," Ghost nonchalantly said as he sat on his bike watching me.

"Fuck. How did I not notice that?" I grumbled as I raked my fingers through my hair. My nerves were frayed, and it was like spiders crawling under my skin.

"Because you're being driven by emotion right now and not your head," Phoenix said as he pulled out a joint and snapped his fingers to light it. The flame seemed to bounce off his fingertips to the end of the white paper until it lit. He took a deep drag and handed it to me. "Take a hit and calm down."

I took two before handing it off to Ghost.

"I'm not gonna sit here getting high when my family is in there somewhere." I motioned down the asphalt toward the turnoff.

"Didn't say we were, but we need to think and have a solid plan before we go barging in there and get *your family* and *us* killed." Phoenix said.

"Phoenix is right," Angel agreed.

"Well, what do you suggest?" I asked, voice laced with frustration.

"You really need another hit," deadpanned Ghost. "Your brain is like, nonfunctioning. Hello, there are cameras. That means I go and look for a way in. Then I come back and get you knuckleheads and we rescue *our* family."

"Fine," I grudgingly conceded before an idea hit me. "Can you call Facet and see if he can tap into their security feed?" I asked Angel.

"Already sent him a message at our last stop to see what he could find out. Last I checked, he hadn't come up with a thing. Now that we have a location, I need to update him. If the security system is hooked up to internet, he'll get in." He sent a text, then waited.

"There was a driveway to another property across the road and before we reached that drive. I think we could pull in and push our bikes into the brush and hide them. Then Ghost goes over, works his magic, then we go play John Wayne," Phoenix said with a smirk as he took one last hit. He held it in and slowly exhaled into the air.

"Well, let's get our asses in gear," I said as I straddled my ride.

Angel reached out and grabbed my arm. I glanced at him with a frown. "We're going to get them back."

Unable to speak, I nodded.

Since Phoenix was the one who spotted the other drive, he led as we pulled back out. Not far down, he turned off on a dirt road that I assumed was private property. We stopped, and one by one backed our bikes into the trees. We gathered loose limbs and broke off smaller ones from the surrounding trees to cover up any chrome that might reflect and be seen from the road.

"I'll be back," Ghost said as he disappeared in front of our eyes. A shiver skated down my spine.

"How the fuck does he do that?" I muttered.

Angel glanced my way. "How do any of us do what we do? It simply is."

"What did Venom say? Is he sending anyone as backup for us?"

"No. Venom, Squirrel, Kicker, and the prospects are holding down the fort. Sabre and Blade are down in Puerto Rico with the brothers down there looking into something with the trafficking shit. Raptor and Voodoo went to look into the gunrunners that killed Halvorson's friend. They're with the Los Angeles chapter right now. All that's available are the old timers, and that's not fair to have them come up here. They're practically retired."

"I knew we should've kept that guy alive that we picked up in Texas," I grumbled.

"Kind of hard when he had a goddamn stroke during our interrogation," Phoenix said with a grin.

"Well, if Blade wasn't such a sick fuck, maybe he wouldn't have made the guy have an aneurysm," I argued. Angel snorted, and I glared at him.

"Not his fault the guy had a weak vessel in his head," Phoenix said before he shrugged.

I sighed.

Time seemed to crawl as we waited for word from Ghost. Though I knew his gift would keep him from being seen, we had no idea what type of people we were dealing with. What if they could see him? Hell, did he show up on thermal cameras? I'd never thought to ask. What if he did and they had them?

My brain wouldn't stop.

"Do you think he's okay?" I asked as I paced.

"Of course I am," a voice whispered in my ear, making me nearly jump out of my skin.

"You're a fucking asshole," I snapped.

Ghost chuckled as he stepped around me.

"What did you find?" Angel asked. We all gave him our full attention.

He took a deep breath, exhaling as he puffed his cheeks out. "That is some serious shit over there. I'm talking cult-type crazy shit. Doomsday Peppers Ranch shit."

"What?" I asked not understanding exactly what he was getting at.

"The bushes are fake. Really incredible ones, but fake. They are on a roller system that moves out of the way. The fence that runs about fifteen to twenty feet in from the road even with those bushes is eight feet tall and electrified. Razor wire at the top of that. Seems to go on forever." He shook his head in amazement.

"So how do we get in?" I asked, ready to explode in exasperation.

"It appears there's only cameras at the gate. Quite a way down the fence line is a spot that is eroded. I think we might be able to shimmy under it. Might be a tight fit for your big ass. How good are you at limbo?" he asked with a smirk.

"Can we dig it out more?" Phoenix asked the question I had.

"One of you carrying a shovel up your ass I don't know about?" Ghost asked with a cocked brow. I flipped him off.

"Let's go," Angel said. As the club's enforcer, he was the highest-ranking member there. We deferred to his judgement and followed him.

When we saw the washout Ghost had referred to, we shot him a look of astonishment.

"You think we're gonna fit through that?" Phoenix quietly asked in disbelief. His eyes looked like they were gonna pop out of his head. "How the fuck did you get in?"

"I didn't, dumbass. I looked for a way in, and I found it," Ghost said as he fluttered his lashes.

"You said the fence is hot and there's a fucking barbed-wire strand running under that below the dirt's surface!" Phoenix said as he propped his fists on his hips.

"Jesus. Bitch, bitch, bitch, bitch, bitch," grumbled Ghost as he rummaged around in the trees. He came back with an E-Tool like I'd used in the army.

"What the fuck? Where the hell did that come from?" I asked in amazement.

"Well, I didn't have it up my ass, but I did have it in my saddlebag." The smartass had the nerve to snicker. He tossed it to Phoenix, who instinctively caught it.

"Why the hell are you giving it to me?" he asked.

"Because you were the one of little faith," Ghost said with a shrug.

That time Phoenix flipped him off, but he crouched down and started digging, careful not to touch the metal shovel to the fence. Sweat trickled down his brow, and he paused to wipe it off with the back of his hand. "You'd think it wouldn't be this fucking hot. We're damn near in Canada," he muttered.

"Thank fuck," replied Ghost. "I hate the cold."

"Yet you live in motherfuckin' Iowa," said Phoenix as he continued to dig. Then he handed it off to me. "Your turn."

I dug with a passion I never had in the military. When I was satisfied that I thought I could fit, I tossed it to the side. It would've been easier if I could grab the fence to push and pull myself through. Instead, I had to lie on my back and shimmy under. The barbed wire caught on my shirt, and I froze. Ghost carefully picked the fabric from the barb, and I continued through.

Once I was on the other side, I listened to make sure no

one was coming. When I was sure it was clear, I motioned for my brothers to go under. They repeated my motions, but once they got to a certain point, I was able to grab their arms and slowly drag them the rest of the way.

We were all through and brushed off the loose dirt. Checking my weapons, I ensured they were all loaded and chambered, then replaced them in the holster at the back of my pants, then the ones at each ankle. Angel, Ghost, and Phoenix did the same.

"Let's go," Angel said.

I gripped his arm. "Hey, I think when we get to wherever they're holding Jasmine and Ehria, you should hang back. If you're hurt, you can't help if...." My words died off—I was unable to finish my sentence.

"I understand. We're going to get them back." His intense gaze held mine as I swallowed with difficulty before I inhaled deeply.

"Lead the way."

We silently made our way through the trees, parallel to the dirt drive. When it seemed like we'd walked miles, the trees thinned, and a large clearing was revealed. There were several large buildings and about twenty-five smaller ones. All were metal buildings, completely nondescript other than some flower beds in front of the smaller ones. There wasn't a vehicle in sight, but one of the long buildings had a bunch of closed bay doors, and I assumed that must be where they were stored.

"I'm going in to see where everyone is," Ghost said barely above a whisper before he vanished. Clenching and unclenching my hands, I twitched and fidgeted. By looking at me, no one would guess I'd been a decorated operative. Then again, I'd never once been on a mission where the subject was personal.

"How do you think he makes his clothes disappear? You

think he has special fabric?" Phoenix quietly asked as he scanned the area. My expression of disbelief was lost on him, because he didn't glance my way once. He scratched the back of his neck with an inked hand.

Absently, I thought about how most of his work was mine. "How are you even thinking this shit at a time like this?" I whispered.

"Need to keep you from losing your shit," he said as he glanced my way and cocked a brow.

"Can you two be quiet?" Angel asked in exasperation.

"Where the fuck is everyone? Unless they have another exit that we can't see, there should be someone here," I murmured as my gaze clocked every detail of the compound.

"It's eerie as fuck," Angel softly murmured.

There was a snap in the brush behind me, and I had my pistol out and aimed as Ghost appeared with his hands up and a cocky grin. "Easy, bro."

I softly snorted. "You're slipping. I heard you. Now what did you find out?"

His grinned disappeared immediately. "See that big building in the center?" he asked as he pointed.

We all nodded.

"All the smaller buildings have windows; those are houses. I don't know why, but everyone is inside. That biggest one in the center has none, and there are cameras all around it. If I had to guess, they're in there. Problem is, we have no idea how many or what we're up against."

I raked my fingers through my hair. "Now what?" I asked Angel. Personally, I wasn't against storming the place, but my logical side told me that was stupid as fuck, because we wouldn't stand a chance in hell, and I could get my family harmed.

"Ghost, do you think you can get inside?" Angel asked.

"Undetected? No clue—but I can try. Didn't want to risk it until I told you guys what was up."

"Here's Facet," Angel said as he pulled out his phone.

A slow grin spread across his face, and his brown gaze lifted to mine. "We're in. He's got their shit running on a loop. As long as no one comes or goes for them to realize something is up, we're golden. What's the best approach?" he asked Ghost.

Ghost walked us through the layout and which route we could use get to the center structure with the least chance of being seen from the windows of the homes. Heart hammering, but minds focused, we moved according to plan while Angel waited in the trees. We all had spent time in the military and it showed. Well, except Ghost, but he had his own skills that made him a badass without formal military training.

When we were close, Ghost disappeared and opened the door a crack. Then it slowly opened enough for a man to slip through. He was gone briefly before he reappeared and waved us in. Fucking spooky as shit.

Again, I cursed that I couldn't touch anything to see if Jasmine and Ehria were okay, but the benefits had outweighed the risks at the time. None of us anticipated she would go missing again. The thing was, if I had it to do over, I didn't think I would've changed it. The ability to touch my woman and my child without gloves like a normal man was something I never thought I'd be able to do.

Now I had to get them back.

Safely.

TWENTY-SEVEN

Jasmine

"SECRETS AND LIES"—RUELLE

"**W**hat is going on?" I asked the woman who had abducted me and my baby. The woman I was now certain was Nico's mother.

"You should not ask questions," she said as she sat a plate of food in front of me. "It's not much, but you need to eat for the baby."

We were in what looked like a conference room or classroom, sitting at the large table. She brought me a sandwich and some fruit with a bottle of water.

Before she could back away, I grabbed her wrist. Her startled gaze lifted to mine.

"I'm not stupid. I'm not going to try to hurt you, but I want some answers." The Jasmine of a year ago would've been cowering by this time, likely nearly comatose. Though she may be lurking in the shadows of my mind, I was no longer that person. I *refused* to be that person again. "You're Nico's mother." It was a statement, not a question.

Fear mixed with sadness shimmered in her eyes for a moment before she softly whispered, "I don't deserve to be called that."

"How can you take his child from him?" I asked, not letting up.

"You think I wanted to?" Tears filled her eyes.

"Well, you did," I said, giving her an "are you serious" look.

She sighed as she cast a brief glance over her shoulder toward the door. "If Alpha hears you, he will kill you. He is angry at me for bringing you."

"Who the hell is Alpha? Why are we here?" I quietly demanded.

"Because the pack has been keeping tabs on my son. Mostly to threaten me, to ensure I stayed in line." When she said "son," her voice wavered. "And Alpha is my husband."

My mouth fell open as I stared. Words escaped me. It wasn't until Ehria leaned forward to grab at the food on the plate that I was pulled out of my shock.

"Nico's father is here?" I asked.

Her eyes went wide. "No! Alpha is *not* Nico's father!"

I paused. "I'm so confused. Can you not talk in riddles and please tell me what the hell is going on? If you kidnapped me and my daughter, why are you locked in here with me now?"

"Alpha is deciding what to do with me," she said as her eyes dropped. "It's a long story."

"Well, it would appear I have time," I sarcastically replied. "We're just chilling here having a good ol' time."

She gave a wry grin as she tucked a silver-streaked lock of hair behind her ear. Though she showed some age, she was stunning, nonetheless. "I can see why my son loves you. He would never have a good relationship with a woman who was weak."

Little did she know, that was exactly how I used to feel. If it hadn't been for Nico and our child, I may never have found the inner strength to work on my self-empowerment and worth. Again, I prayed he would find us soon. My heart was crying for him.

Ehria began to arch her back and fuss. She was getting hungry and tired. Likely, she also sensed my mood.

"Do you need to feed her?" Nico's mother asked.

"Yes. You can fill me in while I do that," I said as I freed my slightly engorged breast and placed my daughter to it. She quickly latched on. As she ate, she seemed intent on our conversation.

"When I was a baby, my parents betrothed me to Amos—Alpha. He was fifteen years older than me, but our parents wanted the match. Mine because Amos was heir to the line of Alphas if he proved himself, his because my family traces back to Genghis Khan on my mother's side. We are a powerful family, but there hasn't been a male in our line for generations. My father thought if he aligned me with the Alphas, we would create strong sons. What they didn't expect was that I would sneak out as a teenager and fall in love with a human. Well, sort of."

"Sort of? And God, that's archaic."

"Who are you telling? Nico's father was named Nikolai Trinidad. He had the same gift as Nico does—he was human but, well, then some. Anyway, when we met there was… magic in the air." Her eyes seemed to be distant as she spoke, and a soft smile curved her lips. "He was stunned when he met me because he couldn't read me. I now believe it was because of my heritage. Regardless, he was the most beautiful man I'd ever met, yet fierce and bold. Back then, we were allowed to go to school in the town. I'd met him after school one day. It is because of me and Nikolai that the children are no longer allowed to leave the property." She appeared sad.

"What happened to his father?" I asked softly as my daughter curled her small hand around my thumb.

"We would meet in secret as often as we could. At first we

simply talked. Then talking led to... more." Her cheeks flushed a becoming pink, and her smile returned. "We had been together for nearly a year. We planned that when I was eighteen, we would run away together. Except I fell pregnant a few months shy of that. I was so afraid. But he promised to keep me safe. One night after my family slept, I left. It was so dark that night. How I evaded the patrol as I snuck through the trees, I'll never know. Nikolai was waiting at the road as he promised. We left and went to Montana thinking we'd be safe and after I turned eighteen, I could contact my parents and tell them where I was."

"Obviously, that didn't work?" I asked with a raised brow.

"No, not exactly. We didn't plan on them tracking us. We managed to live under the radar for the rest of my pregnancy. Nico was born, and Nikolai doted on him. He was so proud of his son, and we were so in love. We got married—that was our mistake and how they found us." She swallowed hard before she wet her lips and continued. "Other than having my eyes, Nico looks just like his father. So handsome. But I digress."

She sighed. "Amos had taken over as Alpha by then. He was cruel and power-hungry. Having something that had been promised to him taken away enraged him. He thought it made him look weak. He found us one day after I contacted my parents. We fled, but he and his men caught up to us in the woods. He told me I was coming home with him and that he was going to kill Nikolai and my baby like he killed Nikolai's family. He felt that because Nico wasn't born like us and I loved him, he wasn't worthy of existing. My husband was beside himself with rage and grief, and he rushed at Amos. What he didn't anticipate was that Amos never played fair. Amos shot him, but he didn't stop. He stabbed Amos in the chest, and when they both fell to the ground... he... Nikolai, was dead," she stuttered.

My heart ached for her, because I couldn't imagine losing Nico like that.

"I thought Amos had died too. In case he had others with him, I packed up as many of my things and Nico's that I could, and I ran. I thought I could start over somewhere. Me and my son."

"But Amos obviously didn't die," I guessed.

"For many years, I managed to stay one step ahead of the pack. When Nico was seven, Amos caught up to us. I was shocked to see him alive. My father came as well. He stopped Amos from killing Nico as long as I agreed to return with them and abandon Nico. I instructed Nico how to get to town. Amos was appeased, because he didn't think Nico would survive in the woods and find his way to town. He also didn't know my sister hid in the trees and watched over him until he reached town the next day. She watched over him for me the best she could without tipping off the pack. Well, she tried. Amos overheard her one day when she was giving me an update on him. He killed her and told me that if I attempted to leave or contact my son, he would kill him." Tears coursed down her cheeks by that time.

"If you had told Nico, he could've protected you," I argued.

She scoffed. "Not against the Alpha's little 'army.' They are ruthless and evil."

"But that doesn't explain why you tried to take my daughter. Surely if he didn't want Nico, he wouldn't want Nico's daughter."

"Because she is one of us. Alpha planted a nurse with your pediatrician because we can scent our own race. Once it was confirmed, he wanted control of her because he is worried she will endanger us if she isn't properly taught. He also wants her lineage."

"I don't give a shit if she's one of you. She's our daughter and she needs to be raised with her parents," I said in indignation. And my daughter's *lineage? I don't fucking think so.*

The beautiful woman looked at me and proudly raised her chin.

"We are wolf shifters and so is she."

Through the conversation, I had begun to suspect and so many things started to fall into place. The little growls my daughter started making. Dreaming of wolves. Nico drawing wolves. Probably the silver ripple we'd seen in her eyes. *Damn.* "I'm not saying you're wrong, because I believe you, but I don't understand how that's possible. Nico is your son, but he's not a shifter. I'm sure as hell not a shifter. How could our daughter be one?"

"Because I am," she said as she pressed her fist to her chest. "Therefore, it passes through Nico, and any female children of his will be shifters. Males would not. We don't know why. If I had been a male mated to a human, it would be likely that Nico would've been born a shifter instead of with his father's gift."

"I still don't get how you could take Nico's child from him. If Nikolai loved Nico as much as you say, what makes you think he loves his own daughter any less? Why would you want to hurt him?" I asked, not understanding how she could go along with something so heinous after what she'd been through.

"Because it was either that or Alpha threatened to bring the three of you here and kill you in front of me and the pack to set an example." Her jaw clenched, and her nostrils flared as I watched her fight a sob. "I'm going to try to get you out of here. We have a plan—" she started.

The door burst open, and we jumped before I could ask her who the hell "we" were. A young man rushed in with a scowl, and I instinctively prepared to protect my child the best I could.

"Father wants you," he said. "I've been trying to convince him the child's mother is no threat. I told him we can kill her after the child is weaned. We need a little more time," he said softly. He barely cast me a glance, but when he did, I caught a flicker of regret in his eyes.

"Play along the best you can and I'll keep your daughter safe," he finally said, addressing me before he left the room.

"Who was that?" I asked as I clutched my infant daughter to my breast.

"My son," she said as her nearly ebony gaze held mine before she stepped out and closed the door.

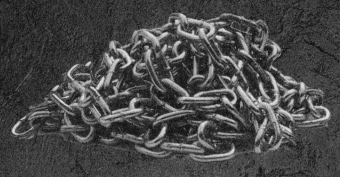

TWENTY-EIGHT

Chains

"DARKNESS SETTLES IN"—FIVE FINGER DEATH PUNCH

When we entered the large building, we saw a large assembly area, complete with seating and a podium. There were several doors along the back wall that I assumed were offices or maybe rooms like we had at the clubhouse, but I really had no clue. There was a big industrial kitchen at one end that opened to the area by a large open window. It reminded me of a church area where they'd have receptions and shit.

There had only been one guy standing guard at the main door, but Ghost had knocked his ass out, shoved his bandana in his mouth, then zip-tied his hands and feet. He motioned to a door next to the kitchen. It was a large storage closet with shelves and shelves of canned goods, and paper- and plasticware. I would've just killed the dude and been done with it.

"Where the fuck is everyone?" I whispered. Ghost pointed across the large area to the last two doors on the right, closest to the kitchen.

"I watched a woman go in the door on the left with food.

Jasmine and Ehria were in there. They both seemed to be okay."
My shoulders relaxed slightly at the news, and my heart soared.
I made personal vow that whoever had taken them was going to
pay and pay dearly.

"The other door?" Phoenix asked.

"Group of men from what I could hear through the door. One
sounded like the leader. He was pissed as a motherfucker, too."

"Phoenix, you and Ghost take the room on the left; I'll take
the one with my family. If no one comes out, fall behind me as we
leave. If I stir up a racket in the room with Jasmine, try to keep
the leader alive. He's mine. But if you have to, take him out. Take
them *all* out." They both nodded at my plan. Fuck, I wished we
had more brothers with us.

Suddenly, the door on the left rattled. We all ducked into the
kitchen and observed as best we could. A man who looked to be
around twenty or so exited the room and went next door. When
he flung the door open, I nearly wept in relief at the brief glance
I got of Jasmine. Ehria was cradled to her and seemed to be okay.

The man went back to the other room and waited at the entrance. A woman with dark hair streaked with some gray walked
out with her head submissively low. Something about her seemed
familiar, but I couldn't quite figure it out. I knew I could probably touch shit in the room and get some answers, but I needed to
be at one hundred percent to get Jasmine and Ehria out of there.

As soon as the door closed, I heard shouting within the room.
We moved quickly and silently.

Phoenix and Ghost stood either side of the room on the left;
I approached the one on the right. Weapons drawn, I motioned
that I was going in. Cautiously, I cracked the door. I knew where
Jasmine had been before, and I hoped she hadn't moved. Quickly,
I swept in and clocked Jasmine and Ehria as the only occupants.

Jasmine's hand flew to her mouth, and a quiet sob was muffled behind it. Ehria rested with her head on Jasmine's shoulder as she slept. Her precious mouth was open, and drool hung off her bottom lip.

I held a finger to my lips to keep her quiet and motioned her to me. She stood. I grabbed my daughter's blanket from the table and I ushered them out of the room. Ghost and Phoenix covered us as we made our way across the expansive room.

We were almost home free when there was a shout of alarm, and about ten men poured out of the room, guns drawn. Jasmine shrieked at the first shot that was fired and crouched down. We returned fire as we moved at a crouch, and I tried to get my family to the door. Between me and Phoenix, we took out half. In quick succession, several more dropped to the floor with blood gushing from their necks.

"Thank you, Ghost," I whispered as I took a shot and ushered Jasmine toward the door.

The young man was holding the older woman back as she fought his hold. I didn't have time to wonder what was going on before she broke free and barreled at the tallest man with slicked-back silver hair.

"Mother!" the young man shouted as he dove for her, but it was too late. Right as the older man pointed his gun at me and Jasmine, she threw herself at him. He fell backward, and she dropped to her knees before toppling over onto him. I pointed my weapon at the young man as he ran toward me.

"Nico! No! That's your brother!" Jasmine cried.

Stunned, I froze. He continued to run toward us, waving his hands toward the opposite side of the room. "Go!" he shouted as he closed in on us. Pushing my disbelief away, I focused on the situation as the young man scooped my daughter up from Jasmine and grabbed her arm to lift her to her feet. "This way!" he said as he ran down the side of the large assembly area.

We raced after him and through a hall in the corner. He pushed open the door and we were outside.

"This is the back exit. If you'd gone out front, the rest of my father's men would've been on you in a heartbeat. Hurry, it won't take long before they catch on." We followed him as he darted behind a smaller building. He glanced around the corner and motioned us on. He pointed to the long building with a line of garage doors.

The building was mere steps away when I saw stars and a burning filled my chest. I couldn't breathe, and I stumbled. "Go!" I gasped as Jasmine shouted and stopped to grab me before I fell. Eyes wide in disbelief, she frantically shook her head.

The man who had helped us—my fucking *brother*—grabbed her arm and jerked her along until Phoenix scooped her up and tossed her over his shoulder. The entire time, she screamed. Unable to keep moving, I tripped again and dropped to my knees.

Something hot and wet ran down my wrist and hand that held my pistol. Glancing down, I saw crimson dripping off the barrel. I couldn't lift my arm. Another shot fired near me, and I scanned the area to see where it came from before I fell face down.

My daughter's pink blanket lay in front of my face, and it was all I could see.

"You fucking piece of shit bastard!" a voice shouted behind me before there was a loud growl. Inside, I chuckled, wanting to say "You're goddamn right, I'm a Bastard," but I couldn't speak, and my vision went hazy.

Pressure hit my back, teeth sank into my neck, and I blacked out from the pain.

Bastard to the core, Royal to the death.

TWENTY-NINE

Jasmine

"RISE UP"—ANDRA DAY

Everything that happened was a blur. I screamed and beat Phoenix's back, demanding he put me down and go back for Nico. He'd been shot and there was a massive wolf attacking him, just like my dream.

Once we hit the building the vehicles were in, he tossed me in the silver SUV we'd arrived in, and I grabbed my daughter from Nico's brother as he passed her in.

"Go get him!" I shrieked as I clutched a crying Ehria to my chest.

"Buckle her in and keep your head down!" Nico's brother shouted at me as he jumped in the driver seat. Phoenix climbed in next, and the tires squealed as we drove forward as the garage door was still opening. We barely missed hitting it as the roof rack scraped the bottom of the door.

Hands shaking, I fumbled to buckle the straps over my daughter as she sobbed and fought. I wanted to look back to see what was happening, but at the moment, my daughter's safety was paramount.

"Hang on!" Nico's brother—I still didn't know his name—shouted as several shots hit the glass, but it didn't break. He plowed into a man pointing his gun at the windshield just as he shot again. The entire time, Ehria cried, and I tried to soothe her the best I could, but tears poured down my face.

"Bulletproof glass? Nice," Phoenix muttered as he breathed heavy.

"What the fuck is wrong with you, Phoenix?" I yelled at him. "You left your brother back there! Both of you!"

"Chill, Angel is there, and Ghost. But if we didn't get you out of there, it would've been my ass."

In shock, I fell back in the seat. "Angel is here?"

Phoenix nodded as he watched the road behind us. Clouds of dirt billowed as we tore down the drive toward the gate that was slowly rolling open.

Relief hit me at hearing my brother was there, but I hoped and prayed he got to Nico in time. I had no idea how many more people were there that they might have to fight off. What if it was too late? I knew there were limits to my brother's abilities. Then I worried that the wolves I'd seen coming around the building would get to Ghost and Angel before they could help Nico.

Mind spinning, breath heaving, I leaned over to press soft kisses to my baby's wet cheeks. She clutched my tangled hair as her cries lessened to whimpers.

"Yes. I know it was sooner than we anticipated and not the way we wanted it to happen!" I heard Nico's brother shout, and I realized he was on the phone.

"Calm down, Maximus. We have things under control." The man sighed through the vehicle's speakers. "What a shitshow."

"Nico and his friends?"

"Busy," the man replied.

"My mother?" Maximus hesitantly asked. There was silence. I watched as Maximus fought for composure. "I'll check in after I get to town."

The call ended, and I bit my lip to hold in my sob. Though she had kidnapped me and my daughter, she was Nico's mother. I may not have seen it at the time, but I believed she'd done the best she could to ensure her children and grandchild were safe.

"I'm going to take you to town. You will be safe there. My friends have taken control of the pack." His words were subdued, and I knew he was working through his emotions. "We thought we could take over before he sent my mother after you, but he did it sooner than planned. I think he may have been suspicious that he had opposition in the pack. By the time we knew, it was too late. We had a plan," he said, and his voice caught. After clearing his throat, he drove in silence.

Phoenix was contemplative as well.

We pulled off at a small motel. "I know the owners here. I'll get you a room to get cleaned up while you wait for your friends. You'll be safe. I'm sorry things went this way."

He got out of the vehicle and went inside.

"Do you trust him?" I whispered to Phoenix.

"Insanely enough, yes," he replied. "But fucking hell, I had no idea Chains had a brother or that his mother was still alive."

"Me either," I murmured.

"Facet tried to find her. Did you know that?" Phoenix asked me as he turned slightly in his seat.

I shook my head.

"Fuck," he muttered as he ran a hand over his mouth.

Maximus came back with a brass key on an old-fashioned motel keychain. He opened the door and looked into the back seat. "I have the room."

Gently, I took Ehria from the seat and carried her inside. Phoenix stayed outside, and I saw him with his phone to his ear. I took in the dated but extremely clean and homey room. Once Maximus closed the door, he dropped into the chair, and his elbows rested on his knees as he buried his face in his hands.

"I'm sorry about your mother," I whispered.

He dropped his hands and stared at me with red-rimmed eyes. "We knew there would be casualties. We all accepted it. I just didn't think…." He trailed off as his gaze fell to his hands.

After a few moments of silence, he stood. "I need to get back. My pack needs me, and I need to check on my brother." He sounded rusty as he said the word.

He glanced at my daughter before he ran a trembling hand over her dark hair. "You're going to need help with her. There are things you won't understand and won't know how to handle as she grows into herself. We had hoped my mother would be the one to be there for you."

The pain in his expression was heartbreaking. I understood, though. Losing your mother is one of the most painful experiences. I was around his age when I lost mine.

Losing Nico would be as bad, but I wasn't allowing myself to think that Angel may not have been able to save Nico. I couldn't. I was holding on to my sanity by a thread, and I was using every coping skill I knew to hold my shit together.

"I'll let you know as soon as I get back."

There was no need to say what he was referring to—I knew. He paused in the open doorway. "I hope you will let me be a part of her life, but I'll understand if you don't want me to."

Without waiting for my reply, he left.

Sitting on the edge of the bed, I cradled my sleeping but sniffling daughter to my body. Eyes closed, I breathed deeply as I rocked slightly.

The door opened, and my eyes popped open, heart thundering. "News?"

Phoenix grinned before he blew out a heavy breath. "He's okay. He and Angel are out right now. Ghost is with them."

Relief hit me like a tsunami, and I nearly fell over. Unable to properly process, I laughed as I sobbed. Phoenix sat by us and wrapped his arm around me.

"He's okay," he repeated as if he needed to remind or reassure himself. I rested my head on his shoulder as I continued to blubber and laugh.

It was hours later when the same silver SUV pulled up out front. Heart in my throat, I stood. Phoenix was napping next to Ehria on one of the beds, with pillows on her other side, but his head had popped up the second he heard me remove the chain lock.

After making sure Ehria was secure, he crawled off the bed.

Tears filled my eyes as I saw Nico crawl out of the back seat, and I ran. Throwing myself into his arms, I cried as I held on for dear life.

"Don't ever do that to me again! Can you *please* stop getting shot?" I mumbled into the plain black T-shirt he wore. He chuckled, and it shook his chest under my face.

"Where's Ehria?" he asked into my hair before he pressed a kiss to me, and I looked up into his beautiful dark eyes.

"Sleeping, and don't you dare wake her up!" I mock glared at him. She'd been intermittently fussy since our escape.

"I won't. Are you sure you're okay?" he asked, searching my eyes for the truth.

My lids dropped, and I took a deep breath that I let out slowly before I locked my gaze with his. "Yeah. I'm okay. Maybe not great, but okay."

With a single nod, he kissed my forehead.

"It's good to see you're okay," Phoenix said behind me. That's when I realized my brother hadn't gotten out of the vehicle.

"Where's Angel?" I asked, fear trickling through my veins. "And Ghost?"

"He's back at the compound resting," Maximus said as he rounded the hood. "Your other friend is with him. Wouldn't leave him. He saved our mother. It utterly drained him, and he's been damn near comatose since. But I promise, he's safe."

"If it hadn't been for you and Ehria being here, I might not have either," said Nico with a chuckle before he cleared his throat. "You know my brother, obviously."

"Well, yes and no," I admitted with a half-smile. "I didn't officially get introduced."

"I'm right there with you, babe," Nico said to me.

Maximus ran a hand through his dark hair, much like his brother often did. If you looked at their features, besides them both being handsome, they looked so very different. Still, they had similar little mannerisms—weird, because they weren't raised together.

"I honestly only found out about you this year," Maximus admitted. "I think my father was afraid he wouldn't be able to stop me from finding you, so he wouldn't let anyone tell me about you. I can promise you, our mother didn't stay away from you willingly."

Nico's jaw ticked, and I knew he was having a hard time believing what Maximus was saying.

"Can we go inside?" Maximus asked as he cautiously looked around. "I'd rather not discuss this out here."

"I'll stand guard outside," Phoenix offered.

The other man who had traveled to town with them stepped up. "I'll wait out here too."

"Thanks. By the way, I'd like you all to meet Dare, my second." Maximus gave a chin lift in the man's direction. That's when

I realized they all had the same green-gold eyes that Nico's mother and my daughter had. Huh.

We went inside, and I checked to be sure Ehria was still okay. Both fists up by her ears, she slept peacefully. Nico's hands slipped around my waist, and he lowered his head to rest his chin on my shoulder. "She's beautiful… like her mommy," he whispered.

I pressed my palms over his hands before I turned to look at him and Maximus. Reluctantly, Nico let me go, and we sat on the other bed as Maximus sat in one of the chairs at the little table by the window.

"For several years, my aunt watched over you. At least until Amos found out and killed her. Mother said he was in a rage and told her that he would kill everyone she loved if she didn't stay away from you." He slouched back in the chair, legs spread and gazing at the ceiling.

It turned out it wasn't one of the bodyguards on the job that had shot Nico. It was one of Amos's people. He and his men were pissed because Ehria was refusing to stay away from us once she knew she was having a grandchild. Turned out she'd been the wolf that I thought I saw.

"My father threatened to kill your baby and your woman if she didn't stay away. At the time, he thought you were dead. That was the night I found out about you. Mother was beside herself, crying in her home when I stopped by to see her. I didn't understand why he hadn't killed my mother over the years. I think it might've been because in his sick twisted way, he loved her. He didn't want you in the pack because he hated that you were another man's child with our mother. That was when we began to officially plan for the overthrow. Dare and I had discussed it in secret in the past, but I was young. I didn't think I would have the support of the pack. After we found out about you, we gathered a group of loyal supporters who would rebel. We had everything ready to set our plan in motion when he sent my mother off and wouldn't tell me why. Then she showed up with you and your daughter. I almost shit myself. It was a complication we hadn't anticipated. I'm so fucking sorry." He leaned forward with his elbows on his thighs and bowed his head.

"Maximus. None of this is your fault. Tell him, Nico," I urged. Nico wrapped his big, tattooed hand around mine and squeezed.

"She's right," he began, and Maximus looked up at him in disbelief. "None of us decide who our parents will be. The fact that you turned out to be a decent man is testament to our mother's influence in your raising."

"You want to know a secret? I'm not sure if I'm ready to be the Alpha," he said with a mirthless laugh before he chewed on his lip and glanced out the window.

"Look, man, I don't know much about the inner workings of the pack—hell, until today, I didn't realize my mother was a fucking wolf. Still, I think you have a good head on your shoulders and you'll do fine," Nico told his younger brother.

"What I can say is I love my pack and I have their best interests at heart. And I pray you're right," he said with a sad smile.

"I know I am," Nico said. "Now, I'd like to get my brothers and head home, if that's okay."

"One of my men will drive Jasmine and the baby home. Unless you'd rather rent a vehicle. I'd understand."

"Maybe you could?" I asked, thinking it might give him and Nico a chance to bond if I could convince him to stay when we got back to Ankeny.

"I would if I could. With the state of things in the pack, it's important for me to be here. At least until I establish my place," Maximus apologized.

"Well, hopefully you'll be able to visit one day soon," Nico said, and I knew there was hope for the two brothers.

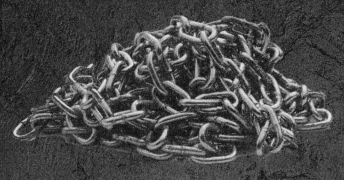

EPILOGUE

Chains

Nerves like I'd never had in my fucking life had me fidgeting and pulling at my collar.

"Stop it. You'll fuck everything up," Voodoo muttered behind me.

"I feel like I'm gonna pass out," I mumbled. He chuckled.

"I'll catch you, Sleeping Beauty," he teased. I rolled my eyes but quickly straightened up when the music changed.

Staring down the aisle, I had a hard time catching my breath at the vision in white. Dark hair tumbled around her golden shoulders in soft curls. A stunning smile spread as she looked at me. Her slender hand curled around the crook of her brother's arm as they slowly made their way closer to where I stood under the ridiculously frou-frou archway she'd insisted on.

I couldn't quit smiling, no matter how hard the damn butterflies slammed around in my guts or how the collar of my monkey suit seemed to choke me. She was absolutely beautiful.

And she was mine.

She reached the front row and paused. My heart tripped. Was she changing her mind?

I needn't have worried. She leaned down to press a light kiss on our daughter's head where she sat in the front row in my mother's lap.

"You sure you don't wanna run?" Voodoo teasingly whispered. I didn't so much as acknowledge him, because my attention was focused on the woman I love.

My brother, Maximus, sat next to my mother. It was still so weird that I had a grown brother I'd known nothing about. The thing was? He was a great kid—man. Things were a little awkward with him, my mom, and me, but we were working on it.

Ehria waved her arms and reached for her mother, but Jasmine smiled and bopped her nose with her finger, making Ehria giggle. My mother leaned down and whispered in my daughter's ear, and she rested her head on my mom's chest.

Jasmine continued toward me until she and Angel were two feet away. Blood rushed in my veins, my heart working overtime as I gazed at my bride.

From the second her hand rested in mine, I barely heard a word the officiant had to say. Voodoo had to nudge me when it came time to say my part. I startled, and my face burned as soft laughter bounced through the intimate gathering.

"Uh, sorry," I whispered, then spoke my vows. I'd written them myself, and I was fucking nervous as hell.

"I, Nikolai Andreas Trinidad, take you, Jasmine Leanna Bearheart, to be my ride or die. I promise to be a pain in your ass but make it up to you every chance I get. You will never question my devotion, though you may question my sanity. I promise to give you lots of babies that are as beautiful as you are and to protect them with my life. I promise to be by your side through the good days and the bad, never wavering and never leaving you behind. I may not always be the easiest man to get along with, but I promise I will love you above all others for the rest of my days." A single glistening tear trailed down her cheek as I finished. She gave a little sniffle before the officiant asked her to speak her vows.

"I wanted to write something flowery and profound that told you the depth of my love. Except every time I sat down to write the words, all I could think about was how you make me feel. So I decided to tell you. From the first time I laid eyes on you, I knew you were the one. Though it took us a lot of ups and downs and a few wasted years, we made it. You saved me in so many ways that I cannot begin to tell you how grateful I am for your strength and your love. You make me a stronger person, and you make me believe in myself. Every time I lay my eyes on you, my heart swells and my stomach flutters. So my vow to you is to always do my best to ensure you know how important you are to me. I will always be your biggest fan and staunchest supporter. Nothing will ever sway my dedication to you and our little family. I will be honored to be your ride or die and to have your babies, though we need to discuss the definition of 'lots,' okay?"

My grin was ear to ear by the time she finished. I wanted to beat on my chest, swoop her up, and toss her over my shoulder and go somewhere I could bend her over and toss her dress up. We wouldn't come out until she could barely walk.

The officiant cleared his throat, pulling me out of my head again. He wrapped the service up with a big, fat bow, and I waited for one single phrase.

"You may kiss the bride," he said, and I framed my wife's face in my hands.

"I love you," I said before I brushed my lips to hers. I intended to keep it PG, but when her lips parted, I groaned, and my tongue invaded her. Her taste drove me crazy, and we quickly lost ourselves.

That was until the whistles, catcalls, and cheering broke

through. With a smile, I reluctantly broke away. She sighed against my lips, and I swallowed her breath, drinking her in. Then I stole one last kiss before the preacher-dude announced we were Nikolai and Jasmine Trinidad.

Jasmine had wanted a traditional wedding with the pomp and circumstance to go with it. Unfortunately, she married into a crazy family of bikers. The sound of roaring pipes as throttles were twisted rang out over the typical music we were supposed to walk back down the aisle to. We laughed as we were pelted with birdseed as we hurried toward the clubhouse where the reception would be held.

Brothers from all over the country were there.

We started the reception line as the guests began to follow us in. I quickly slipped on a thin pair of soft leather gloves in preparation.

"Congrats," Patriot, Rael, Grim, and Bodie said as they each shook my hand. No one questioned the fact that I wore gloves as I shook hands, when it was usually frowned upon. They all knew. Their ol' ladies gushed over how beautiful Jasmine's dress was as they hugged her and welcomed her to the family.

"Chains, you still owe me that ink," said Axel with a grin. He and the rest of the Flagstaff chapter had made the trip up for the wedding. The four months I'd spent with them brought us pretty close, and they were as much my family as my own chapter. They each congratulated us as their ol' ladies hugged me and Jasmine.

"Chains," Jameson said with his usual stoic demeanor when he shook my hand. His ol' lady, Sadie, hugged us both with a whispered "congrats" as they passed.

"My young Nico. I'm so very happy for you," said Madame Laveaux with a fond smile. She framed my face with her beringed hands, then whispered, "You have made me so proud. Now I'm waiting for more great-grandbabies to play with theirs."

She thumbed her hand at Voodoo and Kira.

My eyes went wide as she moved on to Jasmine. Voodoo laughed as he and Kira hugged me. "I take it Granmé told you? We haven't said anything yet, so keep it under your hat."

"Shit," I whispered as I cast a sidelong glance at my wife. She might not be ready for that quite yet. Ehria was a handful. A beautiful, precious, and wonderful handful, though.

Angel was next, and as he hugged me, he whispered, "Remember, you hurt her and I'll still kill you."

As he stood back, he grinned at me and winked. Korrie rolled her eyes at him, obviously having an idea of what he'd said. I could only laugh, because I had no intentions of hurting my wife. Unless it was to smack her ass a little.

One by one, my brothers and their families gave us their best wishes.

The prez of the Tampa chapter, Nycto, and his ol' lady, Eva, were next, followed by Void, Toxin, and his ol' lady.

Spark and Croc even came with their ol' ladies from Australia. Croc hooked my neck so hard as he hugged me, we nearly fell over. It was good to see him again and catch up. I had to tease him about how he was already picking up the accent.

Tarak and Edge were there from New Mexico with their ol' ladies, which surprised me. I hadn't seen them in forever.

Lean was there from Pittsburgh and his ol' lady Mani was damn near making notes. "Thanks a lot, Chains, now she's gonna have me in a monkey suit, too," he said with an eye roll.

"I'm here to help out," I replied with a laugh.

There was such an incredible turnout of brothers, I was blown away.

By the time everyone had run through the line, the drinks were flowing and the music was playing. Guests spilled out into the back that had been set up as overflow with picnic tables and another bar. The perimeter of the area was strung with lights from pole to pole that the prospects had busted their asses to get set up to Jasmine's specifications.

"Can we get the bride and groom to the dance floor?" Ghost said into the mic that was broadcasted through all the speakers.

Jasmine and I made the rounds as we headed toward the dance floor. A smile so big my cheeks hurt couldn't be tamed as I pulled her into my arms.

John Legend came through the speakers singing "Conversations In The Dark." Jasmine caught her bottom lip in her teeth as we slowly moved around the dance floor. The words of the song resonated with me in a way not much else did. We often held each other in bed at night talking softly and sharing our dreams. She was perfect, and I wouldn't try to change her. I would be there when she got lonely, and I wouldn't break her heart. She was my everything.

"I love you so much, Mrs. Trinidad," I said as I brushed a featherlight kiss across her perfect red lips. Her eyes glistened as I pulled back.

"I love you too, Mr. Trinidad."

The song was wrapping up when a squeal caught our attention, and Ehria ran from the edge of the crowd where she'd been watching us. We both stopped, and I leaned down and lifted her as Jasmine kissed her cheek.

"Mommy! Daddy! Dance!" she demanded. Her dark curls bounced as she clapped and giggled while we danced with her to "Thinking Out Loud" by Ed Sheeran. Her tiny beaded purse swung wildly on her wrist. It was hard to believe she was already a year and a half. Time had flown.

I spun my girls as we hit the corner, and they both were all smiles. Never in my life had I imagined this. My heart was so full, I could barely breathe.

"Remember you have something for Daddy," Jasmine said to

our daughter, whose green-gold eyes went wide. Then she fumbled with her little purse as the tip of her tongue peeked from her rosebud lips. She pulled out a folded-up piece of paper that she proudly handed to me.

With a kiss to her cherub cheek, I took it. Every little scribbled picture she made me hung in my room at the shop. This one would be added to the collection.

I carefully unfolded it and immediately stopped dancing. As I stared at the grainy black-and-white image, I swallowed the lump in my throat. My gaze lifted from the small picture to my wife, who momentarily went blurry before I rapidly blinked.

"You're…." I began but was interrupted by my daughter yelling.

"I a big sista!"

Overwhelmed with all the emotion coursing through me, I lifted Jasmine with one arm as the other held our daughter and spun us around.

Best fucking day of my life.

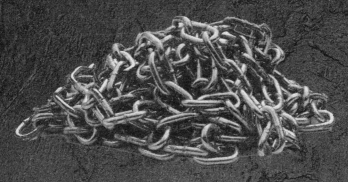

BONUS EPILOGUE

(You didn't think Jasmine and Nico would go out
without a bang, did you?)

Chains

Three Years Later....

I stood in wait around the corner. Silent, I waited for my prey to get close enough that I could take her by surprise.

The second I saw her, my hand shot out to cover her mouth. Her eyes went wide, and I pulled her in front of me as I gripped the front of her neck with my other hand. "Not a peep," I whispered in her ear.

She whimpered, and blood surged through my veins like a fire. Heart pounding, adrenaline pulsing with each beat, I pulled her with me through the open doorway. Quietly, I kicked it shut.

The tip of my nose skimmed the edge of her ear before I nipped it with my teeth. At her squeak behind my hand, I gripped her throat tighter, feeling the vibrations of her moan against my palm as I bit and licked the side of her neck.

"Not a peep," I whispered as I spun us to face the wall. "Palms to the wall. Now."

Immediately she complied, and my dick throbbed in my jeans.

I slid my hands down and around to cup her perfect tits, then slipped one into her leggings. "I fucking love these on you," I murmured in her ear.

She gave a chuckle as her ass pushed back into my painfully hard erection. "You weren't supposed to be back until tomorrow."

"I missed you. So I burned back tonight. Angel didn't complain; he was just as eager to get home."

There would be time tomorrow to tell her about the outcome of our mission. Her father had dropped off the face of the earth shortly before our wedding three years ago, and that made Angel nervous. We were always one step behind him, and it was infuriating both Angel and me. We'd finally gotten a break, but someone else had gotten to him. Not that he would've lasted much longer. He was nothing more than a walking corpse.

Shaking off the memories that had no place in my mind when my hand was cupping my wife's pussy, I bit the slope of her shoulder. "They're all asleep?" I asked as I kissed the bruised flesh.

"Finally, yes." Her reply was a breathless gasp.

"I knew if I let them know I was here, they'd never go to bed," I said with a dark chuckle. Slowly, I slid the stretchy black fabric along with the lace of her thong over the lush curve of her ass. Pausing long enough to squeeze each perfect globe in my hands, I continued to tease her neck.

"Draco fell trying to keep up with Ehria and Angeline at my brother's. He skinned his knee, so he's been playing that up. And Adira is teething. It's been a long day," she said, but it ended in a squeak when I pinched her clit.

Then I lifted her baggy sweater up, and she lifted her hands long enough for me to pull it off. I tossed it to the side and made quick work of removing her bra. It went by the wayside, and I crouched to push the leggings down her perfect golden legs until she stepped out of them. Each inch I revealed, I kissed.

When I stood again, I wrapped her dark hair around my hand and fisted it before pulling her head back. "Have you been good or bad while I was gone?" I whispered, allowing my lips to brush the shell of her ear as I spoke.

"Wha-What do you mean?"

"What did I tell you before I left?"

"Not to touch myself," she breathed, catching on.

"So?"

"I was bad," she admitted, and I growled in her ear. Releasing her hair, I spun her around, lifted her, and carried her to the bed.

"On your fucking knees," I demanded.

She did, and I saw the evidence of her arousal on the insides of her thighs. I swirled a fingertip through her pink slit before moving up to circle her clit. When she whined and tried to rub herself on me, I laid my hand across her ass with a crack. She tensed briefly, but I felt the gush of wetness on my hand that said she loved it. A satisfied grin kicked the corner of my mouth up before I teased her by stroking in and out a few times.

She cried out when I pulled away and stepped back.

"Watch me," I instructed and sucked her arousal off my finger. Her eyes dilated, and her lips parted.

Slowly, I undressed. She was panting, and lust shone in her eyes as she watched, but I didn't change my pace. When I stood naked next to the bed, I took my hard length in my hand and squeezed. A drop of precum beaded at my tip as I slid my hand up and down. When I got to the end, I pinched and twisted my grip, catching the drop and using it and the ones after as lubricant with each stroke. Lids heavy, I gazed at her as she hungrily stared at me.

"Do you like it when I take care of myself and you don't get anything?" Inside, I gloated at the desire that burned in her honey-gold eyes.

"No," she whispered.

"So what do you think I should do to you?"

"I don't know," she replied.

Tsking, I shook my head as I moved to the other side of the bed. She followed my every move. I hopped up on the bed and reclined on the pillow, then went back to teasing her as I played with myself.

"I think you do," I said as I cocked a brow.

She licked her lips and crawled over to me. "What if I said I'd make it up to you?"

"Hmm, how?"

Her tongue went out as she leaned over me and licked around the tip of my cock. When she suckled the head, my eyes rolled back, but I remained silent. Her slender fingers curled around my wrist as she guided my hand for a few strokes, then pushed it off me.

As she did, she swallowed my cock until it hit the back of her throat and she gagged slightly. Not that it deterred her. She drew back but plunged forward again. I let her do that as long as I could stand it, then I grabbed her hair and pulled her head back. She released my shaft with a pop.

"Get up here. I want you on my cock," I ground out.

Triumph flickered in her eyes as she straddled my hips. I held them in a bruising grip as she reached down to line my cock up with her soaking wet core. Right as she started to lower herself, I stopped her. She glared and huffed.

"Jasmine?"

"Yes?"

"Whose pussy is this?"

"Yours," she said on a whine as she tried to drop down.

"You don't finger yourself, you don't use a toy, you don't so much as put it close to the jets in the tub unless I tell you. Do you understand?"

"Okay," she said, and her walls clenched around the tip of my length that was inside her.

I chuckled, then drove my hips up and shoved myself balls deep into her tight heat. She sighed, and I clenched my jaw because I was already on the verge of coming.

"Goddamn, baby," I said through my teeth.

Her wicked grin had me shaking my head. "Can I fuck you now?" she purred.

I smacked her ass again, and her walls tightened around me. "Are you going to disobey me again?"

"Will I get punished like this if I do?" she asked with a mock expression of worry.

"Yes," I said with a smirk.

She rose, then dropped down, her pussy swallowing my cock. Instinctively, my hips thrust up to meet her downward motion. Leaning forward, she brushed her lips over mine. "Then yes," she said before she bit my lower lip. Pulling back enough to stare in my eyes, she ground on me.

With her leaned forward, I released her hips and cupped her tits that were swinging above me. Rolling her nipples between my thumbs and index fingers, I worked them to stiff points before I reached up to suck on them one at a time.

"Nico," she begged as she rode me.

I grabbed her and flipped her to her back in the same

motion as I drove deep into her. Her silky legs wrapped around my hips and curled around my thighs as she met me.

"Harder," she taunted as she panted.

"Your wish is my command," I said with a groan. Each snap of my hips was harder and faster than the last, until I was pistoning into her tight, wet, heat.

Her nails dug into my shoulders, and I fell to my elbows as I buried my face in her neck. Hot kisses were followed by my teeth scraping her sensitive flesh. Gasps, grunts, moans, and the slapping of our sweat-slicked skin filled the room.

"I'm going to come, Nico. Oh my God, I'm going to come," she whimpered.

Those words were all it took to break my control. As my cock began to pulse in her clenching cunt, I roared into her neck.

"Yesssssss!" she shouted.

"Shhh!" I replied as I reveled in the euphoria of our shared orgasm.

My body gave a shudder as I drove deep one last time, and I hissed.

"I missed you," she said, repeating my earlier words.

My lips curved up into a happy grin. "I could tell."

She snorted as she gave her hips a jerk. I laughed but then groaned as I started to slip out of her perfect heaven.

Catching our breath, we held each other. "I love you," I said into her damp skin.

"I love you too," she said as her arms tightened around my back. I lifted my head to gaze at my beautiful wife.

A cry sounded from down the hall, and my head dropped to the center of her chest.

I crawled off her as she pouted, and I chuckled. Wiping my wet dick with my dirty T-shirt, I open a drawer and grabbed some sleeping pants. She lay there staring at me with a Madonna-like smile as I stepped into the flannel and lifted it over my hips.

"What?"

"Nothing," she said as she continued to smile.

With a soft laugh, I shook my head again and padded down the hall to Adira's room. I lifted her from her crib where she stood, holding the bars, crying. As soon as her head hit my shoulder, she stopped. As I went to sit in the rocker, I grabbed some teething gel off her dresser.

I'd settled into the chair when my son shuffled into the doorway. He sleepily rubbed his eyes.

"Hey, buddy," I said softly as I rubbed the gel on Adria's gums, then wiped the excess on my pants.

"I fell today and hurt my knee," he said with his bottom lip stuck out.

I waved him in, and he shuffled over to stand next to me. Adria chewed on her fingers as she blinked her spiky lashes, tipped in her tears. I wrapped my arm around him and kissed his dark, sleep-tousled hair. As I did often, I marveled at the ability to touch someone and not be blasted with their memories. The crazy-ass potion Madame Laveaux had made had indeed worked for all our children after we drank it.

Thank God.

He climbed up in my lap and rested his head on my shoulder as he traced the tattoos on my skin. Adira copied him and laid her head on my other shoulder. We silently rocked for a few minutes. Movement had me raising my gaze to the door.

Ehria stood there blinking slowly. She too shuffled in. There was no room in my lap, so she stood to the side and hugged me and her sister. "We missed you, Daddy," she murmured.

I tilted my head to rest on hers as I smiled.

"I missed you too, baby girl," I said.

"Is there a party in here that I didn't get invited to?" Jasmine said from the open door.

"It would appear so," I said with a wink.

"Daddy's home," Draco said.

"I see this," she said to him as if we hadn't been doing very dirty things ten minutes ago. She approached us, and I appreciated the soft sway of her hips in her knit pajama pants.

"We should probably get to bed so Daddy can too. He's very tired after all the work he was doing," she said as she shot me a smirk.

"But I wanna stay with him," Draco grumped.

"Mimi is going to be here tomorrow. Remember, she's going to make cookies with you, but not if you're tired and grouchy," Jasmine cajoled. My mother had moved down here to help us with Ehria and now Adira.

The genes were being passed on to all my female children, which was why Jasmine and I had decided the three of them were probably enough. We didn't know if we could handle a third little wolf cub in the house, though they wouldn't actually shift until they reached puberty.

Heaven help us all when that happened.

"Buddy, you need to get to bed so you can be rested up. Would you like to go to the park tomorrow?"

His brows rose comically at my question. "Yes!" he said in an excited whisper.

"Me too?" Ehria whispered, keeping with the mood.

"You too, but only if you both get your little butts to bed," I said sternly, trying not to smile. They both rushed out of the room with excited whispers between them. I heard their doors close.

Jasmine gently lifted a now sleeping Adira and set her back

in her crib. She kissed her fingertips and pressed them to her dark, downy head.

"You ready to go back to bed, husband?" she asked with a waggle of her brows.

I held out a hand that she clasped in hers as I stood and reeled her in. "Why yes, wife. I am."

We tiptoed back down the hall, and she welcomed me home again.

The End.

ACKNOWLEDGEMENTS

If you're actually reading this, holy cow—you're dedicated. I thank you first and foremost! KISSES! Okay, now be prepared, this is gonna be a little long.

Chris Fleming was a model, son, brother, and husband. As I said, his star burned bright but burned out too fast. When his light went out, he passed a tiny flame to several individuals to nurture. He lives on in them.

Thank you to all of my readers who keep reading my words. You're the ones giving me a reason to write and hit "publish."

Most of this will be repetitive (if you read all this mumbo-jumbo) because all of you are always in my corner and I love you to pieces.

Thank you to **Pam, Kristin, Brenda, Lisa** for being my betas and letting me bounce ideas off you at all hours of the night. I seriously couldn't do this without you. YOU ARE MY SQUAD!

Kristine's Street Team! Y'all mother-freaking rock! Especially my top promoters, **Whynter, Pam, Chasity**, and **Stephanie**. You ladies continually go above and beyond for me and my books. Never in a million years could I thank you enough. Hugs and kisses!

Olivia, you're the bomb-diggity of editors; the absolute best. You've ruined reading for me at times, but I love you bunches! Thank you for fixing all my oopsies, calling me on the stuff that doesn't make sense, questioning my wording, and for fixing all those pesky commas that I hate. It's your touch that polishes my book babies until they shine.

Penny. Where do I start? My beautiful forever friend. Thank you for always believing in me, even when I didn't believe in myself. <3 Every time I tell you how good things are going and you tell me you're not surprised, I want to cry. Your faith in me is eternally humbling. You're halfway through with nursing school—you've got this!

Lisa and **Brenda**, y'all are the best and I cannot thank you enough for your support, advice, and friendship. And wine. To think it all started with a lunch born from the love of books. 2020 Book Signing events may have went to shit, but we're still doing our thing! Always with wine.

Lou Gray, did an amazing job on this cover! I never would've guessed when we worked on it, that Chris wouldn't live to see its release. So this one is a bittersweet book cover.

Wander Aguiar, this image of Chris is absolutely fantastic. I hope we did your image and Chris's memory proud. And **Andrey** is still tempting me with those emails—I thought we talked about that. With the help of **Chris**'s beautiful image, I like to think we made magic with this cover. **Chris**, this one's for you.

Stacey of **Champagne Book Designs**, never, ever, ever forget—you are a goddess. Every single time, you make each page beautiful. I can't say whether the print or digital are my favorite because I love them all so much. Thanks bunches, and guess what's getting closer? Shameless! It still hasn't set in that I will be there as an AUTHOR! Can you believe it? Craziness!

Ladies of Kristine's Krazy Fangirls, every one of you are the bomb-diggity. You're my personal little cheerleading team and I love you all! (((BIG HUGS)))! I thank you for your comments, your support, and your love of all things books. Come join us if you're not part of the group www.facebook.com/groups/kristineskrazyfangirls

As I often do, I found a way to spin the military into the storyline. As I've said a million times before, I fro this because the military has had such a huge impact on my life. From having multiple family members who served, to being a military brat, to a military spouse, and then working as a nurse in the military system, it's in my blood. With that being said, my last-but-never-least is a massive thank you to America's servicemen and women who protect our freedom on a daily basis. They do their duty, leaving their families for weeks, months, and years at a time, without asking for praise or thanks. I would also like to remind the readers that not all combat injuries are visible, nor do they heal easily. These silent, wicked injuries wreak havoc on their minds and hearts while we go about our days completely oblivious. Thank you all for your service.

OTHER BOOKS BY
KRISTINE ALLEN

Demented Sons MC Series - Iowa
Colton's Salvation
Mason's Resolution
Erik's Absolution
Kayde's Temptation

Straight Wicked Series
Make Music With Me
Snare My Heart
No Treble Allowed
String Me Up

Demented Sons MC Series - Texas
Lock and Load
Styx and Stones
Smoke and Mirrors
Jax and Jokers
Got Your Six (Formerly in Remember Ryan Anthology -
Coming Soon!)

RBMC - Ankeny Iowa
Voodoo
Angel
A Very Venom Christmas
Chains
Ghost (October 2021)
Sabre (Coming Soon!)

The Iced Series
Hooking
Tripping
Roughing
Holding (Coming Soon!)

Heels, Rhymes, & Nursery Crimes
Roses Are Red (RBMC connection)
Violets Are Blue (Coming Soon!)

Twisted Steel Anthology II
Snow's Addiction (DSMC Iowa President)

Pinched and Cuffed Anthology
The Weight of Honor (Coming Soon!)

ABOUT THE AUTHOR

Kristine Allen lives in beautiful Central Texas with her adoring husband. They have four brilliant, wacky, and wonderful children. She is surrounded by twenty-six acres, where her five horses, five dogs, and six cats run the place. She's a hockey addict and feeds that addiction with season tickets to the Texas Stars. Kristine realized her dream of becoming a contemporary romance author after years of reading books like they were going out of style and having her own stories running rampant through her head. She works as a night shift nurse, but in stolen moments, taps out ideas and storylines until they culminate in characters and plots that pull her readers in and keep them entranced for hours.

Reviews are the life blood of an indy author. If you enjoyed this story, please consider leaving a review on the sales channel of your choice, bookbub.com, goodreads.com, allauthor.com, or your review platform of choice, to share your experience with other interested readers. Thank you! <3

Follow Kristine on:

Facebook: www.facebook.com/kristineallenauthor

Instagram: www.instagram.com/_jessica_is_kristine.allen_

Twitter @KAllenAuthor

TikTok: vm.tiktok.com/ZMebdkNpS

All Author: www.kristineallen.allauthor.com

BookBub: www.bookbub.com/authors/kristine-allen

Goodreads: www.goodreads.com/kristineallenauthor

Webpage: www.kristineallenauthor.com

Made in the USA
Columbia, SC
03 August 2021

42707894R00157